Love's Forbidden Flower

DIANE RINELLA

Copyright © 2012/2015/2016 Diane Rinella
Cover art copyright © 2012 Diane Rinella
Cover design by Indie Author Services
Original cover source art © konradbak/Fotolia
The model on the cover of this book, along with the photographer and the cover's designer, are in no way affiliated with or endorsing this product.
ISBN: 0615732623
ISBN-13: 978-0615732626

For those who love in shadows.

ACKNOWLEDGEMENTS

Because words mean little if no one absorbs them, if you are reading this now, thank you. Thank you from the bottom of my heart for allowing my words to enter your life.

My husband, Brian, who has been unfailingly supportive of my dreams and has never once complained when I locked myself away for "just a few more minutes" or spent "just a few more dollars" to complete this project.

Karin, for her faith and for guiding me to fantastic beta readers.

Tori, Hillary, and Sarah, who both gently steered and harshly shoved me into making this book infinitely better.

Joanne, for generously giving far more time than I ever expected.

My friends who supported this effort despite never having read a word I'd written that wasn't on a blog, in an email, or on Facebook.

Those who "had kittens" whenever I slipped some of the subject matter into daily conversation. You gave this story purpose.

The few friends who knew exactly what I was writing about and never doubted I had a genuine story to tell.

Mostly, thank you to those who doubted I could find the time to publish this project. You ensured its completion.

1

Today, somewhere among the roses and petunias, my sanity squirted out of my brain and fertilized the backyard. Why couldn't those heart-seizing moments be experienced with anyone else? Why did they have to be with the man who is the ghastliest of all possibilities?

Obviously I hit my head and became delusional, or I have had so many Thanksgiving leftovers that I've slipped into a coma. Volunteering to play catch with Donovan to help keep his arm loose seemed valiant. But he chuckled before rolling his eyes and shaking his head in mock shame. He then cracked a joke about needing to teach me not to be such a klutz on the field. He's right. I'm truly female when it comes to sports.

After suffering several minutes of desperation, utter humiliation, and ruthless teasing, I surrendered.

He looked to the sky, arms outstretched, shaking his head in disbelief before sauntering towards me while plotting how to finally teach me the basics of throwing a football. At this point, everything still seemed normal.

After tossing me the ball he stood with his back facing me. Upon raising his right hand he said, "Hold the ball like this."

Apparently I failed, miserably.

"No. More like *this*." He made a gesture that reflected my grip precisely. He then gave me his snicker that could charm a nun out of her habit. "You're such a sorry case."

Donovan strolled behind me, put his left arm around my waist, and pulled me close while twisting my hips. It was nothing. We've done it a million times before.

"First, situate your body. Make sure you have a solid grip.

1

Now pull back, like so."

That's when I clumsily bonked him in the face.

"Oh, I'm so sorry!" I laughed. He had it coming for that klutz remark.

"Suuuure you are. Now stay in position." Again he pulled me next to him, but this time he placed his cheek against mine. Hesitation flowed over us as our bodies reacted to the sensuality of the touch. In his racing pulse, his breath, and every cell in his body, it seemed that Donovan desired exploring my mouth with his own. Thoughts of how he must taste wandered over me. Would he be sweet like the cookies I bake that he loves so much? Or creamy and delicious like an expensive piece of chocolate? The kind where even the tiniest morsel could satisfy a craving, yet would leave you desiring more for days to come?

Just as our cheeks glided together, as if in surrender to the intoxication, he gripped my hand tighter and yelled, "Now throw!" He lunged into the toss and forced me to follow along. It was incredibly beautiful—both the moment and the pass.

"I knew you could do it. You just needed the right touch," Donovan yelled while running after the ball.

The "right touch?" How does that translate? Was he messing with me so I'd relax, or didn't he realize what had transpired? Dear God, please let that interlude have been in my head.

He tossed me the ball. "Try it again."

While my body resumed the position, my mind tried to lift its cloudy haze. "One. Two," I released the ball. "Three!" The lopsided pass was far better than I'd ever managed before.

Donovan tossed the ball back to me. "Oh, yes! Lily goes aggro! Almost perfect. Try it again."

The next time, it sailed right into his hands. His expression flipped from wide-eyed to a devious turn of the lips. He ran towards my end of the yard to go for a touchdown. My pride kicked in. There was no way I'd let him get away with that. In the spirit of the game I pounced on him, taking him down to the ground. His head almost landed in a rose bush.

"What the hell? Where did you learn to do that?"

"A woman has her ways," I said playfully. What was I thinking? Clearly I wasn't.

His eyes, with their composition of deep and complicated blues like the waves of the ocean, were magnetizing. Their depth was intensified by his fair complexion and layered, obsidian hair that is reminiscent of the feathers of a raven. My breathing ceased as his eyes drew me in, transfixed.

"Hey, Lil. I'm kind of pinned here."

At least that's what I think he said. That pesky haze still cluttered my brain like murky pea soup. He must have sat up because his hand caressed my face like a whisper while those incredible eyes came closer. "Hey, you all right?"

My head rattled away the clouds. "Yeah. I'm fine."

"We'd better call it quits before one of us breaks the other."

As if nothing extraordinary happened, he aided me to my feet, and we went inside, wordlessly.

For the remainder of the evening, we tried to act like all was normal, but it was obvious something was amiss. Our usual dinner banter was strained to the point where Mom joked that we might turn into normal siblings—ones who often don't get along. But that will never happen; we're too connected. How we can often say so much to each other without a word only fazes others. To us it's a simple skill we possess, like writing in cursive. How have I never noticed how freakish that is?

But dinner was middling. It was after that I made a fool of myself.

"Hey, thanks a lot." Donovan said as he slipped into my room. "You almost got me in massive trouble." He appeared slightly indignant, and a little uncomfortable, as he leaned casually against the doorframe with his arms crossed.

"What?" I dropped my pencil onto my math book and mocked his characteristic eye roll. "Okay, how?"

"You had to tell Dad you tackled me." Donovan plopped onto the foot of my bed so heavily that my book bounced and my pencil flew onto the floor. Attempting to look scornful, I lowered and pinched my brow, then motioned for him to pick up the pencil.

"I did, fair and square. Did he really give you a bad time over that?" I swiped the pencil from his hand while hoping Dad was kind, yet knowing the truth. He's always far too hard on Donovan and expects him to be the quintessential manly son at all times. Also, I should have known better. At five foot eleven, Donovan's got a good seven inches on me, so of course Dad was upset. No excuses, even when it comes to his sister.

"Just a little. He did that voice again. The one where he's all, 'I am trying to sound like I'm kidding, but I also want you to know that I am serious.' I think he's afraid I'm going soft right before the big game, and I'll disappoint him."

It was then that the stupidest thing I'll ever utter sprang from my mouth. "That's silly, Donovan. I bet you'll never go soft, and if you don't watch your moves, the next time I pin you, I may do more than damage your ego."

My insides clamped. Maybe he heard it the way I hope I intended it.

His eyes sparkled as he absorbed my words. Since this afternoon those eyes have become my obsession. "Goodnight, Lilyanna," he practically sang. He left with a grin that said it all. Donovan knew exactly how I feared I meant it. I might as well have written it on the bathroom mirror and taped his toothbrush next to it. I'm seriously screwed!

It's nonsensical. There'll be no enchanted moment where one of us discovers the other was adopted or abandoned by aliens. Though my thoughts should sicken me, all I want is to sneak into his room like I did when I was little, put my head on his shoulder, and have him tell me it's just a bad dream. But this is reality, and nothing about the glow burning inside me since being captured by his eyes feels nefarious.

But how illogical is it really? Aren't you supposed to fall for your best friend? The one who listens to you with undivided attention, no matter how ridiculous you're being? The person who will instinctively drop everything to put his arms around you when you're hurt, even if you've yet to utter a word? Donovan is all those things and countless more.

I've got to stop reading Mom's romance novels. They're making me delusional.

2

Sanity is overrated—or so I tell myself as I lumber down the stairs while still in my bathrobe and heading for the coffee pot. I've the best attitude I can muster, despite my stress-induced insomnia. My only desires today are for business to be as usual and a little java jive injected into my veins to start things rolling. With the right attitude, my delusion over yesterday's events will fade and life will be back to normal by noon.

Donovan is leaning against the kitchen counter and sipping coffee. He shoots me a look like I'm a zombified monster who ate my own brain and has been up all night puking it all over myself.

"Dear God, little sister. What happened to you last night? Did you sneak out and get into a fight? Please tell me the other girl looks worse."

"My pillow turned into a rock and threw itself at me."

"So, uh, I guess this is a bad time to remind you that I need to leave early today, and you have about five minutes to get ready if you want a ride."

Is he kidding or just checking to see if I'm still off my rocker from some abominable concoction I must have been slipped yesterday? "Crap!"

His laughter follows my sprint up the stairs. "Just because you had such a bad night, feel free to make it eight minutes."

The fall weather in upstate Rhode Island sends a chill through me as we exit the house. Though I've lived here all my life, fall's colors never fail to stun me. What is autumn without nature's paintbrush? How would it be to live where the seasons impose little change? The thoughts send my mind to remote places, like a deserted island, just big enough for two—

"Are you sure you're all right?" Donovan asks while opening his car's passenger door for me.

"Yeah, I'm fine. Just too much on my mind last night."

He shuts my door, and then strolls around to the driver's side. He's either not getting my drift or is using his patented poker face.

Our chatter is uncharacteristically reserved as we pull out of the driveway. I have about two seconds to create conversation and avoid a silence that screams of uneasiness.

"I kept thinking about life after graduation. Being stuck in a classroom is not for me. I'm not going to college. I'm going to pastry school."

The pause is deafening.

"What, no smart ass comments?" I ask.

His eyes stay on the road. "Lil, I know you absolutely hate school and would probably rather join the military and fight in some made up war than go to college, but are you really sure this is what you want?"

"Absolutely. You've seen how my baking skills have evolved. I'm so far beyond being Betty Crocker that I can't imagine not doing more with them. I can either suffer through four years of college, and be miserable, or go to pastry school for a year and come out ready to hit the ground running and happy. Do you really need to question which choice is better? Besides, if I go to college, I may wind up like Mom and become a disgruntled career woman who gives up everything to have children. Instead, I can have my own bakery while raising my family and live life on my terms. When you come right down to it, that's what I really want."

"Dad's going to kill you. I sort of can't blame him. With your grades and how mature you often sound, it's easy to peg you as an English major. Then again, you're the one who can do no wrong. It is the son who always disappointeth."

"Donovan, you know that's not true."

Still he avoids looking at me. "No, Lily, I don't know that. I really don't. You just don't see it, do you?"

He parks in the school lot. The touch of my hand on his arms stops him from exiting the car. "I see it Donovan. I just don't want it to be true. He needs to see you like I do."

Finally, he faces me. "Well, my darling sister, I don't know how anyone sees me anymore. Anyway, pastry school is a great idea. You need to do whatever it takes to be happy and not listen to what others say. Then again, *you've* always been good at that. Have a good day." He exits the car. "I'll see you at home tonight. I have practice this afternoon."

Yep, Donovan starts off concerned about me and ends up being annoyed because of Dad. Things are normal, though usually he would stay and open—

Donovan opens my car door. "I'm sorry for giving you a bad time this morning," he says.

I smile and double pat him on the cheek. "Don't break anything at practice."

⯑

Leaning on the kitchen counter seems to be the only thing keeping me upright. Lack of sleep, the day's boredom, and my pondering this morning's revelation have brought on pure exhaustion. My knack for always knowing my needs on a deep level surfaced again through my announcement about pastry school. Now I have a year to convince my parents that college is not the end-all-be-all. I'd have just as much luck telling Dad I'm joining the circus to perform in the motorcycle ball of death.

A clamor from down the hall jolts me, and the side door burst open. "Jinx!"

"What? What are you talking about?" I shout back to Donovan.

"You. You're a jinx! Remember what you said when you

got out of the car this morning?"

"Not a clue."

"You said, and I quote, 'Don't break anything at practice.' " Donovan rounds the corner into the kitchen. He's sporting a shiner on the right side of his face and a small gash on the other. He laughs at my stammer for words. "It's fine, you should see the other guy."

"Yeah, right."

"No, really. I got off easy. Peter broke his leg. Or rather, I broke Peter's leg when he broke my fall. How do I look?" He holds his arms out to the side and flutters his eyelashes. He reminds me of a blood-battered Cupie doll.

"Purple."

"I was hoping for dashing or heroic. Do we have any frozen peas?"

"I'll look and meet you upstairs," I announce while heading for the freezer. It figures. Just as things seem normal, he had to walk in looking all wounded and sexy. Damn! How have I never noticed how gorgeous he is before?

My feet thud on each step as I trudge up the stairs. Who did I offend in what life to deserve my predicament? This just sucks!

Donovan stands in his bedroom while admiring his black eye in the dresser mirror. "Impressive, huh?" he asks.

"Yeah, I'm sure all the girls will think so."

"They already do. I had half the cheerleading squad crying over me."

"Great, The Bimbo Brigade. Yeah, that *is* impressive." I smack the bag of peas in his hand before placing it over his eye. "I'll go get something for that cut. Did Peter really break his leg?"

"Yeah, he sure did." There's an obvious sound of remorse in Donovan's voice. "Honestly, even though it was an accident, I feel horrible about it."

When I return, I find Donovan sitting on the bed with his elbow on his knee. His head is hung with the peas pressed against his eye. I bend over and raise his chin to face me. In some ways I feel that I am consoling a sensitive, little boy who has been picked on. "Hey, these things happen. If it was an accident, then it wasn't your fault. It could just have easily been the other way around."

"Yeah, but I only play football to keep Dad happy. It actually means something to Peter, and he's out for the season now. This may have killed his free ride at a decent college. Accident or not, I'm still a part of that."

I sit next to him and swipe antiseptic on his cut. He winces. "Were you the only ones involved?" I ask.

"No, another guy landed on me. I accidentally used Peter to break my fall, but it was my landing on him that caused the injury."

"Again, it's obviously not your fault. There are so many things that happen to us in life that we can't let ourselves feel guilty over those that we couldn't have possibly controlled."

"Yeah. I suppose you're right."

He's locked into my grey-violet eyes again and has the same gape as yesterday—like he's beholding something fascinating for the first time. His hold on me causes a muted gasp, and I inhale his shower-fresh scent. It's disappointing. His aroma is always best after his cologne has absorbed into him and allowed him to create his own, apprehending musk.

Wait. When did I notice that?

My mind circles back to the thought of him in the shower. I've witnessed him in just a towel countless times, but how he looks like a glistening marble statue that would make Michelangelo jealous of God's tinkering is suddenly ornamenting my thoughts. The full view must be breathtaking.

"You know, Lily, you have really turned into a lovely lady. When did that happen?"

His lips call to me, making me confused and embarrassed. My glance shies away, and I notice his hand on my knee. It then recasts onto his arresting eyes as he slides his arm around me and draws me closer. My heart hammers.

Disparagingly, his eyes break their hold. He brings my head onto his shoulder, violating the tone of the moment but not the sentiment. I glimpse up at him and softly kiss his wounded cheek while he toys with my long, chocolate-brown locks. As his fingers trace my jawline, our foreheads gently meet.

"Hey, is anyone going to feed me?" Dad yells from downstairs. The interruption is both a welcome relief and an intrusive disappointment.

3

Donovan and I often sit at the same table in the den while studying. For years this time has segued into rousing conversations, be they serious, heartfelt, or laced with ridiculous banter. But this time it feels weird. It's been a week since his accident, and our awkwardness is unnerving. Excuses to explain away my anxiety fail; someone messed with this chair, the room feels warm, or the lamp has been moved. Why am I using a pencil? Is my eraser smaller? Like a lot smaller than yesterday?

The reason for my discomfort becomes apparent when I look up. Donovan is staring at me like he needs to talk. I need to talk to him too, but I'm just as closed off. For the first time in our lives, we dodge a pressing subject as I attempt to break the ice. "If you're trying to figure out how to ask me to do your trig homework for you, the answer is no." I swear when he goes off to college we'll be on video chat two hours each night just working on his math assignments.

"I gave up on it a few minutes ago," he says.

My eyes roll back into my head.

"I know. I'll get back to it in a minute. Actually, I'm failing miserably at moving on to a sample college admission essay I need to write."

"What's the topic?" Why am I buying into this? He's probably making up something ridiculous just to keep me on edge.

"That's the source of the writer's block. The only guideline is that the essay be based on personal experience and the insight that it brings."

"So, what are you feeling insightful about?"

"How if I screw this up, Dad will probably send me to military school. Unless I was a girl. Then he'd tell me a C is a perfectly acceptable grade and buy me something pretty because a daughter can do no wrong."

"You're such an ass." I resume my studies in minor annoyance.

"Call 'em as I see 'em. But seriously, I'm stumped."

He really should know better than to hand me the open can of worms to dump on him. Maybe he is not dodging me after all. "How about the importance of communication and what happens when people fail at it?"

"And tie it to world affairs?"

"No. College admission essays are to be personal. You're just like me. When you can't communicate to your satisfaction, you turn into a wreck. You can eventually handle anything as long as you know what you are up against. It's when you don't get the information you need, or can't express yourself, that you have a real problem."

"You make it sound so easy," he says, his voice slightly cracking as his fingers tap his notebook.

I don't know how much more tension I can take before I throw caution to the wind and spill my guts. My new tone reflects that we should talk about something deeper. "It is, and it isn't. But if I have all the information, even if it's something that hurts, I can face it."

Donovan peers down at his assignment. His fingers glide back and forth across a pen that sits on the desk. "What if you're in a situation where you've always been able to talk to someone, and you have something you want to share, but you're afraid if you do, it would ruin the relationship?"

I pull my chair around next to Donovan's and take his hands into mine. We mastered intimate conversation years ago, but it feels different now. "You and I have always shared everything, no matter how personal or awkward, and there's certainly no reason to stop now. There's nothing you can possibly say that would damage what we share."

"You can read me like a book."

"You always have that same power with me. I can only do it most of the time."

"Why, Lil? Because when you get emotional your inner voice shuts off and your real voice loses it filter? I'm well aware of what happens when you get emotional. It ain't pretty."

"Gee, thanks."

After shooting me a wicked smile, he pretends to resume his studies. But then he swallows deeply, letting his true emotions seep through. "Given that little fact, I guess I don't have to tell you what I wanted to talk about."

"Actually ... you do. Often I can read you like I'm hearing words you don't speak, but lately I think you've been blocking me out."

With a subtle nod his eyes hood, sending pain into my heart. He squeezes my hand, and as his eyes peer straight into mine, his softened features convey he is in search of the very depths of my being. But the honesty is short lived. I am certain no one else could ever see the veil he is slipping over his emotions. "There is something I need to talk to you about."

After taking a poignant breath, he sprouts the grin of a joker, which I quickly remove from his face. "I'm not finishing your trig homework."

Donovan scrunches his eyes with a groan. "Damn it, Lil! I thought you said it's turned off."

"Some things are still obvious. Like how you're such an ass." My annoyance with him propels me away, but I am more irritated at myself. I can't tuck my emotions aside, although lately I've wanted to more than ever.

Donovan tugs me back into the chair. He leans in as if the empty room has ears. "Really, there's so much more to say. I just don't know where to start, or even if I should. It's all pretty overwhelming." He gazes down at my hand and strokes it before kissing it gallantly, pressing it against his cheek, and looking at me with puppy eyes. "But seriously, can you help me with my trig assignment?"

I give him a smile of resignation before reaching for his math book and letting the elephant in the room lie.

4

The carnival ride started two weeks ago, and a decent night's sleep still evades me. If I could just put the puzzle together, maybe peace wouldn't be so fleeting. The thing is, I've no idea how the completed picture should look. I am also uncertain if I have all of the pieces, and if they go to the same puzzle.

But seriously, whom am I kidding? This labyrinth of perplexity shows I'm falling in love. No matter how wrong anyone says it is, my feelings cannot be altered. I wish it were merely lust. I could accept that and move on. But love complicates it. Not only does it ensnare me, it makes me want to jump into its clutches and surrender.

I push the worldview of my feelings being gross, evil, and deviant away for the sake of self-preservation. Being traumatized by a moral situation is pointless if the condition does not exist. Without verbal confirmation, it is still possible that Donovan's feelings are a fabrication of my distorted perception.

Again looking like an accident victim, I enter the kitchen in my bathrobe. Donovan is alone and eating breakfast. He gets a good look at me, and concern fills his eyes. "Lily, are you all right? I mean it. Do you need to talk about something?"

I shake my head and reach for the coffee. Has he not heard his words and seen his actions over the last few weeks? Again I wonder if I have been misreading what I think are signs. If so, I am a moron of epic proportions.

Our chemistry tingles my skin when he steps behind me, places his hand on my arm, and nuzzles his cheek into mine. Softly he says, "I understand. I want to help you with your problems, but I don't know how."

My problems? I've been reluctant to talk too, but ... Am I just imagining what we are going through, or has he fully popped into denial? Is he scared of facing us or of hurting me? I fear the worse case scenario: there's something causing us to completely fall apart, and he can't read me any more either.

"Donovan, I'm fine," I say reassuringly. I am going to catch my breath by claiming I'm sick, staying home, and spending the day baking. Once that is done, you can rest assured all will be dandy."

"Mom and Dad are going to know you're not sick, since you tend to go on baking binges when you're stressed."

Ugh. Doesn't he see I can't pretend this situation doesn't exist? There are bigger issues than concern over if Mom and Dad know I am playing hooky.

Frustration over how the person I have shared everything with still can't talk to me, or at least let me open up to him, causes my cool demeanor to warm. "With all that has been going on, *that* is what you're concerned about?"

I feel him back away emotionally while physically maintaining his intimacy. It messes with my head. "I'm sorry, Lil. If there's anything I can do to help you through—whatever it is ..."

There *is* something he can do—he can face his emotions. However, the still-healing gash on his cheek that he got weeks ago tells the real story. He doesn't even want to play football. He's doing it for Dad. When will Donovan live his own life?

I set my coffee on the counter, and then slip my arms around him. It catches him completely off guard. When I pull back, I take his hands and stare into his eyes. With sisterly love I tell him, "There is something that you can do for me. You can admit who you are and what you want, so that someday you can be the one standing here on the verge of a meltdown because you're trying to figure out how to make everything you want and love work for you. When that happens, maybe we can finally talk. Until then, we'll just keep loving each other."

I cap the hug off with a squeeze, and then avoid eye contact when I grab my coffee and head off to my room.

❧

"Eat this." I nearly assault Donovan as he comes in the door by slipping a piece of mint into his mouth.

"What the—? What is this?" He looks at me like admission into an asylum should be considered. He's probably right.

I huff as my shoulders drop and my chin thrust forward. "Really? You don't know what that is? It's fresh mint."

"Like the stuff they make candy canes out of?"

"No, like the stuff they *pretend* to make candy canes out of."

"Why are you shoving a tree in my mouth? Usually when you do that, it's something good."

Before heading back to the kitchen I tell him, "It's not a tree, it's a bush. Remember that flavor. It might be hard to accept because it's different, but that doesn't mean it's not special and should be ignored."

Tonight, I am taking a chisel to the iceberg. We need to have some kind of normal conversation, because something important is at stake. If we are constantly on guard, I fear we will lose the bond we have had all of our lives.

After dinner, I bring out glasses of water with lemon slices and place one in front of each of us. "Please cleanse your palates." Everyone looks at me like an alien ship has just dropped me off.

"Well, she did say she was sick this morning," Donovan cracks under his breath. "Maybe she really has a fever."

Dad sounds half serious. "Should we be worried?"

Mom seems intrigued almost to the point of giddiness. "Oh, be quiet boys! You know how passionate Lily gets about things. I can't wait to see what she's doing."

I go to the kitchen and return with a tray of Crème Brûlée. Each test subject gets two, distinctly marked ramekins, along with spoons. They probably think I'm crazy. Frankly, I am. I'm downright batty and know of nothing else to do, so I am going back to a project I started long ago. Donovan has always been my driving force. He not only encourages me, he absorbs my every word and emotion. He files them for when I need to be reminded of something or if he just wants to taunt me. I need that back in my life.

I ask for everyone's participation. "Please, tell me the difference between the two, which you think is better and why. Cleanse your palate when you switch between them."

Eyebrows rise all around the table as each subject takes a bite of the first one. More skeptical looks follow as they switch between the two desserts. "Well?" I ask. They keep tasting and looking at each other hesitantly. Do they expect poison to kick in? It's not like I have never experimented before. "What, not even a wise crack? Nothing?"

"They are both very good, dear." Leave it to Mom to be half encouraging.

"Is there a difference?" Dad asks. "This one is really good, but it's strange. Where have I tasted that before?"

I shake my head in amazement. Dad is also beyond hope. "All right, Donovan, your turn to tell me I'm crazy."

He puts down his spoon, leans back in his chair, and flips his head to remove the tuft of hair that's fallen in his face. He scoffs at me, but then his smugness disappears. "The first one is like a passing fancy; it tastes like a bargain peppermint patty and has a, well, I don't know the word, but it's kind of fake—like a cheap date you waste your time with. The second one you want to savor; it has a smoother consistency, and you used fresh mint. It's the real deal."

Mom and Dad sit dumbfounded as Donovan proves his point about the quality of the desserts by tilting both ramekins. The second dish is empty while the first has only a single bite gone. Raising the bad one toward me he states, "There is no way I am falling for this." He then looks to the real deal. "This one is special, and I'd be a fool not to appreciate it." I can swear he follows it with a silent, *"You do get what I am saying, right?"*

I'm floored by his metaphor. And yes, I know what he is really saying, because I know Donovan. I express my happiness the only way I can.

"Yes!" I jump out of my chair, run around the table, hug him from behind and plant one firmly on his cheek. "Finally! Finally someone in this house getting a trained palate!" I'm bouncing so much there must be a trampoline built into the floor.

Dad's glare at his son is incredulous. "How the hell do you know what *fresh mint* tastes like? What kind of red, white, and blue-blooded man knows what fresh mint even is?"

Donovan is all too happy to one-up Dad. "I actually paid attention when Lily practically shoved a piece if it down my throat today."

"She did that to me too, but I thought it was just some weird woman thing."

"Edward!" Mom scorns her husband.

"Well, you women do get a little crazy," Dad says. He sounds only half serious.

"Why didn't you give me some mint too?" Mom asks. "It's not fair that the boys had an edge, *even if one of them did squander it.*" Mom shoots Dad a "Shut up, Edward!" look.

I take my seat across from Donovan while eating out of the one ramekin intended for myself. "You cook all the time, Mom. Mint's a culinary staple so you should already know how it tastes."

"Well, Lana?" Dad asks.

"Don't get yourself in any deeper, Edward. You're in a lot of trouble for that woman crack."

Donovan hasn't taken his eyes off of me. My heart rate skyrockets when he shoots me a smile and says, "Sorry Mom, but denial doesn't alter the truth. Sometimes you can know what something is, but you need the right guidance to truly appreciate it."

"Speaking of tasting things," Dad says, "how's your taste of superstardom since you scored those touchdowns in the big game? I bet it's really made you a hit with the ladies, 'ey Donnie?"

Donovan winces. His eyes lock onto his spoon. "Can we please not talk about this?"

"Come on, son, let your old man live vicariously for a moment. How many of those hot cheerleaders gave you their numbers and which one, or rather, how many, are you seeing this weekend?"

Mom drops her spoon into her ramekin with a punctuating *clank*. "Edward! That is revolting! Please leave him alone!"

Donovan's eyes flash to me before returning their gaze to the table. "Well, Dad, in all honesty, there's only one girl who can get through to me right now, and she's certainly not a cheerleader. However, she is the loveliest lady I've ever seen."

"Hot dog!" Dad exclaims. "When do we meet her?"

"Edward!"

"All right. All right. I'll leave him alone."

"It's fine, Mom. All things in due time, Dad. She's very special, and she's worth treating right. I'm having a hard time getting my courage up with this one."

5

"Come on, Lil. We're going to be late."

Donovan is practically pulling me out the door. I wish he'd hold on to those horses a little.

"Late how?" I ask. "We're just going to pick up Sally before you dump us off for Christmas shopping at the mall."

"We said we'd be there in five minutes, and I don't want to spend my morning waiting around for Elizabeth Taylor and her friend, Dream Date Barbie."

"Geez, okay." I put on a coat, gloves and hat as rapidly as I can. Donovan is already standing at the front door. There must be an invisible elf holding a match under his butt.

When we reach the car, he opens my door. He's almost bouncing while waiting for me to sit. It's freezing out, but does he need to run to stay warm? I can't wait until I get my license in a few months so he won't have to schlep me around anymore—not that the attention is unwelcome.

Throwing open his door, he tosses his football jersey in the back like a dirty rag into the hamper. He's far too happy to only be going to a holiday party at school for the teams. He must have another agenda.

Once out of the driveway, we begin our journey in the wrong direction. "Hey, don't forget that we need to get Sally."

"No, we don't."

"Um, yeah, we do. That's the plan. Remember?"

"I'm well aware of *your* plan, but you have no idea as to mine."

"Oh, no. What are you roping me into now?" I ask while whipping out my cell phone.

"Who are you calling?"

"Sally. I have to tell her you've been tackled too many times and are having some kind of episode."

"Put it away. She knows we aren't coming. She's my partner in crime. Well, one of them."

"So you have flipped, and we are pulling a Bonnie and Clyde. I wish you had told me. I'd have worn a more appropriate outfit. Do I get a Tommy Gun?"

"You are full of questions today. Can't I just surprise you?"

Judging by the dazzle in the sapphires on his face, his master plan must be a big one. The speedometer on my heart reads faster than that of the car as we accelerate down the freeway, heading out of town. "Am I being kidnapped?"

"Would you like to be?"

Yes, please.

"Don't answer that. We are going to Pawtucket. There's a bakery there that has a special class this afternoon on holiday desserts or something. I saw it listed a few days ago and managed to get you in with a little financial help from Mom. Ok, every penny came from Mom. She loved the idea. She wanted to come too, but I told her there was only one opening left."

Now I'm the one bouncing. I can't believe I get to do this and just love that Donovan is the one making it happen. He is always looking out for me, but this is over the top. "Seriously? This is amazing! How long is the class?"

"Four hours, and it's in their kitchen. It will be great experience for you since this is what you want to do with your life. Maybe it will give you more ammo when you finally approach the parental units."

"This is so sweet. It's a lot of driving taking me there, coming back for the party at school, and then picking me up again."

"It would be if I was going."

"What? It's the big holiday party for all the jocks. They've been trying to figure out how to spike the punch for weeks."

"I really don't want to hang out with those guys."

He's never been fond of his teammates, but this party is a huge deal. Taking a pass on it is unimaginable. "So, what movies are you going to see while you wait for me?"

"Well, see, there is a catch. You need a partner to take the class, so you are stuck with me. I'll try not to embarrass you too much."

"No way! You're telling me that you are blowing off a big party to celebrate how great you are to take a pastry class with your little sister when Mom would have done it? Who are you?" God, he really has hit his head too many times.

"Sounds rather chivalrous when you put it that way. Just remember, Mom thinks I'm going to that party."

This is just too good to be true. He supports me in everything—but, seriously? "Wait a minute. What do I have to do in return?"

"Absolutely nothing. Just don't let Mom and Dad know I missed that party to bake a cake. Dad will turn me into a unic."

"There has to be a catch."

"No catch. I swear. You deserve something special, and I'm glad to be a part of it. You're getting to know another side of yourself, and I want to get to know it too."

Can my heart possibly melt anymore? I want to jump into his seat and kiss him. Instead, I opt for crossing my arms and squinting sideways at him.

"Fine. If you really want there to be a catch, you can make me your special cocoa tonight while I watch cartoons."

Ah, yes. The things Donovan loves. Cartoons and quality treats. He's always been sweeter than anything I'll ever make, and he knows I'd do that for him anyway. "That's right. There's a Looney Tunes marathon on tonight."

"Yeah, I can't wait," he says while drumming on his steering wheel.

"You want little marshmallows in your cocoa?"

"You have to ask?"

ॐ

Donovan opens my car door on the way to school the following Monday, revealing a white rose sitting on the passenger seat. White roses have always been my favorite flower. Often I wish that Mom and Dad had named me differently so people wouldn't always buy me lilies. I love getting flowers. Donovan seems to be the only one who has ever understood my preference for roses, specifically white ones.

As I pick it up to inhale its aroma, Donovan muses, "Huh. I wonder how that got there?"

Actually, I do wonder. This came from a store, and, even with the attached water tube, it's unlikely it would have survived this well all night in the freezing car. Donovan must have bought it yesterday and sneaked it into the house, then put it in the car when he scraped the ice off of the windshield this morning.

A surprise awaits him too. While home alone yesterday afternoon, I baked his favorite cookies—oatmeal with raisins, cinnamon, and coconut—my personal recipe. He goes mental over them. Stashing them in his locker before lunch will be a nice little thank you for our adventure on Saturday. He's likely forgotten that he wrote his locker combination in his math book at the beginning of the year. Snagging it yesterday while he was out was as easy as baking a frozen apple pie.

As we pull into the school parking lot, my friend, Sally, and her brother, Jason, are getting out of his car. Sally has been my best friend since she moved here two years ago. Well, she's my best female friend. Though she and I are definitely close, no one can hold a candle to Donovan when it comes to whom I turn to when life gets complicated.

Sally runs up to the car; eager to talk to me about the call she got last night from a boy she had a disastrous date with on Saturday. Why did she open my door? That's Donovan's job. He has done that ever since he got his license and started playing chauffeur. Damn it, Sally!

My ear gets talked off on the way to class about the call, and the apology Sally received. "Lily, I just don't get it. What kind of boy comes on to you like that, gets rejected, says you are a waste of time, then calls the next night and asks you out again?"

"Probably one that hopes you'll succumb next time. You did tell him no, right?"

Sally is a naturally pretty blonde with big green eyes, a trim figure, and a cursed voice that makes her sound like a cartoon character. Unfortunately, the combination leads boys to think she is dumb and easy. She's actually one of the brightest people I've met, though she sure never sounds it.

"Of course I did," she says. "I should move to France. When I was there over the summer the boys were just as bad, but at least they had adorable accents."

Sally's travel experiences are jealousy inducing. Every summer her parents take her and Jason abroad. Their parents are both doctors in a private practice, so they can afford to take full advantage of their free time. My Dad does well in the insurance industry, and Donovan and I certainly have no complaints. But although my family has held passports for years, the farthest I have been away from Rhode Island is Disneyworld, when Donovan and I were little. He spent the entire trip running around in mouse ears and asking where Bugs Bunny and Snoopy were. We were too young to understand that not all cartoon characters live in the same enchanted village.

As we take our seats for the first class of the day, Sally notices the rose sticking out of my backpack. "Hey, where did you get that?"

Why must the beautiful truth be hidden? "We had to stop at the drug store on the way to school and they had these by the register. It seemed like a great day to treat myself to something pretty."

"Speaking of treats, how was your little surprise on Saturday? I couldn't believe when Donovan called and asked me to help him. Jason would never do anything like that for me. Did you make anything yummy?"

Mmm ... Saturday. In some ways it seems like it was an apparition. Four hours in a kitchen with Donovan should have been hellish, but he really surprised me. That may be because he let me do all of the work. At first I thought he was afraid of screwing up, but then it became apparent that he wanted me to embrace the moment without him in my way. He was valiant in tackling the mundane tasks like measuring ingredients and washing our equipment, but he stepped back and let me take the reins on everything else. Because of him, I truly learned that in a bakery is where I need to be.

"Yeah, there were quite a few things I had never done before, like actually getting a cake to roll properly and making a Yule Log. It turned out amazing and mine was the only one that did. The pastry chef there was happy to teach me a bunch of additional stuff. Poor Donovan actually sat around and waited an extra hour for me. It was incredible."

Sally sighs. "He's so perfect. I wonder what he would be like to date?"

Don't even think it, lady! He's off-limits.

6

With a stretch and a moan, my eyes open to a sweet, yet freakish, sight. Sitting on my pillow is a teddy bear with a Santa hat not on its head, but stretched over it with holes cut out to expose the bear's eyes. Around its neck is a silver necklace with a football pendant. As I play with it, I discover a note tucked under the hat reading, *"Something to always remind you of the day you made me fall."* The words bring my heart into my throat.

The bear has given me a new fondness for the day. I infuse a little more Christmas cheer, Lily-style. While I prepare the final touches on some homemade hot chocolate, Donovan comes down the stairs as if the wispy aroma has traveled to his room and elevated him off his feet.

"Wow. Are you making cocoa again? We're all going to get fat."

"Not just cocoa, special Christmas cocoa."

Observing eyes are sought before he whispers into my ear, "Special, huh? What magical herbs have you put into your potion?" He then backs off before grabbing cups. "Actually, don't answer that. I may not want to know if you are also serving it to Mom and Dad."

"Okay, I'm not sure what to make of that comment. There's only a little mint added, so don't go getting any funny ideas."

"What is it with you and the fresh mint lately?" Donovan sets four cups beside me for the cocoa.

"Fresh nothing. It's Christmas morning, and I already have to help Mom cook. Extract exists for a reason. Oh, thanks, but I only need three cups."

"Can't be bothered to suck it up and drink the fake stuff

with the peons, eh?"

"Please. You know better than that. Real extract is in here, not flavoring. Sugar has overstayed its welcome with me. I'll have juice instead."

The thick chocolate cascades into the cups before I garnish them with marshmallow and deliver them into the living room where our parents sit. Donovan walks up behind me with one hand behind his back. "Pineapple or orange?"

"Is this a challenge?"

"Of sorts. Pineapple or orange?"

"Orange." I generally prefer pineapple, but orange juice just sounds better today.

He pulls his arm out from behind his back and hands me a glass of orange juice. "Thought so."

"Does this mean you two slow pokes are finally ready?" Dad asks. He reaches under the tree to hand Mom one of her gifts. You'd think by his enthusiasm he actually got her something different this year. Yeah, right!

Dad always gives Mom an array of gift cards and wise cracks, "I know you're just going to go crazy shopping over the next few weeks no matter what you get today." Mom buys Dad new clothes to wear to the office, while Donovan and I find him the wildest, yet most fashionable, ties imaginable. To everyone's surprise, Dad actually wears them, saying they make him feel *hip*. It's always a challenge to see how bizarre we can go without spilling over into the realm of tastelessness.

Donovan ceremoniously bestows a gift upon me, plopping it on my lap with a thud. Did he get me a telephone book? Maybe it's a Bible with all of the passages about the wrongness of my thoughts of him highlighted for easy reference.

To my joy, it's the most thorough book of advanced pastry techniques I've ever seen, with over nine hundred full-color pages of photos, demonstrations, and formulas for just about everything I could want to make.

When I pry my view away from the tome, it's easy to

appreciate how gorgeous Donovan looks leaning against the mantle. His eyes have more spark than the roaring fire beside him. I force myself out of my stupor before heading toward the hall closet and lugging out a box half my size to present to him. He looks at me sideways with a skeptical little snicker before turning his attention to the card.

To Donovan, Because I believe in you and your dreams. Love, Lily

Beneath the wrapping resides nearly every penny of my savings account now in the form of an acoustic guitar—something Donovan has asked for every Christmas since he can remember and has never gotten. Dad feels it would take Donovan away from sports and always says, "Only hippie freaks who smoke a lot of pot and boys with long hair, tight pants and low morals play guitar." Maybe Donovan wants one so he can dangle it over Dad's head and taunt him.

I indulge in Donovan's expression as he revels at the instrument. It's like he's seeing the world for the first time. "It's perfect, Lil. Thank you."

Our parents' silent disdain makes me proud. Donovan has received from me one of many things they've never given him—unconditional respect for his personal desires. It's a Merry Christmas indeed.

As I'm about to drift off to sleep Donovan slips into my room and stands at the foot of my bed. "Did you have a nice Christmas?"

"Almost perfect." Rolling over, the pendant around my neck is revealed.

"Almost?"

"I used to wonder, 'What's he waiting for, Christmas?' There's no need to wonder anymore, as even though I think that note I got was a confession, I'm still waiting."

"Lily." His whisper is accompanied by his patented eye roll. "We can't do this right now. It seems eyes are always on me, and neither one of us needs that kind of trouble. Besides, we know this isn't really right. We need to stop and think about this. Once we start we'll be changed forever."

"We also know it's not really wrong. Some people search a lifetime for someone they can connect with, and yet so early in life, here we are. How can something as beautiful as us be wrong?"

He looks a little ill before forcing his big brother expression to return. Still, his tone is bleak. "Lily, promise you'll never give up on me. No matter what happens or doesn't happen. You're the only one who's ever really cared about me. Please always believe in me, no matter how much I'm struggling or what it's over." Taking my hand, he kisses my forehead, and leaves me to my dreams. "Good night, lovely lady. Merry Christmas."

My senses awaken me to find a figure sneaking away from my bed. Catching him off guard, I grab him by the pants, pull him down, and pin him to the mattress.

I whisper, "You're lucky I realized it was you before I pulled out the baseball bat I keep under the bed. What are you doing in my room?"

Donovan returns the murmur as he waves a note at me. "Trying to slip a message under your pillow. I changed my mind because I was afraid you wouldn't find it, but Mom would."

"What does it say?"

"Why don't you unpin me and find out?" He must be enjoying this as much as I am. Mr. Football Hero could easily break free of my wussy hold if he didn't want to be here.

"Umm ... No. What's it say?"

"You have *got* to be kidding me."

Restricting his ability to move, I sit on his hips and snatch the note.

It reads, *"New Year's Eve."*

"What does this mean?" My hand holds it for him to see as if he doesn't know its message.

"Will you please get off me?"

I descend my face directly in front of his with our noses

31

almost touching. "Do you promise to tell me and not run off?"

"Yes!"

I lie down on the bed and snuggle into Donovan. I play dumb so I can enjoy the moment for all it's worth. I know exactly what the note means, and he's well aware of that fact. But now we are relishing this part of the courtship. It's suddenly become that rare time of anticipation in our relationship—the time when we know we will evolve.

Without thought for his actions, he rolls to face me, slides his arm around my waist, and holds my body while engulfing my spirit. "It means that your words keep getting to me. You're an incredible woman, and I want to spend every moment possible with you. At some point I need to face that. Lily, I don't know if we should do this, but maybe on New Year's Eve I could take you to your friend's party, and then we could go to Joe's awhile. When Mom and Dad are gone, we'll come back here for some time alone and start to figure this out."

I'm enchanted by his considerate tone. "That sounds really sweet."

Donovan pulls me closer and gently strokes the back of my head. "Really? This whole situation is so strange, and if we're going to let things happen, it has to be for the right reasons. We should never look back and think the whole thing was some kind of perverse mistake. The last thing I want is for you to feel I had any notion of taking advantage of you."

The moonlight shining through my window illuminates his eyes, and I'm completely enthralled by his gaze. "You're so amazing. No wonder I'm falling for you."

His stuttered breath whispers over my lips. "I don't want to hide from myself anymore. Lying next to you feels so comfortable and right. The moonlight is bringing out the violet in your eyes, and I feel like my heart is going to come out of my chest. It would be so easy to give in without another thought."

He brings my head towards his, our lips nearly meeting. My heart pounds in anticipation.

Suddenly he pulls away. "I need to do this right. If we ever do surrender to it, I want you to know how much you're respected. You're not just some girl; you're someone to be treasured. New Year's Eve, okay?"

"Definitely."

Donovan slips out of my room. I know I should question if this is right, but how can something that feels so wonderful be wrong?

7

Finally, the big night is here. I was beginning to think Father Time had been run over by Santa's sled and would never snap out of his coma. After spending the morning baking brownies for the party at Gina's, the bulk of my afternoon was spent with Sally, doing each other's hair and nails. Now I truly feel like I'm Elizabeth Taylor.

I came dangerously close to bursting while talking to Sally. Fibbing about a crush on Jim Douglas, who will be at the party, and the hope for some New Year's Eve magic seemed to work as damage control.

It's a bummer that Sally can't be at this bash. Though I'll have Donovan with me, and we won't be there long, it would be nice to have her around. Her familiar presence would make him feel less out of place among a bunch of underclassmen.

With an hour and a half to go before our charade begins, Mom is abuzz with commentaries at dinner about how I'm spending my evening. She's almost begging for an invitation to my teenage party so she won't be stuck with Dad's stodgy friends. Dad seems grumpy. He probably doesn't want to be with his friends either. How sad is that?

"Oh," Mom says, "and there was this one party where the boy I was dating had a fake ID and had bought a keg—"

"Lana!"

"Well, Edward, do you really think kids today are any different? We've raised ours to do the right things. It's not like their friends aren't like the kids we grew up with."

I expect to exchange a snicker with Donovan, but he's lost in his own thoughts. The Human Eating Machine barely took any food and hasn't devoured a bite. All he has done is create little mounds with it—only to then separate each morsel, making his plate look like a puzzle of atoms. He continuously repeats the process of building up and tearing down. His expression brands the sight as metaphorical.

As Mom and I clear the table, Donovan lags behind, taking in the destruction on this plate. He then brings his carnage into the kitchen and dodges past me with his head low. He tilts the plate over the wastebasket and looks as if he's watching his life's fortune flush down the drain. After setting his plate in the dishwasher, he heads off.

My gut churns over the display. Donovan gets a little despondent when Dad reams him for something lame, but I feel this upset has little to do with Dad's ideals.

I have my hands in dishwater when Donovan reenters the kitchen and speaks to me from the other side of the room. "I'm taking off now. Mom and Dad are going to drop you at Gina's. I need to get to Joe's early and help him set up. Happy New Year."

What? This isn't the plan. We're not supposed to leave for almost an hour. Maybe he feels the scheme is a little too obvious, and it brought on the doldrums during dinner. I'm sure he will meet me at Gina's later. He'll probably send a text message.

The hour passes and my transformation into a princess is complete. For as dolled up and mature as I look in my deep violet dress, stilettos, and updo, feelings of toddlerhood grip me upon exiting the backseat of my parent's pumpkin mobile. As they drive off I sneak over to the side of Gina's house and ring Donovan's cell. The call goes straight to voicemail. I leave him a message, asking what the new plan is, before heading inside.

Mountains of coats, gloves, and purses almost cause me to stumble through the foyer. The place is so packed that the path through the living room and into the kitchen is barely maneuverable without dropping my plate of brownies. Three guys stand in the corner while futzing with a keg, unable to grasp the concept of a tap. Now I really wish Sally was here.

My cell phone still reflects a lack of reply from Donovan while the morons at the keg wonder if they need an ice pick to open it. I flee the kitchen on a quest for familiar faces.

Gina waves wildly and tries to dodge her way over like she is about to burst with news. "Lily! I thought you'd never get here. I have a message for you."

I knew Donovan wouldn't fail me.

Gina's dress is flattering as the emerald green accentuates her lime eyes and dark features. She made a great choice. "Hi, Gina. Happy New Year. Great dress!"

"Thanks, you really like it?" she asks with a crooked beam darting out of her eyes. There seems to be a source of alcohol other than the keg.

"I do. You look fantastic. What's the message?"

"Jim Douglas is looking for you. I think he likes you."

Ugh. How is that for irony? Sally probably got the word out, thinking she was doing me a favor. He's cute, but there isn't an interested bone in my body.

I visit with my friends before excusing myself to the bathroom. On the way, I peek into my purse only to find there are still no messages.

Well, when in Rome … I'm relieved that someone got a clue with the tap and didn't attack it with a fire ax. I start partaking in a small cup when none other than Jim Douglas approaches me.

"Hey, Lily. I was wondering if you were coming. How was your Christmas?"

I tingle at the memory of the amazing day that filled me with hope for the New Year.

"Oh, the usual. How about you? Did you get everything you wanted?" I repress a gag while taking a sip of beer. I've heard of two-dollar wine, but if they paid more than that for this keg they were robbed.

"Not quite. I did pretty well, but I'm hoping to make up for it tonight. You didn't bring a date, did you? Maybe we can hang out a little." He asserts himself by touching my arm and playing with the short sleeve of my dress like his only thoughts are of removing it. This guy is as transparent as egg whites. For his sake, I hope he doesn't possess their other characteristics as well.

"Sounds great, Jim. Oh, my phone is buzzing. Will you excuse me?" Talk about saved by the bell. Donovan never fails me.

I feel tricked when I look at my phone. The buzz was a text from Sally wishing me a happy New Year. While returning the sentiment I notice that it's eleven forty-six. If Donovan is going to show, he doesn't have much time.

My eyes begin to sting. It's time to stop kidding myself. Denial has been my best friend tonight, and it just ran out on me. It's far too obvious that the man who, in sixteen and a half years, has never let me down, has just stood me up.

I grab my coat and slip outside to call Donovan one last time before conceding to the truth. The phone rings a long time before going to voicemail.

"Donovan, it's Lily. It's obvious that you aren't coming. If you want to chicken out, I get it, but at least tell me. You've never left me hanging before. Please don't do it now. Not over this. If there has ever been a time I needed you to talk to me, it's now."

My body shivers as I lean against a lamppost and watch the fog in my brain respire through my mouth. The party holds nothing worth returning to. I'm less than two miles from home, and I just want to curl up in bed and cry. I take off my new shoes that beautifully match the outfit I was so proud of. My feet turn numb as I head down the snow-covered sidewalk.

Shortly into my journey, my phone buzzes with a text from Donovan.

"I can't do this. I'm sorry, but it's over. Happy New Year."

Countdowns blast from the houses around me as I sit on the curb and stare at the message. I almost wonder if someone stole his phone and is putting me on. The Donovan I know would never do this to me. Maybe my love has broken him. My tears show it certainly has broken me.

8

The end of January is a crappy time for a heater to go out. Even with thick PJs, a robe, and two blankets over me, I'm still an icicle. Hopefully this warm milk will help me sleep. If I had half a brain, I'd sneak into the liquor cabinet and dump some brandy in it. At least then I might not care. Then again, if I can just make it back to my room without tripping over all these blankets and rolling down the stairs like a giant strawberry only to have my brain ooze out as I crack my head open, then I shouldn't complain.

I start to enter my room and Donovan emerges from the bathroom. He looks more miserable than I do. "Man, it's cold! Can't you sleep either?" I ask.

"No." His tone feels like a venomous sting.

"Want something to keep you warm?" His blood-curdling glare is an unwarranted response to my innocent question. His face drops upon seeing my steaming cup. Then, as if a button was pressed, his expression snaps back to being dismal.

"If you want warmth, maybe you should get a dog," he growls before returning to his room.

"At least the house has an excuse to be cold!" I slam my door, thus probably waking the whole house. Considering Donovan's recent attitude it should be of no shock to anyone for me to be upset over something he's said. It's bad enough that I'm such a barbaric creature that would succumb to letting myself get all zigzagged by some guy, but to allow that creep to be my brother is seriously mental. What the hell is my reasoning? Especially with the way he's been acting. And to think that men have the audacity to say women are nuts. Men are testosterone-driven whack jobs!

Ever since Donovan bailed on New Year's Eve, he's turned into the prick of the universe. Now, between guitar lessons, sports, and God knows what, Donovan disappears almost every night. When I do see him, it's like playing Russian roulette as to if he'll be sweet and tender, or mean and almost vindictive. Is he is tying to destroy my spirit?

My life sucks. Seriously. Screw my life! I don't want to face tomorrow. The last thing I want is to deal with Donovan. If he's a jerk again I'll likely strangle him—while driving even—until his face turns blue and his eyes pop out! If he's nice, he'll make me feel secure and fuzzy inside; then, I'll try to get him to talk, and he'll revert to being a dick, and I'll be back at the notion of strangling him. I'm screwed.

When morning comes, I brace myself before bolting downstairs. I expect to see Donovan in the kitchen, eating his breakfast. Instead, my mom, who often switches between trying to be a nineteen fifties' housewife and my giddy best friend, greets me with false cheer. "Good morning, darling! Oh, you don't look well. Did you have a bad night with the heat out?"

I reach for the coffee, intending to take my cup upstairs as quickly as possible. "Good morning, Mom. It was very bitter and sharp last night."

"Oh, I'm sorry, dear. Grab some breakfast, and let's get going. We should leave soon."

"We? I thought Donovan was driving?" Has it really come to this?

"Oh no, dear. He left early. Didn't he tell you he had an early practice? We can go, and I'll let you drive. It's been too long since we had mother and daughter time. Let's make up for it this afternoon and go buy all the stuff we wanted for Christmas and didn't get. Doesn't that sound like fun?"

Actually, it sounds impossible. No mall sells what I wanted, and if it does it's located somewhere off of the Vegas strip or in the pits of Hell.

At least the upside of all of this is that Mom is letting me drive. It sucks that I can't drive with Donovan while he's still seventeen. It's actually less safe this way, as Mom's hounding gives me the jitters. She warns about every bump and pothole in the entire state.

When we arrive at school, I bolt from the car and try to shiver off the anxiety Mom gave me. Gina runs up. "Did you see the big commotion going on in the park across the street?"

Geez, just what the doctor ordered—more drama. About twenty people are gathered, and a lot of screaming and cheering is going on. Sally hangs toward the back of the crowd, sees me, and runs over. "Lily, you need to get over there fast. No one has been able to break this up."

"Why would I want to get involved in someone's fight?"

"You don't know? Donovan and David Watts have been going at it. David insulted the football team yesterday, and Donovan challenged him to a fight this morning. He's beating the crap out of him. No one has been able to pull him off."

What? Donovan never fights and certainly wouldn't care about an insult. His team pride is minuscule.

I sprint across the street—almost getting hit by a car in my anxiety. When I reach the front of the crowd, Donovan looks fiery as he repeatedly bangs David's head onto the ground. Thank God this isn't on concrete. I throw down my books and try to pry Donovan off of the guy. Donovan jumps up and almost swings before realizing who it is and halting.

I've already ducked, and choose to stay frozen until I'm sure it is safe to raise my head. His eyes look hollow as he bites his lip and looks to the ground. He can feel my heart sinking.

Donovan takes a moment to look at the bloody man lying on the grass. David seems to be shaking off the effects of his abuser. Thank God.

With a flip of his hair, Donovan storms away.

What the hell is happening to him?

My day continues downhill. After forgetting the dissertation that half my night was spent struggling over, the snoring that woke me during my trigonometry test was my own. This is the real clinker though. I'm in no social mood, but Sally insists that a little privacy and some good conversation will ease my tension. Thus, she's dragged me into a deserted science lab to eat our lunch. The gesture is sweet, but the room reeks like a chemical toilet. I'm afraid to set my food down for fear of what's been annihilated, or possibly even bred, on these counters.

"What are you doing this weekend? Anything fun?" she asks before taking a bite out of a vile-looking baloney on white sandwich. Why do so many people have mediocre taste in food?

After taking a peek at my own blasphemous meal, I push it aside. "Not really. Mom wants to go shopping this afternoon, which is code for wanting to talk. So if that's any indication, I might as well stay here and pray for Monday to come mercifully fast."

"I know what you mean. My mom drives me crazy too. I thought you and your mom got along though." Sally looks at her sandwich in disgust and discards it for an apple. There's hope for her yet.

"We do, but she's been acting oddly. My whole family's been whacked out of their minds. I should have the water checked."

Sally's Betty Boop-ish voice suddenly sounds abrasive. "Speaking of your family, what's the deal with Donovan? He used to be such a great guy, and now he's turned into a total jerk."

"Just because he got into a stupid fight doesn't mean—"

"It's way worse than that. He's totally changed. Remember when we both got dumped right before the Sweetheart's Dance last year? Donovan could have asked anyone, but instead he took us both and was totally sweet. He was the nicest guy in school, but now he hangs out with the shady creeps from the team and is completely rude.

41

Jason said he's been like that since after Christmas break. He also said Donovan humiliated Alana Langton. It used to be if he wasn't interested in someone, he was still nice. This time, he was just horrible. When did your brother become such an ass?"

Can't I please get through the day without any more Donovan madness? "I've no excuses for him," I say, curtly. "Can we talk about something else?"

"I'm sorry. This must be what's been bugging you for the last few weeks."

"Yeah. Talk to me about anything else, okay?"

Lunch is survived by pretending to be happy about the silly things we discuss; like crushes on movie stars and celebrity gossip—stuff we have no real interest in. On the way to class, I duck into the bathroom in need of a moment to shake off the brick of reality that Sally just did a roundhouse on my face with. The notion of us talking about the same Donovan is unfathomable.

Inside a stall, I slam my head back against the divider. What's wrong with me? This is my brother and not some breathtaking celebrity that I don't share genes with. How is it that this is finally sinking in? It makes me feel ill. Is this how Donovan feels and why he's turned? It would explain an abundance about his behavior if he's so repulsed by his own desires that they've lead him into an internal civil war.

I almost hope that I'm just delusional. I don't want Donovan to feel this horrible way. But if he thinks I'm crazy or deviant, he needs to do some self-exploration into his own actions and find his real emotions tucked away.

Enough already! World be damned! If anyone finds my feelings wrong, gross, disgusting, or immoral, that's their problem. The only opinion that deserves my respect is Donovan's. It's not our fault we have the same parents. Screw everyone else!

But Donovan won't share his feelings, and it causes depression to swarm over me like killer bees.

Please God, no matter what it is, someway, somehow, send me the truth. Don't let me go to my grave not knowing.

&

I get into the driver's seat of Mom's car while pretending that everything is in tact, despite the madness that surrounds me. Whatever my derailed mom has in mind, be it an ambush or an inquisition, I'm as ready to get this over with as can be.

I'm actually praying for an ambush—one that tells me what the crap Donovan's deal is. A drug problem would almost be welcome news. Maybe he's been the victim of a mad science experiment. Or possibly Dad has finally put him over the edge with talk of him not being manly enough, and he's given up and in the middle of hormone therapy for a sex change operation. Whatever the reason for his madness, it may well be why I've been summoned.

The conversation begins with the predictable questions. The all-important one being: "Where shall we blow our diets?" Herein lies the trap, as this is where "The Talk" will happen. I suggest an ice cream parlor. Since it's nowhere near a mall and doesn't serve that ridiculous stuff referred to as frozen yogurt, it's the least likely place to run into my peers.

Once seated, it doesn't take Mom long to put on her "concerned mother" face and begin. "Lily, I hope this doesn't feel like an inquisition, but let me just come out and say it so we can get this over with. I know there is something you are struggling with. Honey, I don't want to press, but please, whatever it is, let's talk."

Damn. It's exactly as feared. That's all right. I'll throw her off her guard in a heartbeat by telling her the truth—sort of.

"Men suck!" Dashes of truth fly out while I fabricate numerous details to avoid the reality that would likely make Mom's brain hemorrhage, sending her into convulsions, and causing her to die on the spot. I speak of a boy named

George, claiming he was named after George Harrison. It will totally suck her in. British men are her weak spot—especially ones who were in their twenties when she was a child.

I met George in the fall. It was amazingly romantic when our eyes met. He always paid so much attention to me and made me feel special. Just when it seemed safe to care, he backed away. Now he's seeing someone else and the whole thing is just devastating.

Mom's big reaction to the drama is, "Are you sure that is all? It seems like with how you've been acting there should be more."

"Gee, Mom, thanks for belittling my grief," I groan, slouching in my seat and tossing my spoon into my cup of half-eaten ice cream.

"I'm sorry, dear. It's just that you've been upset, and your father and I are concerned. You used to be so good at talking to me about things."

It's true. We used to talk a lot about what she thought was everything. We've always had a good mother/daughter relationship, but the last few years she's been a little too interested in being one of my peers. She is not very good at being ageless, though she longs to be. I actually feel for her and wish there was a way to help, but I don't have her answers.

Agony over Donovan is causing my emotions to surface regardless of my desires. I've no choice but to accept that if I can't stop them, I'd better control where they go. "No, Mom. For stuff like this Donovan was always there, no matter how stupid or serious the problem. But now he's become so mean. I just don't know what's happened to him."

My tears from last night attempt to resume. I seem to be all cried out—though my eyes feel streaked with fire.

"Darling, a man isn't the right person to talk to about matters of your heart. What about one of your other friends? Have you—"

"Are you kidding? The last time my heart was broken, Donovan found me sobbing outside and let me scream into his shoulder because he knew I needed it. And when I said I'd lost my heart forever, he told me he could fix everything. He ran into the house. When he came back, he said he had found it and stashed it in his drawer, since he didn't know who it belonged to. Then he put one of those stupid candy hearts that everyone gets a box of on Valentine's Day in my hand. God knows how old that thing was. It said 'Miss You' on it, and he claimed I needed to eat it in order for it to work again. It was the stupidest thing ever. He even held it up in front of my face and talked in this goofy voice about how it wanted to come home. I ate that damn heart just to shut him up, and by the time I swallowed that disgusting thing I was almost entirely fine.

"But he didn't stop there. He gave me a lecture on self-worth, and how I should never be the girl who cries over some lame guy because I deserve better. We've always been there for each other. Damn it! I need him again. He won't talk to me, and I don't understand why. I had the best friend in the world, and now he's slipping away."

I divert my eyes, ashamed of how much the sister in me loves the brother in him. Mom clutches the napkin she's been using as a tissue, fidgeting with its edge. "I—I had no idea that he could be so sweet or that he had become so distant. He and your father have been very busy getting him setup with a college. He's also been forcing Donovan to get some academic assistance and is really harping on him about his grades and making career decisions. You know how your father can be. That's probably all it is, but I actually hoped you would know more. Lily, is your being upset really just over George dumping you and you not being able to talk about it? Are you sure that—"

At least now there is insight as to Dr. Jekyll and Mr. Hiding; but I know Donovan, and there's a lot more to it. Now another problem commands my attention—the one right across from me. The nervous look still on Mom's face sold out the true nature of her questioning long ago. Since my answers are not to be found, it's time to end the charade and spit out what she seeks.

"MomIamstillavirgin."

The color returns to her face. Yep, that's what it all came down to. My heart can be shattered, and I can be without my best friend, but as long as I'm still a virgin, all is right in her world. In fact, Mom now looks almost radiant. "Is there anything else you want to talk about?" she asks.

"Yes." The twinkle forced to invade my eyes sells my lie. "What exactly are we shopping for?"

Mom's luminosity tells she wants to charge something pretty and shiny to Dad's credit card. "I hear there's a dance coming up. Shall we get you a new dress?"

I agree and force an upturn of the lips despite the stake that Donovan jabbed into my heart. But Mom's content as she walks with the swing of a fifties teenager and grabs my hand. "Got a date yet?" she asks, sounding more like a teenybopper friend than a mother.

"No, but there are a few boys I have my eyes on. I just haven't decided which one I am going to bewitch into taking me."

Thoughts of continuing the charade cause my gut to grip and twist, and I force down the sick in my stomach. Can I maintain the charade and keep my breaking point at bay?

History has shown it is hard it is to hide my emotions. Heaven help us all when I fail.

9

I practically scream under my breath, "I can't believe you're taking one of the Bimbo Brigade to the Sweetheart Dance!"

Donovan snips in my ear, "What was I supposed to do, take *you*? No, that wouldn't be awkward at all."

"No. But do you really need to take *her*? Let alone announce it at dinner like it is an applause-worthy accomplishment?"

"What's wrong with her? Just because she's totally hot and completely brainless is no reason for her not to have a date with a guy who pretty much can't stand her. I thought you'd be happy I'm taking someone I despise. Besides, what's wrong with Brittny?"

"Well, for one, her name is Brittny. Two, she's a total slut. Three, she's brainless. Four, that blonde hair on her head is bleached. Five, I hear she bleaches it elsewhere. Six—Oh, wipe that smirk off your face!"

"Please, keep going. Don't hold back on my account."

"Ugh!" I storm out of the den, slamming the door with intense reverb.

An hour later, Donovan sprints past my room to announce that dinner is almost ready. He tries to dash away while ignoring my call for him to stop. But when I grab his arm, saying that I'm serious and talking can't wait anymore, my touch halts him in his tracks.

I drag him into my room and close the door. "We need to talk about what's happening. You've changed and not just toward me. Others have noticed it too."

His expression morphs as he stares down at me with eyes that are icy with condescension. "Lily, what are you talking about?"

47

"I know you've been hanging out with some sketchy people and you keep coming home battered. Every time I see you, there is a new bruise or gash."

"Lily, get serious. What the hell is your problem?" He sneers while bolting for the door.

Feeling every bit of my being becoming weak, my mouth forces out the subject closest to my heart. He's roller-coastering; meaning if I stay strong there is a chance of getting to his core. I'm learning him all over again. "Then why are you pulling me so close only to shove me back so hard? I don't understand why you're becoming so cruel. It is like you—"

"Lil, look. You and I, we can't happen. Nothing has happened. Nothing can. It's time you faced that." He stops me from interjecting. He's about to shatter my heart, again. "No, Lil. You *have* to listen." Swallowing his pride, his emotions mutate before me. With both of my hands in one of his, he caresses my hair with his other. "You need to find a guy who you can really love and who will care for you. Don't give your love to just anyone. Make sure he's worthy." He leans in and delicately kisses my cheek, allowing his lips to linger before pulling away.

My lips pinch together to mute my true emotions. I'm hurt. I'm angry. Worst of all, I'm swooning, but I can't let him see that. My agitation requires acceleration so his will remain low. "What, like that bimbo is worthy?"

"Really, Lily. It's not what you think, and it's not what I want, but it has to be this way."

He couldn't possibly have meant the words that are now stamped into my mind. He's my shelter, my sanctuary. How could the power of our emotions possibly evade him? I exaggerate the size of the lump in my throat so I can ride his sea-saw. Besides, if I can stay focused on keeping him calm, maybe I won't break. "No. No, it doesn't. You know it doesn't."

"Yes, Lily. It does." Placing his forehead to mine his tears sting as they trail down my face, merging with my own.

The fragments of two hearts that have been shattered into millions of pieces lay on the floor before us.

ॐ

Mission accomplished, in spades. My date for the dance is one that's going to make Donovan greener than mold. Al's attractive, popular, smarter than Donovan, and a senior. He's also on the football team and gave Donovan a run for his money as to who's the better player. As a result, Al may just steal that scholarship Donovan hopes he'll get.

My stomach churns. I can't stand being petty and horrible, but my shredded insides are bringing about desperation. How can I sit here and watch while he is moving on? Especially since he is throwing it in my face.

Man, I hate Brittny! She makes me feel like my claws are popping out, and I want to gouge the girl's eyes. She's just too skinny. Every time she's near I mutter, "Eat a sandwich!" under my breath.

The fact that she's a first class, Grade A tramp also has a lot to do with it. She always wears ridiculously short skirts and too much make-up. What Donovan sees in her is beyond my comprehension. However, he did say he asked someone he couldn't stand. But then again, she's a slutty tramp and Donovan's a hot teenage man. The thought of Donovan with Brittny and her sleazy, nonexistent morals is just abhorrent.

She'll probably look like a whore, and Donovan hates that. I possess the unfair advantage of knowing what he likes; just enough skin and makeup to be alluring and for a lady to show off what she has without looking like she wants to sell it. My classic, yet somewhat criminal, strapless little black dress exposes just enough cleavage, leg, and curves to make him pant for more.

I emerge from the bathroom, and Donovan stutters to find words. "Wow! You look amazing. Umm, uh, are you going out?"

"Yes. Maybe you heard that there's a dance tonight. I believe you have a date." Or rather, a prostitute.

"Yeah, but I, uh—I didn't realize you were going."

Donovan looks itchy. Does he have a rash? Can I get that lucky? "Yes, I have a date and everything." My voice sounds bubbly.

Slipping away now proves to be the perfect tease as I notice him slowly gawking over my figure—his eyes drifting from my curves to the seams in my stockings, down to the rhinestone bows adorning the back of my heels.

"Wow. Uh. That's er, um, great," he says while raising his eyebrows and shaking his head to discard the sin from his mind. "Who are you going with?"

Could he be more panicked? My increased confidence bursts forth as I look straight at his gorgeous face and beam, "Oh, Al Thompson asked me. He's kind of cute, so I said yes."

Donovan's jaw abandons his face and just about shatters on the hall floor. "Al Thompson? From the football team?"

"I forgot he played football. I guess you know him." Boy, do I ever think I'm clever!

"Do I know him?" Donovan not only rolls his eyes at me but his whole head. "Lily!"

"What?" Seriously, this is great!

He looks like he's about to go into convulsions as he throws his hands into the air and talks toward God. "Lily, this isn't funny. God! Why Al? Of all the guys in the world!"

Have I blown it? Is Al some kind of lunatic? Does he kill babies? Does he eat live bunnies? What could possibly be so upsetting about him? "I don't understand," I mutter.

Donovan latches on to my shoulders. For a moment, I'm convinced he'll beg me not to go out with this horrible alien creature that performs beastly acts. "Lil, remember when I was in the first grade, and I got busted for jumping in the mud puddles at school and covering someone in filth when it was a total accident? Al was the guy who ratted me out and said I nailed him intentionally. I missed out on cartoons for a week because of him."

I burst out in laughter over Donovan's little tizzy and the karma that is kicking him in the butt. He's upset because he missed out on cartoons over ten years ago? I thought he was my older brother, not a toddler. My date selection could not be more brilliant!

"All right, all right. That's enough." A smirk shows through his scowl. Drying the streaks of hysteria from my face, he attempts to fix my smudged make up. "At least for once I'm drying happy tears. I guess the universe decided to check me to the boards on that one. You might want to touch this up yourself. Although, since it is Al, I kind of like the idea of you going out looking like Alice Cooper."

"Cute. I'll go touch up. He should be here any moment."

"Hey, be careful, okay? I'm not too sure of this guy. I don't want you to get into a bad situation."

"I'll be fine. I kind of need my hand back though." Donovan's been holding it since right after he grabbed me by the shoulders.

"Oh, sorry."

"Yeah?" I walk away with hips in a full and gentle swing, holding the saunter just long enough for him to notice before I turn my glance back to him. His eyes are locked on my figure. "I don't think you are."

The school gym is alive with lights and sounds emulating from a giant pulsating cocoon that creates trapping boundaries. Didn't streamers and balloons go out of style decades ago? They live on here in numerous burst of color giving life to the chamber of near darkness that is lined by bleachers and couples who really should get a room. It is almost haunting how the place is lit enough to see halfway across it, but effort is required to look for something, or someone, specific. Masochistically, I could seek out Donovan, else it's almost as easy to let the sea of faces blend and to try to forget he's here.

My date selection is an interesting one. When Al picked me up he did everything the way a gentleman should; he rang the doorbell instead of honking the car horn, was polite to my parents, repeated the time I needed to be home like a trained bird, and held my doors open. He was even considerate enough to ask if I wanted vodka or brandy in the flask he brought for me. Oh, and did he tell me how stunning my ass looks in this dress? Al is so charming that I've triple-checked that I have enough money for cab fare home and verified my cell phone is fully charged.

We've been here less than thirty minutes, and I'm already beyond bored. Al's friends are idiots, and he's the cream of the scum crop. I feel like a hood ornament as he parades me around introducing me as "D-boy's lil' sis." Yuck! There's no way Donovan likes being called D-boy. When this madness is over I'm going to bust out with that one frequently and at awkward moments. It's become one of the many things Donovan is never living down.

"You lookin' for something, baby?" Al asks with a slur as I eye the room. My first thought is of a fire escape.

"I just thought I would see what my friends are up to."

"You mean those cute little *chickas* I saw you with the other day? Well let's find 'em!"

We walk about five feet before we run into another group of guys from the football team. "Hey, it's Al and D-boy's lil' sis!"

Random Jock #1 asks, "Where's that bro of yours?"

Random Jock #2 replies, "I saw him in the corner earlier with Brit-neeeey!"

"Whoooooooo!" The Jock Squad squawks in harmony.

"Hey, Al. You still got that extra flask on you?" I ask. Actually, at this point, I'm not too proud to beg.

"Absolutely, my fair lady. This one has brandy. Would you like the one with vodka instead? I still have about half left."

Wow. I never realized what a gentleman a lush could be.

"Brandy's great." Shoot battery acid would be great. I've no qualms about downing half of it quickly.

The burn of the alcohol creeps down my throat, nearly causing me to gag. But if I'm going to suffer through this horrendous night, I might as well not care about it. It doesn't take long for the brandy to kick in, and just as it does, D-boy and Slut Face stroll by.

"Heeey D-boy!" There's that delightful harmony again. The sound of the accompanying high-fives is even more sickening, but the sight of D-boy and his date makes me think gastrointestinal anthrax is kicking in. Hoe Bag's skin tight, low cut, black and red striped cotton sling that she calls a dress barely covers her ass and shows the outline of every bone squeezed underneath it. At the sight of me, Donovan quickly drops his arm from Brittny's nearly non-existent waist as if he's five and Mom caught him stealing cookies.

D-boy cowers while making excuses to leave, but Brittny obviously has other intentions. Clinging like a black widow's web, she rubs against Donovan while talking to the other boys. It's like her personal experiment in their voyeurism, and they're eating it up. Now I've had it! In Donovan's full view, I pull out my flask and take a long sip, trying to maintain my composure as the alcohol blisters a trail downward. Instead of awaiting his reaction, I excuse myself to the ladies room. "Be right back." I wink at Al. "Miss me."

Walking away with my head high and hips in full wiggle, complete satisfaction is achieved as I hear all the attention, via catcalls, turn in my direction. D-boy squirms as the tide of domination turns.

Ten minutes later, while trying to clear my brain and focus on the hands of my watch that seem to have multiplied, I realize how long I've been fuming in a stall. Once I brave enough courage to return to my date, D-boy and Scum Bucket are long gone. Which is worse—having to watch that vile display or not knowing what Donovan is doing? Polishing off the last bit of brandy, I take a good, long, sour look at my date. It's time to make lemonade.

I give Al's arm a tug. "Hey, Al. Come on. Let's dance."

"Nah, I really don't like to dance."

"You will with me." As if the pant in his ear was not enough, the look I give that makes him quiver like bacon hitting a hot skillet seals the deal.

Al's dance skills make him look like a duck impersonating a turtle. My impending actions with this creep make me itch. With my arms around his neck, I gyrate in the vicinity of parts of his anatomy that are best not pondered. It's the most disgusting thing I've ever done, but how else do I break free of Donovan's hold? After all, if he can get his jollies, why shouldn't I?

Al maneuvers his right leg between both of mine, rubbing it against my crotch. I'm compelled to flee but suck it up and make his ear my new focal point. Not enough of the alcohol has kicked in to make him sufficiently attractive for me to actually want to do this. Just as enough courage is mustered to hone in on Al's lips, a hand sharply yanks me away. Thank God!

"Come on, Lil. Time to break it up." Donovan is trying to keep his cool, but his terse voice sells him out. Removing myself from his hold is easy. Of course he would not anticipate resistance. He expects me to follow him like a good puppy.

"Donovan, I'm fine. Please leave me alone."

"You don't seem fine. You need to go home."

His forcefulness makes me undress him with my mind.

Wait. That self-righteous bastard! Did he really say, "*You* need to go home?" and not "*I'm* going to take you home?" What am I supposed to do, walk?

"I'm not going home. I'm fine." The slur in my voice almost makes it inaudible. I turn to go back to Al.

Donovan puts an arm around my waist as if I'm a delicate doll made of glass. His tenderness is killing me, and he knows it. He always sees through me, which makes me a little paranoid about how earnestly he's taking this situation.

Therefore, I must believe him when his words penetrate me with all the love of a big brother. "Lily, I don't think you know what you're doing.

My brain starts to whirl. Donovan's right, but it's too late. Pent up emotions are about to control my voice. My cottony tongue somehow manages to slur the words in a whisper so soft my own ears can barely discern them. "Donovan, tonight I'm going to lose my virginity, and it will be either to you, or him. You get to decide which, but you have to do it now."

My insides quiver as I walk away. Is he calling my bluff? Is he so annoyed that he gave up and left, only to pick up the trollop in retaliation? Al's just about to slip his arms around my hips when I'm swept off my feet and plopped down out of the way. Donovan's eyes are so ablaze that they actually look scorching. "Don't you dare touch her!"

"Come on, D-boy. I'm your friend. Cut me some slack. You don't want to hurt me." Al's sentence sounds like the smear of a bug that has been stepped on and dragged with the bottom of a shoe.

"And you don't want to fight me Al, 'cause I'll kill you." The gathering crowd cringes as the resonance in his voice proves Donovan means every bit of it. This is the new Donovan—the one who turns into the Incredible Hulk. It's the polar opposite of his true ego that existed as little as two months ago. Did I unleash the monster again? I'm so disoriented that I can't do anything to stop it.

I used to wonder what my breaking point was. Now I see I found it when Donovan broke character so dramatically he put on a show of dating someone whose morals go against the grain of his being. I figured the world had spun out of control for him. Without realizing what I was doing, I threw myself in the same predicament.

But what if this isn't it? What if this is the tip of the iceberg for me?

Thankfully, Donovan shows he still has his priorities. Without hesitation, he swings around, swoops me into his arms, and leaves the gym with his damsel.

I'm nuzzled in Donovan's arms when we arrive at the car. He feels heavenly, like on Christmas night when we were on the verge of wonderment. But my heart sinks as he opens the car door and places me inside like a piece of coral—fragile yet jagged. "Noooo. Please don't let me go."

"It's all right, Lil. I'm going to take you home. Let's get you buckled in all nice and safe. You're going to be just fine. And if you're lucky, I won't kill you before dawn."

Halfway home, the haze is forced away enough to snuggle my head into his shoulder. "Please don't take me home."

"Where am I supposed to take you?" His tone tells me he's deservedly angry, yet feeling responsible for my actions and doesn't want to hurt me anymore. It plays into my wasted, one-track mind.

"Take me someplace where we can be alone. Take me to the top of that hill over there, and hold me all night. Wake me with gentle kisses and caresses in the morning. I just want to love you, and you won't let me. Why won't you let me?"

"Lily, you know I can't do that." In my stupor, his voice is like satin, making his harsh words seem hopeful, but the alcohol rushing through me makes me irrational.

"No. No, I don't. You have yet to give me a single good reason."

"Lily, please stop."

"No, you stop!" Losing control of my sanity, I yank the steering wheel. Donovan needs to pull over and talk to me. But I've caught him off guard, and the car swerves wildly. My heart goes into my throat, and I quickly regret ever setting my sights on Al.

When he regains control, Donovan pulls over and grabs me by the shoulders. His eyes pierce through my soul while his hands rattle my body. Now I fear he will be the one to lose all control. "Are you insane? Stop and think for two seconds about what you're doing! Dear God, how wasted are you?"

I'm too gone to question the best way to handle him now. Instead, I start screaming all the things I've wanted to for months. "Maybe you're the one who needs to stop, Donovan! You need to stop and think for two seconds about what you're doing and face reality! Stop being mean and angry all the time! Stop fighting with everyone! Stop breaking my heart every time you come home wounded! Stop hiding from me! Stop hiding from yourself! Just let everyone see who you really are!"

Again, the seesaw works. Resentment shows in Donovan's eyes, acknowledging that I'm right. Pulling me close, he captivates me while delving into my soul. "Lily, I am so, so sorry. Please forgive me."

His pulse is thundering with a desire that cannot be suppressed, no matter how hard he tries to hide his pain. Finally, I've won the war. His amazing, oceanic eyes that glow in the moonlight turn their gaze upon my lips. His lips part, and suddenly I'm headbutted unconscious.

ಌ

"Rise and shine sleepy head!" Donovan's perky voice springs from an obnoxious blob that whips open my bedroom curtains.

"Uuugh. Stop singing so loudly! Who brought in a spotlight?"

Donovan is what he probably thinks is charmingly flippant as he strolls over with a glass of water and two aspirin. "How's my sweet and innocent little sister today? Oh, wait, I don't have a sweet and innocent little sister anymore."

"Don't be mean," I moan in absolute agony, covering my face from the sunlight with my pillow.

The bounce as he sits on my bed makes my stomach flip like a pancake, and the thought of pancakes almost makes me sick. Mercifully, Donovan lowers his snippy voice as he lays into me. "You're the one who got totally wasted, dirty danced with a sick perv, gave me an ultimatum, and then practically forced me to leave my date to drag your sorry ass home."

I can't lift the haze in my head. Everything I say sounds like it's muttered in slow motion by a grizzly bear. "Wait. What did I do?"

"Let's start with what you think you did. Tell me that, and then I'll fill in the blanks."

"Ummmm, I got wasted? Al had two flasks. Mine had brandy. I think I finished it. I danced with him. Is that it?"

"Noooooo. That's definitely not it."

Suddenly I gasp and almost spring from the bed, but a ton of bricks hits my head and snacks me back down. "Oh, gross! Please don't tell me I slept with Al!"

Where is my garbage can?

"As tempting as it is to make you think so, no, you didn't. You did, however, almost do the nasty with him on the dance floor. Don't worry, I got to you before your clothes came off, but not by much."

"Oh God! How'd I get home?"

"That would be your brother in shining armor. You don't remember the ride home?"

"Not a second of it. What happened to Al?"

"Why do you care? Don't tell me you actually like that guy." Judging by his tone, the look on his face must be incredulous, but my eyes are still too blurry to tell.

"Oh, man! He's so gross. I don't know what I was thinking."

"Ready to be really disgusted? I dumped you on the sofa and then went back to get Brittny, but I should have saved the gas money. She'd already left with Al who should be waking up at her house, oh, about now."

"Ewww! That's disgusting! I guess I ruined your night. Sorry." Actually, no—I'm not. He deserved it as much as I deserve this hangover.

"It was a pretty bad night. Sadly though, you actually

saved it. Brittny's a skank! I can't believe I was going to sleep with her."

"What? No way!" He's serious, and that's not Donovan. He's no angel, but how could he even consider giving his virginity to a tramp? When it comes to romance, he's down right old-fashioned. Our situation's affect on him is unbelievable.

"Yeah, I actually was. But I will be eternally grateful to you, and your stupidity, for me not having gotten an STD." Donovan lowers his voice and places his lips near my ear. "Lily, we're a mess. We have to handle this better. Do you trust me?"

"You know I do."

"Then please believe that I know what I'm doing. I was wrong to throw Brittny at you. I didn't know what else to do. We need to go on with our lives as a normal brother and sister."

"You have yet to really talk to me. It just seems like if I understood better, it would be easier. Oh, man! Why does my head hurt so badly? I just want you to come out of hiding."

"I can't, Lil. I can't tell you what I'm feeling, and I can't be with you. Not now. I don't know when." His voice returns to what others must perceive as a normal volume. "You're just lucky Dad left for his business trip early this morning and missed the drama. But if you pull another stunt like this I'll turn you in. Get some sleep."

Once there is time to process everything, my heartache will return. Right now the guy using a nail gun on my head needs to go away.

"Wait! What ultimatum? And why does my forehead hurt so much? Did you headbutt me?"

"Yes, after you almost ran us into a tree."

Oh, dear God.

10

My life is unrecognizable. Donovan's smart. He's set up his life with military regimentation so it's easy for him to escape me and everyone else. Mondays and Thursdays he's off studying with a tutor. On Tuesdays he disappears to guitar lessons. Wednesdays his new girlfriend, some cute girly-girl named Lisa, comes over to study in his room where their obnoxious giggling is barely covered by the loud music they play. When the weekend comes, Donovan disappears almost entirely.

Ever since the morning after my drunken escapade, he's scarcely said a word to me. When he does, I've no idea what to expect. Often he sits across the table at dinner and sneaks looks at me through sad and longing eyes, yet there are other times when all I do is say "good morning" and he shoots me a glare that makes my blood chill.

Donovan's being invariably on edge and Dad's increasingly macho attitude are putting Mom constantly on her guard, making me apprehensive about everything. I can't remember when I've had a decent night's sleep, and my appetite disappeared weeks ago. My head feels eternally in a fog while the curves that I've always been so proud of slowly vaporize.

Dad keeps raving about the lovely Lisa with the adorable face and perfect body. If it goes on for another second, I'm going to lash out at him not only for his crudeness, but also for his lack of respect towards his wife. Dad treats Mom like a second-class citizen, and I don't understand why she accepts it. She was a Litigation Paralegal until she married in her late thirties. How she went from being self-sufficient to subservient escapes me. I should speak my mind, but my hands are wildly shaking. Maybe it's because I have to tell Donovan that dinner is ready.

For the last few days, Donovan's been a walking encyclopedia of dickdom. Steering clear of his wrath seems to be impossible, as he strives to be nasty to anyone within barking distance. The thought of approaching him gives me the willies, like looking at a furry spider.

In hopes of avoiding a fight, I write a simple note stating, "dinner is ready" and slide it under his bedroom door.

Instantly, Donovan emerges from his lair and starts roaring. "What the crap, Lil? Can't you even be bothered to tell me?" He crumples the note and savagely throws it on the floor. The action calls my attention to a sizeable contusion on his arm. Again? When did that one happen?

"I don't want any problems tonight, all right? The last few days have been rough enough."

"Oh, like your life is so freakin' hard! Poor little Lily, the fragile flower that can do no wrong. Trust me, you have no idea what a hard time is."

"I am sick and tired of never knowing what to expect with you! Yesterday, when I interrupted your concentration, you yelled at me and then shot me nasty looks all through dinner. I should have known better. It has to be incredibly hard for you to form a thought, let alone get it down on paper!"

"Well, now who's being Queen Bitch?"

He's never used language like that with anyone before. But Donovan's words are not nearly as painful as the spikes shooting from his eyes that vividly scream he feels I'm the most revolting thing on the planet. I'm unable to deal with any more insults, or yet another melt down, so walking away seems to be the best solution.

"Lily, wait—" He sounds regretful as he clutches my arm to stop me. He damn well should.

"Oh, are you going to fight *me* now? Why not? You've fought practically everyone else. Actually, save it until tomorrow so you can finally finish pushing the envelope and get expelled. You can lose your scholarship and be stuck home all the time. Then Lisa can start coming over on weekday afternoons too, just like your little session on Saturday."

"We didn't know you were home. Lisa never would have left my room like that if—"

"Just shut up! I think you've rubbed her in my face sufficiently. It's pitiful how you think you have to hide behind a girl you can't even pretend to love just to get me to go away. Once more, from the look on her face, I'm guessing you never finished the job. You're pathetic."

ॐ

My emotions are a ticking time bomb that's about to go off at any second. How dare Donovan suddenly announce at dinner he's leaving for college summer classes the day after graduation, which is tomorrow! Barring immediate clarifying conversation, he's leaving me hanging without resolution to the problems that plague us. That filthy bastard!

"Hey, can you turn down the volume on the freak out?"

Donovan's complaining because I'm making an utter racket while furiously cleaning the house. I really don't give a crap who hears. But now that I have his attention, I'm ready to roar.

"Excuse me?"

"You've been in the foulest of moods lately. What's the deal?" He sneers as he runs his eyes down my body.

"Foulest of moods? Well, at least your vocabulary has improved. That's quite a jump for you."

"What the?" He repeats the snooty look he gave a moment ago. His personal lexicon may have upgraded, but his range of body language still requires work.

"You want to know? I'll tell you, but I can't possibly believe that you're so stupid you haven't figured this out yourself. You and I used to be so incredibly close."

He changes his tone for fear of what I may say aloud. "Lily! Please lower your voice!"

I may be at my wits ends, but he knows me better than anyone, or at least he is supposed to. Of course I am not going to say anything stupid for our parents to hear. My volume continues. "All of our lives we were always there for each other, no matter what happened."

"Lily, I'm begging you. Please, please stop. At least yell at me quietly."

I continue discreetly without losing my drive. "One day, things changed in a rather unorthodox way, and you didn't seem to mind. Then, suddenly, you became a distant, self-serving asshole. It's bad enough you wouldn't talk to me about the changes I thought we were both experiencing, but now you never talk to me about anything. So, can you at least tell me if you're totally repulsed by my feelings? You have to see what I'm confronting. So many times it seems you feel the same way, but you won't say anything outright. I still catch you fixated on me, and I have to tell you it doesn't exactly feel like you're turned off—and now you're running away from me."

His eyes shut. They are accompanied by a hesitant swallow. "How did I ever let this happen? I'm not repulsed, but you're right. I am running."

"Then why won't you talk to me? We've always talked about everything. Crap, Donovan, you've told me some serious secrets and several have to be far more embarrassing than anything you're holding back now. Damn it! Everything else aside, I miss my best friend!"

While fumbling for words, he looks at the ground, the ceiling, out the window. Finally he speaks. His voice is laced with resignation. "Lily, you're right. You know me better than anyone else in the world, now and probably ever. Just remember that. If you really, really remember— Just look deep inside me, and you will know. Someday I will tell you everything. *I promise.* Until then, please don't stop believing in me. You're still the only one who ever has, and I know that more now than ever."

"Oh, stop with that believing-in-me crap! There has to be more going on than the obvious. You're either sad or angry, and you're constantly getting into fights. It's like you're a version of you from an alternate universe. What am I missing?"

"If I could tell you, I already would have," he barely mutters. Upon leaving the room he looks back at me through hooded eyes. "I'm so sorry."

"No! You don't get to do this. I'm tired of you treating me like crap one minute and then being all emo the next and make me feel sad for you—all without explanation. It's unfair and abusive. You can either man-up, and tell me what the hell is going on, or you walk away for good. I mean it. I'm done!"

Donovan stares at the carpet in silence. He leaves me with no choice. "Fine. You've lost me. You've lost your sister. You've lost your best friend. Clearly, you are no longer the person I used to know."

My remaining courage thrusts me out, not just from the room but, as far as I'm concerned, every aspect of his life.

11

In the middle of the night following his graduation, Donovan covertly departs, but not before sneaking into my room while our parents sleep. It might be best to remain tranquil, as if facing a grizzly bear. Before words escape me, he softly puts a single finger over my mouth and kneels on the floor near my head. Moments pass in silence. Finally he smiles, and with a gesture for my muteness, removes his hand.

The sparks of love and life have returned to his eyes, bringing more air into my lungs than they have been capable of handling for months. Finally, his voice sounds like his own, not that of the monster that's possessed him for the last six months. "Lily, I *promise* there will be a time when I will tell you everything. Meanwhile, you need to know that you are beautiful, lovely, and perfect. You do *not* repulse me. You scare me, but you certainly don't repulse me." His charming grin is back too, along with the happy version of his annoying eye roll, which is now delightful again.

He toys with my hand. The smoldering fire in his eyes that I have waited so long to see again has returned. "It may be a long time until you hear from me again. Just please never lose faith in me. Be patient and give me some time and space. In addition to everything else, you are truly my best friend. I'll be back soon. Meanwhile, live your life to the fullest. Don't hold back for me or for anyone, especially Mom and Dad. Don't let them talk you into anything. Scratch that, I know no one can talk you into anything." He chokes back emotion. "That's one of the things that makes you perfect." Donovan kisses my forehead and begins his departure.

"My turn?" I ask. Actually, I'm not asking. We both know there's no way I'm letting him slip out like this. I have more than earned the right to speak my piece.

He returns to his previous position on the floor while hoping this isn't another bullet to dodge. I stroke his raven locks as my fingers have done so many times before. Surprisingly, he lets me—and he's enjoying it—though I can tell he's a little afraid I'm about to smack him.

"I will never, *ever* lose faith in you. But I can't go on like this forever. The only reason I have tolerated you is because I know who you really are, which is confounding, because, for the life of me, I can't figure out what's going on. It's far more complex than indecision about me. I know something is wrong on a very deep level, and that's why I lost it the other day. But that doesn't mean I am giving up on you. *Not now. Not ever.* I'm going on with my life, but I'm going to make you keep your promise. Just know that when you are ready to talk, I'm here."

My lips repeat his closing gesture of a kiss on the forehead. As he begins to leave, I stop his hand from slipping away. "Donovan, that thing you're not saying that we both know you're thinking and feeling, I'm not going to say it either, but I'm thinking and feeling it too. I've accepted it. When you are ready to hear it, I'll be ready to say it. I just hope that when you get through whatever it is that's causing you so much pain, that we'll be together in the end."

"Never change who you are, Lily."

He grabs his bags and sneaks out the back door. Memories flood me of the time I lost my heart and Donovan brought me a candy one. Can I make something resembling a spirit out of candy? Regardless, my Donovan is long gone and will remain so until his spirit returns. Prayers for him are released to Heaven before I sigh relief. It's time to get on with my life.

12

Escape from the house couldn't come fast enough, partly because of my newfound enthusiasm and partly in avoidance of my parents' complaints regarding Donovan giving them the slip. Enigmas and clandestine emotions are behind me. I will resume living earnestly and impassioned like before, even if it's without my best friend and confidant.

To commence my new life, I will indulge in something decadent for breakfast, not chemical laden floor scraps from a drive-thru that contain more grease than my new car will. Well, my new-to-me car. Without Donovan to schlep me around, I will soon be given the keys to a respectably used, cute little red Bug that currently sits in our driveway. It's calling to me like a siren. Just one more week, then turning seventeen will free me of the Rhode Island Public Transit Authority.

I'm getting a job. My mind needs distractions and there is only so much baking I can do at home as an escape. Besides, Dad is getting fat. A morning of reading the want ads, sipping great coffee, and eating something enticing is the perfect birth to my new existence.

After grabbing a copy of the newspaper, I head to Josette's French Bakery. They have the best Pain Au Chocolat for miles. Nothing sounds more perfect. That is, until the handwritten sign in the store window beams at me like a classic neon treasure.

Part Time Help Wanted—Kitchen Staff.

I bolt straight in and request to speak to Josette.

Josette is a very pretty, mature lady with deep brown eyes, flowing dark brown well-dyed hair, and lovely, yet slightly loose and faded, fair skin. Her Americanized, French

67

accent is welcoming, but her charm falls flat when I learn that professional kitchen experience is required. Howbeit, true to my nature, and on this of all days, defeat is a word whose definition escapes me. I'm getting this damn job!

Josette possesses a warm glow that makes me feel at ease. If I can just get my foot in the door, I can win her over. "I admit I'm inexperienced, but may I please ask what type of professional kitchen experience is required for such a position? I plan to attend pastry school upon graduation, and if I had that experience now, would that be sufficient?"

"Yes, or if you had worked in any place that required you to understand how to properly handle and store food."

"Do you mean rules like the danger zone for food is between forty and one hundred and thirty five degrees Fahrenheit; raw unshelled eggs have a maximum refrigeration life of four days; and that all food should be covered as close to the surface as possible to prolong life, lessen the chances of contamination, and help maintain freshness?" Ha! Let's see how shocked she is now.

"Yes, that is exactly the type of thing I meant. How do you know all of that?" Josette seems to take a liking to me. Is that creaking noise in my head the door of opportunity?

"I'm very serious about my art. However, I understand that you need a solid foundation, such as understanding the basics of baking chemistry. But for fun, I recently started designing with Biscuit Jaconde."

That should get her. What other American, teenage girl knows what Biscuit Jaconde is? Then again, if it hadn't been for Donovan's encouragement and then his becoming a self-absorbed dick, forcing me to study instead of dealing with him, I wouldn't know a quarter of what I do.

"Interesting," she says. Is she seeing potential? Damn it, sure as fast food is disgusting this is going to work!

"Josette, what if I came back at this time tomorrow with samples of my work? If you like what I can do, would you consider me for the position?"

"You do know that I am not hiring for a baker, right?

There would be some of that in time, but you would start with regimented basic duties, like cleaning."

"I am very fine with that. I really want to start paying my dues."

Josette's face seems to come aglow. "Very well. I can't wait to see what you bring. Keep in mind, I will be very honest, and I know my competition. If you bought it somewhere, I will know."

"I will be sure to add my special touches so that you will be immediately certain I made the items myself!"

"Very well then! See you tomorrow."

಄

Summer is blurring past. Within two weeks after winning Josette over and scoring the job, a key member of the kitchen staff unexpectedly, and rather dramatically, quit. This left the bakery in a total uproar, poor Josette frantic, and me temporarily promoted.

I love everything about my job; from the grime I scrub off of the floor to my talented coworkers—even the ditsy one. Though totally exhausted, I'm grateful that when night falls, slumber immediately cloaks me leaving no time to ponder the emotional upheaval of losing what I consider most precious.

But true happiness is still a little evasive. Serving as a painful reminder of my bereavement, Donovan neglected to call on my birthday. Since the start of my existence he would commence that day with an obnoxious act. Last year he rigged my alarm so it played the most gawd-awful thing I'd ever heard—a version of "Happy Birthday" barked by dogs. The year before, he set off the smoke detector. When I scampered downstairs in a panic, a cup of cocoa and a stupid grin awaited me.

Donovan has always been here in ludicrous ways, but this year his only contact was a card and a book by one of France's top pastry chefs. The card merely said, "To My

Sister On Her Birthday." Its simplicity was disturbingly out of character.

Finally, Josette has hired a replacement, and my job has reached a sane pace. Josette constantly expresses her gratitude. She even told my parents I possess the drive of two people and am deserving of more than she can pay. It's high praise coming from someone who holds both my personal and my professional admiration.

My parents also repeatedly express how impressed they are with my dedication, genuinely giving me the confidence to announce my plans for the future one night at dinner.

"Mom, Dad, I'd like to discuss something very important to me." I set down my fork and place my hands in my lap. Ice runs through my veins while remembering the time Donovan said he didn't know what he wanted to do with his life and how unglued Dad became over him not having his future mapped out by the time he was sixteen. Dad will likely show as much disdain for my situation.

"I've known for a long time what I want to do with my life, and these last few months have proven it. I work very hard each day, yet at night I go to bed with a smile on my face. I haven't even touched upon all of the good stuff, and, despite that, I'm always excited to go to work, no matter how tired I am. Josette is willing to write a glowing letter of recommendation so that I can attend a premier pastry school."

My words seem to hang in the air.

Dad looks pained. In a command for attention, he clears his throat. "I suppose you plan to do this while attending a university or some other college."

"Yes. I plan to take business classes on the weekends and then keep that going once I start working. Eventually I will open my own shop."

Mom's face gives way to a proud smirk, while Dad silently processes what seems to be bad news. Setting down his fork and folding his arms, he sits back in his chair. "You know, sweetie, had you said this a few months ago, I would have started screaming that you were crazy and throwing your education away. When you took that cockamamie job you say you never should have gotten, I thought it was kind of cute, and I was proud that you got a job without us asking. But you have worked really hard. I don't agree with your choice, but you have earned my respect, and I feel I have to honor your decision."

Leaning forward, he points a finger at me as if to punctuate his words. "However, I insist, and I mean insist, that you devise a solid plan to go to college. No matter how successful you are in this cooking thing, I want you to at least get a basic degree in General Ed, even if it is just an associate of arts. You are too smart not to broaden your horizons. I mean it, Lilyanna. You need to come up with a solid plan to do both. You do that, and you have my support and blessing."

"Really, Daddy? You believe in me that much?"

He puts his hand firmly on mine, "Yes, dear. I do."

I'm totally floored. I expected a confrontation and a night of lying in bed wallowing deep in my misery. But respect from Edward Beckett? That was never foreseen. Then again, I'm female and will be "cooking," so it's likely that in Dad's mind I'm setting myself up to be the perfect housewife. Either way, as long as I continue to play my cards right, success is mine!

After everyone goes to sleep, for the first time since he departed, Donovan's room calls me inside. I lie on his bed, and his essence that still graces the pillow encases me. Maybe I should swap his pillow for my own so I can feel closer to him every night.

Donovan, what happened to you? What happened to us, and all of our different incarnations? Did you really need to let them all go?

The ability to share my good news is only a call away. But he asked for space, and I need it too. For the first time in weeks, my spirit allows my brain to ruminate over him, wonder what he's doing, and most importantly, who he really is.

God, please send him back to me filled with words of resolution. Even if you don't condone my struggles and damnation is upon me, please help me to understand so that I can achieve peace. As for Donovan, please help him find happiness, even if it hurts me. Meanwhile, would you please send me a diversion? You sent me to Josette and in that gave me the ammunition to tell my parents about pastry school and gain acceptance. Thank you for that. Now would you please send me the next thing that I need in life? I don't know what it is, but I'm sure you do. Thanks.

13

A rush of euphoria shoots through my body as the alarm sounds—as if lightning has zapped away shackles that have emotionally restrained me for months. With a huge spring in my step, I can't get to work fast enough.

Just as my workday is scheduled to finish, Josette approaches. "Lily, can you stay late and watch the front of the store? I have to run a few errands."

Exchanging my dough-encrusted apron for a clean one, I head to the front with a tray of fresh Biscotti. Upon walking through the double doors into the shop, a delightful voice instantly sweeps me off my feet. Its source is absolutely adorable—about my age, five foot seven inches tall, incredibly thin, has the cutest, shoulder length, disorganized soft brown hair, a sloped nose, and puppy dog eyebrows that slightly slant inward over bright blue eyes as soothing as the sky.

Try as she might, Jennifer at the counter can't understand a word the poor guy says.

"I said, do—you—have—an-ny—crump-ets?"

I can't help but giggle at his frustration, which he returns with a snicker. The animated way his head bounces as he speaks with his hands firmly planted on his hips has me captivated. "My dear, please tell me that *you* understand me. I know I'm in a foreign country, but I do speak English, or so I thought."

Jennifer is lost. "I can't understand you. Are you from Canada?"

"Oh, Jennifer! He's from England. Judging by his accent, I'm guessing maybe near Manchester. Am I correct?"

The stranger throws his hands in the air. "Finally,

someone who understands me! And yes, Manchester. How could you tell?"

"My mom was a little girl when the British Invasion hit, and she crushed heavily on all the English boys. She always says the happiest music came from Manchester. I grew up listening to Herman's Hermits and the Hollies while being grilled on trivia. I can't tell you how many times she's dragged me to see Peter Noone in concert. She's a little embarrassing."

"I know what you mean. I have the queen of the 'little embarrassing' mums meself. I sure am glad you came along when you did. I was on the brink of throwing a wobbly with this bird."

For the first time in months, I'm beaming, inside and out. It's like an eraser is being taken to the emotional scars on my soul. "I'm sorry to tell you that we don't make crumpets here. Is there anything else that I could interest you in?"

"Bollocks." He looks down at his shoes as if embarrassed that the answer to my question is a little inappropriate. He then peers at me with eyes that reek of innocence, meaning he might be nothing but trouble. "Well, maybe you could tell me your name."

"It's Lily. Well, Lilyanna really. But everyone calls me Lily."

"Lilyanna is very lovely. I'm Christopher."

He eyes the shop, as if what to say next is written somewhere. "Do you work here daily?"

"Most days, until school starts, and then I'll be here on weekends. I'm usually in back, so if you come by you should ask for me. I'll see what I can do about those crumpets."

His endearing smile returns. "Ah, don't toy with me, pet."

"No really. Come back at the same time in two days. Let me see what I can come up with for you. No promises it will be any good." My heart gallops. Where is this forwardness coming from?

"Really? All right! I'll see you in two days, Lilyanna. Can I take you to tea then? Sorry, I guess it's coffee here. I'm kind of 'fresh off the boat' I believe your expression is."

"Either would be lovely."

"I'll see you then!" He fumbles with the door before shooting me a look in admission of his lack of grace.

As soon as the door closes, I turn to Jennifer and beam, "He's *so* cute!"

"Who? The scrawny guy with the marbles in his mouth?"

"Yes, Jen. The young Manc who just left here. He is a-dor-a-ble!"

જી

My excitement might be a bit too elevated as I proceed to give myself a crash course in crumpets. Christopher's totally got me swooning. Two days after our encounter, he returns to the bakery and asks for Lilyanna.

"Who?" Jennifer replies.

"Bollocks, not you again. Lil-y-an-na."

"What's a millytanya? Never mind. Hey Lily, that foreign guy is back. Can you help him?"

My laughter rings throughout the back of the bakery and into the shop as I nearly race to the front. "Hi, Christopher. I'm almost done. See if you can grab us a table outside. There's usually a quiet one around the corner that no one ever sits at."

When I return to the back of the store, Josette is also amused by the antics. "Tell your friend not to feel bad. It took her over a month to understand me. If she was not my cousin's daughter, I would have never let her stay." Josette pulls a tin holding a crumpet off of the stove with a pair of tongs. Dumping out its contents, she examines it. "I think you have this right. I have not had one of these in years, but they seem to be what I remember."

I give the woman who has become a close friend a big hug. "Thanks Josette. And thanks for letting me do this."

"My pleasure. I owe you a few favors after all you have done for me. Just let me know if there is anything else I can do. You deserve someone to make you happy."

Snatching the plate of hot buttered crumpets and two cups of freshly brewed tea, I try not to look too eager as I practically sprint to meet Christopher.

I set the plate in front of him. "Bob's Your Uncle!"

"Blimey!" he marvels. "Tea and everything? Just a moment, I thought I was treating you to tea."

"Welcome to America. After dealing with Jennifer's ridiculousness the other day, I figured the people of this country owe you."

His azure eyes are big and wild. Dear God, I want to bottle that color and inject it into my veins so it can forever tint my heart.

"Well, kindly tell the rest of the citizens that I apologize for my poor attitude towards *some* of their people. I'm Gobsmacked!"

"Really? I've never had these before, so I've no idea if I made them right."

Stopping short of his first bite, Christopher tilts his head, swaying his locks into his eyes. "Just a moment, luv. How is it you've never had crumpets yet you made these?"

"I'm brilliant."

"Indeed," he chuckles. "Bob's Your Uncle! Wherever did you hear that?"

"We get the BBC here too, you know. Besides, my mom's insane. Again, you've been warned." Prayers are sent to heaven as I take my first bite of crumpet.

"Really? How soon until I meet her?" Christopher goes a little red as he sets down his tea. "Sorry. Is that forward? I've been told American girls are more forward and independent than British girls. I don't know how to act."

Relief pats me on the head as I swallow my bite and find it pleasant. "This American girl is very independent, but not very forward. You can meet my parents when you pick me up for a proper date."

He smiles through his embarrassment. "Help me here. I would love to take you on a proper date, but I hear there are rules about how far in advance you are to ask, and that women get upset if you assume they are immediately available. You American ladies are very complicated."

"Just ask," I whisper.

"All right," he mimics my quiet demeanor. "Would you like to join me on a date this Saturday for dinner?"

"I would love to."

"Lovely. Why are we whispering?"

While looking around covertly I retain my hushed tone. My smile builds. "Because I'm a complicated American, and I'm trying to confuse you."

"Blimey!"

ℂ℁

"Honey, your date will be here soon. How are you doing?"

Mom's jealousy has kicked in, and she hasn't even met Christopher. Upon hearing he hails from Manchester, she was practically fanning herself and started making cracks that if he looks like Peter Noone of Herman's Hermits, she's running off with his father. Compelled to make it worse, I told her he plays guitar and looks more like a Hollie than a Hermit. In Mom's world that's the most torturous thing I could ever utter.

Now that Donovan is gone, she's more content. We both needed relief from the winner of the Mr. Alternate Universe pageant and are looking for ways to be happy again. One of hers is grilling me about Christopher. Nothing awkward has been asked—yet. The most prying she's done is inquiring about his mom, whom he just moved here with in escape of Christopher's father and their messy divorce. Overall, Mom's been easy to deal with, which is optimal since Christopher and I haven't even had our first date.

"Come in, Mom," I reply.

She observes my reflection in the mirror as she steps up

behind me. "Lily, you look lovely."

Her words are a symphony. Lovely is exactly what I'm going for. After months of problems that would challenge any adult, being seventeen is perfect. I don't want to appear a stunning woman or be a tramp and get laid to forget someone. I want that precious time discovering the world with someone I don't have to hide with. I want to be seventeen while I can.

"Do you really think so Mom?"

"You certainly are dressed for the part. This pink and lavender sundress hugs your curves gracefully while maintaining a lovely flow. I love the waves in your hair. They make me want to grow mine long again. You need a necklace."

"I have the pearl pendant you gave me."

"That would be perfect."

Then the doorbell rings, precisely on time.

When Mom and I arrive downstairs, Dad already has Christopher under the interrogation lamp. Dad has never shown respect for my dates. Apparently, he mimics how his father disciplined his own children, so it's conceivable that this is how Grandpa acted with my late Aunt Audrey's suitors. No wonder why the poor woman died young and single.

"And remember, young man, no unsafe driving. No necking!" Dad badgers.

"Dad!"

"No going more than five miles away from this house! And have her home by ten!"

"Edward, please!" Mom scolds. "Be nice to the poor man."

I try to make proper introductions and get past the madness that has transpired. "Mom, this is Christopher. Christopher, this is my mother. I see you've met my father."

"Yes, we've been having a rather pleasant conversation about your well-being. Here, I brought these for the two of you."

Christopher presents Mom and me each with a pink rose wrapped with fern and baby's breath. Finally! Someone who doesn't think they are clever by giving me lilies! Dad has a reserved look of appreciation. Mom, however, seems conflicted as to whether she should try to fight me for Christopher or shove me out the door with consent to elope.

"This is very sweet of you. Lily, I'll put yours in water and set it on your nightstand. You two have a good time." Mom then has a moment of sanity. "Christopher, please have Lily home by eleven, right Edward?"

Our dining options are limited to fast food, one Mexican and one Italian restaurant. There is also a fish and chips place that I assure Christopher if we venture to my dad won't instantly know we went too far and call out the mob. But to his credit, Christopher has made reservations at the Italian restaurant because he heard true Italians own it and thought I might find that enjoyable. He also printed a list of movies with show times that end early enough to get me home before Dad can freak out. Something seems wrong with this picture. Maybe he's a ploy for an underage porn racket, and I'm being abducted.

The menu is full of saliva-inducing faire, including the off-limits Pasta Puttanesca. Its spiciness is heavenly, but since the name means Pasta of the Whore it is probably best not consumed while on a first date. How many times has Brittny ordered it? She probably uses it as code. Then again, can she even read the menu?

My taste buds finally settle on pork in an orange Marsala sauce. After Christopher's grilled chicken arrives it occurs he's chosen the blandest item on the menu. Crap! I forgot about the old adages regarding the Brits and their lack of taste in food. Mentally, my fingers and every bone, vein, and artery in my body cross in hopes that it's coincidence.

After dinner we pass on the movie and opt for mini-golf, since there is a place barely located just this side of the forbidden zone. Christopher's golf skills are akin to the talents he possessed the other day in the bakery when opening the door after meeting me. He is, to use his wording, a bit daft at times when it comes to coordination. How he manages to play guitar is inconceivable. He must not be very good.

Pensiveness washes over Christopher as he sets up his shot on the fifth hole. When he finally goes for his stroke it is one of grace. The ball sails perfectly into the cup—the cup of the eighth hole, that is.

"Bugger!"

My smirk is insuppressible.

Leaning on his club, he shakes his head and covers his eyes. "At least I'm succeeding at providing you with follies this evening."

"Hey, this time you actually hit the ball."

"Thanks loads for pointing that one out, luv." He chortles as he dashes off to reclaim his ball.

I love how his hair bounces as he runs—making me want to fondle it. But he's been the perfect gentleman, and I don't want to jinx this night. High hopes fill me for many more like it.

"I believe that is what you American's refer to as a screw up," he says upon his return.

"I believe that is what I call a brilliant shot. I'm scoring you a hole in one for that."

"Not on your Nelly!"

"Fine, I'll penalize you one point for going off course and score it two points. It's worth it for the entertainment value."

His approach behind me is just close enough that I can feel the brush of his shirt against my skin. It's attention commanding and makes me crave more. "I'm afraid to ask, but what's the score now?"

"Twenty-two to eleven."

Christopher smacks his head into his hands.

"How about I let you blame it on these Yank courses? They must be slanted funny."

"I think I'm just out of my element. It's been yonks since I've done the likes of this."

"What do you normally do on dates back home?" I ask as we begin our journey to the next hole.

"I practically live in clubs, but I've yet to find any places here for live music. I think I'm going to have to venture out a bit."

"Your mom lets you go to clubs? My parents will barely let me go to a concert. Unless it's something Mom drags me to, and then it's some guy who's got a good ten years on her."

"Mum likes those blokes as well. Large age differences are common in my family. I appeared after Mum thought it was impossible for her to have more children."

"My mom got off to a late start having kids, so she is also a bit older than most parents. I would love to go to a club show and see what it's like." I set the ball up for my shot.

"That gives me something to aim for with your dad."

"Good luck with that. My mom is your ally." I take my shot and watch the ball do its loop-de-loop before stopping its run just outside the hole.

"I sort of got that impression."

"Don't let him get to you. I take it your dad is different if you get to go to clubs."

"Yes, I suppose he is. He appreciates seeing talent. But I have some older mates that take me as well. I'd actually rather be with them, but that's another story."

Christopher tends to long for home quite a bit. I feel for him. Making such a change at this stage in my life is unthinkable. "Sorry. I didn't mean to hit on a sore subject."

"It's nowt, luv. I just really miss me mates." Christopher takes his stroke and somehow manages to shoot the ball with a sideways curve through the loop, bank it off the side of the course, into the back area, and knock my ball in before his bounces off the green. "Bollocks!"

I nearly choke while trying to suppress my laugh. "Wow, another impressive blunder!"

Christopher throws his hands up and shakes off his error. "Do you listen to music much?"

"That's a trick question. My mom is always playing her old records, so I'm surrounded by it. The only time I actually get to listen to my music is when she's not home."

Christopher lets out a little chuckle. "She and Mum would get on well. Mum's tastes have definitely evolved, but she adores the classics. She was quite the hanger on at one point."

Is that code for groupie? The thought of her being a bimbo gives me a little shiver, which compels Christopher to run to his car and grab his jacket for me.

I can't refuse his gentlemanly offer. Maybe this is crazy, but I want to test the waters and feel his aura little better. When I put on Donovan's coat just before Christmas, the love and sense of protection emanating from it was consuming and reminded me of how much he challenges me. It evoked thoughts of him feeding me mango on a deserted island. The warmth of Christopher's jacket makes me feel like life with him would mean I wouldn't have a care in the world. An instant sense of respect and comfort surrounds me. Thoughts of living in a magical land abound.

After a beautiful night of Christopher keeping his hands to himself, which is admittedly a bit of a disappointment, he makes a point of bringing me home at ten-thirty, perfectly pleasing both Mom and Dad. He walks me to the door, and I'm hopeful this was the first of many dates.

"Christopher, I had an amazing time."

"Me as well. May I call on you again?"

Seriously, how adorable is that? "I would love it."

"Very well. I'll ring in the morning and set a date."

A tingle lingers after he kisses my cheek—like a magic wand has been waved. He starts to leave, but I give his hand a little tug and regain his attention. "The other side is jealous." I flush as I say it.

Christopher goes a little red himself. He kisses my other cheek, only to pull back and capture my eyes with his own.

My heart tries to convey that a little more affection would be welcome, and his lips grace mine so delicately that his kiss flows around my body like a wisp of a rose.

Mom's fascination with British men must be hereditary.

My legs seem to have disappeared. I soar into the house and up to my room. Before I can close my door, Mom races in. She reminds me of a giddy teenager and practically forces me to sit on the bed with her. "So how was it? Come on, Lily! Dish!"

"I had a great time, Mom. Christopher is fantastic. What did you think of him?"

She seems surprised by the question. "You really want to know?"

"Yes. What's the big deal?"

"I'm just glad that after going through a distant period, and after that horrible date you had a few months ago you refuse to speak of, that we are talking about this." She smiles emphatically. "I like him. I really like him. He has a great energy, but also warmth. He seems perfect." Then she adds one last, very excited, comment as she starts to leave. "And you're right. He does look like a Hollie!"

I totally understand the swooning. Maybe I can make her night even brighter. "Hey Mom, how about we stay up and watch that Herman's Hermit's movie you love so much? The one that starts in Manchester."

The little girl in Mom just about comes unglued. She squeals, "I'll go get the DVD!"

14

I'll never have a better summer. The chaos at the bakery fuels me, and spending every free minute of the last month with Christopher has fused my heart back together. Given this, the thought of school sounds more excruciating than ever. I want to enjoy my youth, but that doesn't mean I desire to be trapped in a restrictive classroom like a child.

Thankfully, one blissful week of summer remains. Josette recently realized my vacation has been spent in the bakery. As a result, she concocted a little surprise and gave me a week off—with pay. Her accent never sounded lovelier than when she said, "Go grab that adorable bloke of yours and get him some sun. He is too pale!"

Christopher is the perfect companion. Between his charming wit and his occasional awkwardness, he never fails to put a smile on my face. The fact he somehow manages to be both adorable and totally sexy doesn't hurt matters. I thought it impossible to find that combination in one person. It's unfair to the rest of mankind.

How Christopher's living room can contain so little, yet appear this muddled baffles me. He is constantly cleaning after and caring for his mom. There's something very dysfunctional about their relationship that I've yet to understand. I figure it's due to her emotional state regarding the impending divorce. She's been a disaster. One minute she's crying her eyes out and the next she's dolled-up and headed out on the make. It guts Christopher, and he tries to avoid conversation about the whole mess.

I've lost track of how much time we have spent cuddling on this sofa. It's generally sweet, but right now his eyes are locked into mine in silent confession. Our lips meet, and he kisses me more profoundly than ever. In the past few weeks he's given me some fantastic kisses, but these are lingering and filled with an ecstasy that makes my head foggy. He fondles my heartstrings, but I'm just not ready to go down this road for reasons I don't want to confess to myself.

Christopher's never been this forward. I resist just enough to come up for air. "Wow. Not that I'm complaining, but I thought you said you wanted to talk?"

"I'm sorry. I do want to talk to you. I also wouldn't be brassed if we didn't say a word and kept going like this." His next kiss steals my breath both in rapture and apprehension. I gasp at the enthusiasm, and he shies away. "I'm sorry. I'm a tad nervous."

A tad is not an accurate description. He looks downright afflicted. The Christopher I've come to know and love is usually very happy and comfortable, albeit a little daft.

Wait. The Christopher I've come to know and *love*?

I brush the notion aside to address the issue at hand. "Hey, are you okay? You know that you can talk to me about anything, right?" The genuineness of my words surprises me. Suddenly I see how much he's come to mean to me. Am I all right with this?

"Can I? Can I really? Because that is kind of what I want to talk about. I feel like a clot with no idea where to start."

"Whatever it is, just say it."

He catches a little air before knocking me on the floor with his confession. "Lilyanna, I'm starting to develop some pretty strong feelings for you, but I'm rather confused. Most of the time it seems you feel the same, yet others you're so distant it's as if you're pushing me away. I just—Lilyanna, I really think I've fallen in love with you, and I need to know how you feel, if you even know."

Oh, dear God! My eyes must be like saucers. He sounds like me with Donovan, but he's actually stating his feelings. Why did I never lay the cards on the table with Donovan? Words are a mighty instrument. Is this why if I tried to talk to him rationally, he'd flip in the other direction?

"Lilyanna? Are you all right?"

My head snaps back into the moment. "Did you just say you love me?"

"I think I do. I'm not sure. Well, I know I love you. But I'm trying to figure out if I'm *in* love with you. I want to stop for a second and figure out what we're really feeling before we go down a path we may not be ready for."

The truth becomes apparent. Somewhere down the line we became inseparable. We don't just go out on dates and make out; we actually spend quality time together. We've shared how we feel about pretty much everything but each other. We've been kissing more and more passionately, yet he's barely attempted second base. But just because we haven't gotten very physical doesn't mean we haven't become emotionally attached. Would he even understand the second base analogy? They don't have baseball in England. They have cricket. Are there bases in cricket?

"Lilyanna, I'm sorry. I obviously shouldn't have started this conversation. I don't want you to feel pressured into anything, but when you're ready, I want to be ready."

Without warning, my moment of truth burst forth like water from a broken fire hydrant and floods me. "I started falling in love once, and I got very, very hurt. I had barely recovered when I met you. I'm scared, Christopher. I'm falling in love with you, and that scares the crap out of me." Christopher doesn't need to know I'm still in love with the mystery man, just that I'm falling for him. It rips me apart that Christopher may never have me truly to himself.

He shows no hesitation in sharing his feelings. "I want to spend every possible moment with you in any way you'll allow. I want to take you on dates, watch the telly with you, listen to music and kiss you over and over until we know how we feel and decide what to do next."

Christopher's openness is a welcome contrast to Donovan's shadowed emotions, and it's sweeping me off of my feet. I close my eyes a moment to savor the experience. "That sounds perfect. I want to be closer to you now more than ever. Do they have bases in cricket?"

His normal demeanor returns, and his skull dances with his words like a bobblehead. "You want to play cricket? That's one I didn't expect."

"Let me rephrase. Do you know how to play baseball?"

He looks at me blankly.

"Do you know what the expression, 'Getting to second base' means?"

He's clueless as to where I am going with this.

"Never mind. Just kiss me—a lot—and let me show you. But Christopher, once you figure it out, don't get any ideas about getting to third."

"You Yanks are a strange lot. Why can't you just speak English?"

"Shhh." I find myself taking his hand and placing it over my pounding heart. He raises his gaze to look deeply into my eyes that are still affected by my revelations. My hand guides him to the pearly, top button of my rose-hued blouse. He hesitates before taking over, kisses me, and goes to the next button. Again he pauses and kisses before continuing, as if seeking permission for each advance. Upon reaching the last button, he caresses the contours of my face before sweeping me up to free me from the garment and tenderly kissing down my neck, following the trail the buttons last held.

My spine curves in suggestion that he continue. He toys with the clasp of my bra, as if expecting resistance. Languidly, he removes it. I pull him down and writhe under him, placing myself in a prime position to feel his excitement. Shuddering a tender exhale, his downward kisses resume until he nuzzles my bosom and slides his hand over my breast, kissing it. "Second base," I whisper.

His gaze reflects both an impish grin and a respectful look acknowledging this is a far as he has permission to go. He rests his head on my chest and smiles.

"I've got to learn more about American Baseball."

ღ

My vacation is covered in pretense. Each day I wake ridiculously early, fictitiously leave for work, and park my car around the corner from Christopher's house. I then climb through his window and cuddle next to him until his mom leaves.

Christopher finds my antics adorable, yet somewhat daft. He's of the strong opinion his mother wouldn't care if I burst through the front door in lingerie while boldly announcing that I'm about to send her son's brains to the moon. Apparently she has rather liberal morals sexually and expects the same of her five sons. However, modesty has the best of me. Besides, since he moved the chest that holds the gardening supplies under it, crawling in his window is too fun to pass up.

The more I witness Christopher in even mundane activities, the deeper I'm falling. My emotional and sexual desires for him are driving me a little crazy, and the madness is leading to things getting progressively hotter. But right now the heat has dissipated. Christopher's hands seem to be all over me, and not very coordinated about it. Suddenly he stops floundering and pulls away. "You know, when we finally get to whatever base that last one is—"

"You mean, shagging?" I boast brightly, toying with his distress.

"Yes, luv, the old slap and tickle. Look Lilyanna, I'm trying to do the right thing here. When we do get to that point, you know that with me being so inexperienced things are not exactly going to be perfect, right? I want you to be comfortable guiding me to all of the right places and into doing the right things so that I can take care of you. It will be your first time, right?" He turns his attention to the floor.

"Yes." How is this a big deal?

"I just want to be sure that your first time is better than mine was." His cringe reveals fear that I'll soon bash his head in. He then tries to answers questions before they can form in my mouth. "It was a huge mistake. Before I left home I'd been sort of dating someone, and she wanted to give me a 'going away present.' Oh, it was fine during, but after I felt horrible. It was all very cheap and common, and I left the next day feeling even more gutted because of it. I don't want to do that to you."

I've been so wrapped up in my own past that Christopher's had never occurred to me. Facing that he also had a life before me brings on jealousy and reinforces my previous revelation that I'm falling in love with him—not just jumping into bed to forget and move on. Somewhere this all became real.

"I'm sorry," Christopher continues. "I wanted to tell you sooner, but I haven't been able to figure out how."

It's time to mute the whispers of my past. I surrender into his puppy eyes. "Now I know why I'm falling in love with you. You are all the wonderful things that are essential in my life. What I need most is honesty and you are so good about giving me that. Please continue to be honest with me no matter what it is about and even if you think it might hurt me. If you really want to take care of me you'll do yourself a favor and release your past."

He doesn't know how to proceed. I save us from our miseries with a grin of mischief. "I have a wonderful idea. Let's start finding all those little places on me, so that when the time comes, you know exactly where to go." Christopher's expression becomes a mix of wide-eyed excitement and bewildered anxiety. I love how it changes to one of delighted surprise when I unfasten my jeans. I slide his hand into my pants for him to feel the glorious and creamy effect he has on me. My breath flutters at his touch, "Third base."

"There are only four, right?"

"Yes."

"Thank God."

As the sun reaches its apex on the final day of our week together, Christopher and I curl in bed, lost in overwhelming emotions. While previously I'd been tortured with overpowering thoughts of lust, last night I dreamt only of how beautiful it would be to share myself with Christopher.

I break the silence with words that slide out effortlessly, "Christopher, I love you." My eyes cannot unlock from his. It brings about a feeling of security.

"I'm in love with you too. I actually knew it a few days ago but feared you weren't ready to hear it."

There's something different about him—something making him stronger and more self-assured.

"Christopher, I'm ready for that next step."

"Are you going to give me another analogy about baseball that I can't understand?" he softly quips.

"No. I want you to make love to me."

"Lilyanna, are you absolutely sure that you're ready for this?" He chokes on his words. Clearly he wasn't expecting a confession of true love and my surrender to him was more than he hoped for.

"Yes. Do you really love me?"

"Truly I do."

Our passion knows no resistance, no inhibitions, no fear, and no haste. I relinquish every bit of my trust and being to Christopher, knowing he's sure to respect me. At the whisper of his touch, our garments seem to melt into the ether. My legs part. I await the infamous pain that shocks some, but all that matters is the beauty of him merging with me.

He tries to control himself and often diminishes his actions to stare into my eyes so as not to move too rapidly. His caresses are filled with so much tenderness that they are almost painful and tear at the depths of my heart. As the climax of his body washes over him, I feel myself radiate. He takes one last moment to admire me before focusing all of his attention on my obtaining complete pleasure.

Gently he slides two fingers into me, locating the precise spot I guided him to yesterday; the spot that makes me tense at the beautifully wicked sensations he sends spiraling through my body. Placing his palm in the perfect position to extract divine sensations, he lightly pulsates while his fingers caress my inner being. A mad urgency flows through me. As we revel in my tremors, he holds me as if to protect my fragile heart from my body's violence.

The loss of my innocence is veiled in beauty and without fear of dark consequences. As we coil peacefully I feel I'm lying on rose petals. Christopher spends the rest of the day telling me how much he loves me, how he never wants the day to end—how he doesn't need anything in the world but me.

I'm in awe of how captivating and unselfish he genuinely is. All of my apprehensions have dissipated, and I can't possibly imagine lying here with anyone else.

15

My alarm rudely interrupts my slumber, and I groan in disdain. "Noooo-hohoho. Make it go away!"

The contempt isn't for the alarm, but for the day it rings in. It's the first day of my senior year, and I'd rather move to Siberia than face the next nine months of torture.

In the kitchen, my perky mom is of little help defusing the misery. "It's going to be better this year, Lily! All the good stuff happens, and you have a fantastic boyfriend to share it with. You should be excited. Is Christopher excited about starting his senior year here in America?"

"Not really. We both wish we could ignore that ugly building and keep our lives the way they've been for the last month and a half."

"Don't you mean like how they have been for the last week?" Mom asks as she sips her tea, proud of her coyness.

The coffee pot beckons. I'll need all the help I can get as we venture down the road of lectureville, and caffeine is the closest drug available.

"I stopped by the bakery last Thursday. Jennifer said you had the week off and was probably with some guy from New Zealand. I assumed she meant Christopher. She's not very bright, is she? Should she really be handling people's food?"

Busted. "I didn't say anything because I really wanted to spend quality time with Christopher. Josette surprised me with a paid vacation, and it came just as he and I decided that we really needed to get to know each other better before things went too far."

"That makes a lot of sense. Actually, I'm really glad that you two had time together. I've been concerned that you have missed out on too much with how hard you've been working. I was just surprised that you were still getting up so early when you didn't need to. You seemed well rested though and very, *very* happy. Are you very happy?"

Mom's transparency makes me embarrassed for her. "Mom, just ask the real questions."

"Will you tell me the truth, or are you going to say what you want your mother to hear?"

"The truth, but only if you promise not to judge Christopher or me. I think you can figure it all out anyway, so let's get it over with."

I plop down at the kitchen table and attempt to relax, but tension bites me. "Wait. Where's Dad? I don't want him to walk in on this conversation. He would totally freak out, especially since he's not too crazy about Christopher in the first place."

"Edward left for work early. It is not that he doesn't like Christopher, it's more that Christopher is not the kind of man he wants to see you with permanently. You know how your father is, and Christopher's a little..."

"Scrawny? Not a jock? Comfortable with himself? Human?"

"All of those. Okay, questions. How about I ask them all at once, and then you answer the way you want. I will accept any blanks as things you don't want to talk about. Fair enough?"

"Very." Is Mom crocked?

"You left early every day last week. Where did you go? Just how much time did you spend with Christopher? Do you love him? Does he love you? Is he treating you right? Are you sure you know what right is? And do I need to get you on birth control?"

This conversation is of little surprise. I am also not shocked that she waited until now to have it. Ever since things have gotten stressful with Dad, she's been big on me being independent. Apparently I'm not the only one who fears I'll turn out subservient like she did.

She gave me the chance to have my freedom, so she deserves honesty in return. Also, after months of stress from hiding my emotions, I'm ready to spit out some truth.

"I went to Christopher's every morning, and we spent the day together doing whatever it was we felt like doing. We had a very long talk the week before about our relationship. At the time we weren't sure of our feelings, but by the end of the week we both knew that we're in love. He's very respectful to me, which is why we had such a big conversation the week before, and why we spent so much time getting to know each other before we—before we took things further. And yes, we were safe, but birth control is probably a good idea."

Mom sits motionlessly with her broad eyes locked on her cup. She releases a gratified sigh.

"Okay, Mom. I know you said you'd now mind your own business, but I'm giving you another shot. Anything else?"

Mom puts her hand on my arm and smiles at me through dampening eyes. "Thank you for trusting me enough to tell me these things. I really appreciate your honesty right now."

Now? "Mom, you know that I've never really lied to you, right? There have been times when I was uncomfortable with your questions and glossed over the answers or tweaked them to sound less upsetting, but I've never given you a solid lie."

"I'm very glad to hear that. So, I get more questions?" Mom asks. She takes another sip of tea.

"Sure, Mom." Dear Lord, please don't let me regret this!

"How about a comment instead? You don't get to ask questions. Just take it at face value. Men are very odd creatures. I know that women are complex, but men just don't make any sense. Women can be manipulative, but men can be selfish and deceiving. I'm not saying there aren't men who can be trusted, but you can never really be sure who they are, even when you think you know them. I'm glad Christopher is good to you, but make sure you don't get so wrapped up in who he is now that you will be forgiving if he changes."

Pondering all that Mom's words could represent with respect to the fact that she's been miserable and fighting with Dad for months, the possibilities make my skin feel violated by worms. "Mom, is there something that you would like to be honest with me about?"

"Remember, we had a deal. No questions."

"I'm breaking it. Are you all right? I'll respect your privacy, but I need to know if you're okay."

"I'm fine, dear. It's just that sometimes people are not at all what they seem once you start really digging. I don't want you to ever be caught off guard like I was." Mom stands and puts her cup in the sink as she vacantly stares out the kitchen window. "Now go pick up that adorable boyfriend of yours. You don't want to make him late on his first day."

16

The list of reasons why school is my nemesis is huge. If you analyze it, it all boils down to two things; feeling trapped in a classroom, and being surrounded by juveniles.

This year, immaturity has found a new dimension, and it's all Christopher's fault. Well, not his really. It's more like God's for making him the endearing creature he is. How had it never occurred to me that if I found Christopher to be adorable, then the rest of the female population would too? Of course they would. Those blue eyes and crazy accent are to die for!

Sally and I approach Christopher's locker and stare at the all-too-common sight of his female entourage. "Again?" Sally asks. "It's been over a month. Are they never going to get the hint that he's in love with you?"

Christopher fumbles with his books. He has no cute smile. No charming wit. Nothing that at all implies he's enjoying this display of attention.

"It doesn't seem likely. This same thing has happened every day for weeks. You know, watching him squirm never gets old," I half-seriously say with a wicked grin.

"He's lucky you're so good-natured about it."

"That's because I'm so happy. With him, I don't have a care in the world."

"You're so incredibly lucky. Is he good in bed?" Sally asks with a gleam in her eyes.

I buoyantly look at my friend. "How long have you been dying to ask me that?"

"How long have you been sleeping with him?"

"Touché." My gaze turns to the awkwardness in front of me. "He's amazing. In *everything* he does."

"Really? 'Cause it doesn't seem like it would be that way."

"I know, huh?"

In his attempt to avert the flock, Christopher clumsily, and rather comically, sends his books flying to the ground. At the sound of my chuckle, his eyes turn heavenward. Nearly tripping over the disastrous pile of books, he dashes to me. "Lilyanna! For once the Queen has saved me! How are you, luv?" With pleading eyes that scream for rescue, he boldly kisses me, grabs my hand, and drags me to his flock before scrambling to retrieve his books. "I believe these are friends of yours. They've been ever so nice in offering to show me around. Don't we have plans?"

"Yes. Remember you promised we would have a quiet lunch together under that big tree near the gym. I brought you Summer Pudding." I hold up a brown paper bag.

"No wonder why I love you so much!" He crams his books into his locker and grabs me by the hand. "Well, thank you, ladies, but I must be moving on. Cheerio." As quickly as his dash began he abruptly stops, spins around, and gives a sheepish wave to Sally before shutting his locker. Like a shot, we're off again.

"Thank you, luv. I believe that is what you Yanks call 'an amazing save.' I just wish there were really Summer Pudding in that bag. You toy with me cruelly."

"Who's toying?"

We don't get far before two of Northland High's lamest jocks, who are tired of their girlfriends always gushing over Christopher's adorable accent, start laying into him.

"Come on, Lilyanna. Time to go." Christopher tries to walk away, but one overstuffed dimwit, reeking of alcohol, blocks him. Sally valiantly runs up to assist, as if she can possibly help. These guys are big and can easily take us all down. Now the jerk starts in on me. Apparently I'm the real target.

"Go ahead and run off with your little slut. My brother can tell you all kinds of stories about her."

My legs lock, and I realize who he is. It's Al's little

brother, Bob. I was really hoping that night was gone forever. I don't want to admit even a second of it to Christopher.

Bob keeps his focus on me. Clearly he feels he has the upper hand. "What're ya gonna do now that you don't have your dick of a brother to protect you anymore?"

His words push me to my limit. The very mention of Donovan still ignites a fire. How dare this creep bring up Donovan? How dare he harass Christopher? Worst of all, how dare he mention anything that could make me any less in Christopher's eyes? No one is allowed to ruin my happiness and certainly not at Christopher's expense! I have far, far too much pent up frustration to take it. This jerk has no idea what he's up against.

My eyes lock into Bob's. My mandate is laced with venom. "Are you so insecure that you have to drink and push people around? We both know the real reason for this little visit is retaliation on your brother's behalf. You obviously know who my brother is, but have you forgotten how he almost ripped your friend's heart out and fed it to him? Have I told you I have my brother's temper? If only a fragment of your feeble brain functions, you will stay away from Christopher and never, ever speak of Donovan again!"

"Lilyanna dear, I really think we should leave." Christopher and Sally both pull at me, but I'm not budging. This guy has got me where it hurts, and he's not going to win, even if I wind up in the emergency room.

Bob laughs. "Oh, you have your brother's temper all right. But what'cha gonna to do with it, slap me to death?"

I break loose from Sally and Christopher's grips and get in the jerk's face. I know his weak spot. It's the same as everyone else who knew Donovan the second half of his senior year. "Laugh now, creep. My brother won't be gone forever. You've seen how protective Donovan is of me. Just imagine how he's going to react when I tell him about this little interlude?"

Bob turns green around the edges. My eyes narrow, and

with a low hiss in my voice, I complete my mission. "Everyone knows how close we are. He's only a phone call away. I'm sure he has nothing better to do this weekend than defend his little sister. He'd be here in a heartbeat."

Victory is mine. I turn to Sally and Christopher, whose faces have lost all of their color. "Now we can go." Without a peep, Bob let's us walk a way.

During the silent drive home, Christopher recurrently gives me sideways glances, and his mouth keeps opening and then closing. Is his pain because I'm hurting? Or is it because I've hurt him?

Inside Christopher's driveway, I sit with the engine running and the parking brake on. I need to stay but fear he wants me to go. Finally he reaches over, turns off the engine, and gets out of the car. "Come on. Let's get you some tea." He comes around to the driver's side and opens my door. "Come on, Lilyanna. I think you need me now."

"Really? It seems I don't need anyone."

"Quite the contrary." He grabs my arm and gently tugs. I fall into his arms with tears streaming down my face. "Come on, luv. Let's go inside."

Christopher sits me on the sofa and kisses my forehead before leaving to put on the kettle. His frustration chimes through me as a ruckus comes from the kitchen, like a disastrous mess is being cleared. I've only met Christopher's mother a few times, but it's obvious she's still having a rough go of it. Poor Christopher never says much but seems to have his hands full already, and now he has to care for me too. Life is certainly not fair to this sweet, displaced man who constantly strives to make himself, and others, happy.

Christopher hands me a steaming cup and sits beside me. His eyes are focused on the cup, and while his features are soft, his grip looks tight. After a moment, he sets it down and wraps an arm around me. He sweeps away the hair that is falling into my face. His gentle kiss touches my cheek. He seems all too used to dealing with moments like this. "Talk to me. Please."

The carpet holds my gaze. "I'm sorry. I should've let you handle that. I didn't mean to imply you couldn't."

"It's nowt, luv. Really. I've no concern about that. I am now a tad afraid of ever upsetting you, let alone meeting your brother. I might be starting to understand why you haven't talked about him much if just the threat of him scares yobs like that." It's not Christopher's best attempt at ice breaking, and his face shows no humor.

"Donovan's not really like that. He's been going through some tough times and—Oh, I just don't know where to go with this." And certainly there is no desire to. Donovan's evil twin is highest on the list of reasons for my past evasiveness about him. The notion of anyone thinking Donovan is anyone other than his true self tears at me. Thanks to Bob, Christopher is learning an ugly truth that will change no matter what my personal cost. The need goes far beyond my recent complexities with Donovan, though I'd be lying to not admit they're a huge factor.

"Obviously you two are very close."

His words hit my gut. "We were. The term best friends doesn't do it justice. Something really bad must have happened because he went from being this smiling and charismatic person to mean and angry all the time. For seventeen years he was gentle, loving, and amazing, then one day it all changed, and he won't tell me why."

"Maybe he doesn't know himself."

It may just be his nature but something keeps Christopher at bay. Donovan knows how to console me. If he were here, I'd be cradled in his arms after he had wiped away my tears. But this is Christopher, and he doesn't comprehend my needs, and it confuses the hell out of me.

"No, he does. He's told me he can't talk about it, which is ridiculous considering the things we've shared. Now everything's changed. He's throwing up roadblocks, and I haven't heard from him since he moved. Then today that jerk is awful to you and starts attacking Donovan. As much as I love how you wanted to walk away, I couldn't let that creep demean the two people I love and treasure most."

"Your brother is very lucky. I'm very lucky. Try not to fret too much, luv. Donovan will talk to you in time. When people are that close for that long they never really leave each other."

"Sounds like you speak from experience." I grab his hands and use them to brush away my tears. I can't tell if the action is out of his nature or if something has stopped him from doing it voluntarily. It's the only way out of part of my distress. The action changes something in him, and his lips curl. Christopher pulls me in and reclines us onto the sofa. He's learning to read me. I forget that people need to do that.

"I've seen it for years with me parents, but that's a long story. Also, I miss everyone back home like crazy. If some yob attacked them, I'd get a little knotted too, especially if I knew they really needed me and wouldn't let me be there for them."

"So, how much do you hate me now?" I ask.

"None at all."

"Fear me?" I smile.

He backs away a little in jest. "Oh, well, now that's another story! But I love you more than I fear you."

Bringing me close again, I rest my head on his shoulder. "Hmm ... we've got to get rid of that fan club of yours."

"You mean those pesky birds?"

"Yes, your female posse."

"Blimey, I've tried to figure that one out since school started. I'm glad you don't let them get you stuffed. I guess you can't be all that mean." I smack his arm, and he grabs it while exaggerating the pain. "Ouuch! Okay, really. Any ideas?"

"Well, they always attack you at lunch and after school. Let's keep the books for your afternoon classes here and come home for lunch. That will eliminate part of it."

"Yes, but if we come to an empty castle we may never

leave."

"I don't see the problem."

"Cracking!"

17

Thanksgiving looks like it's going to be a real turkey. Thank God I'm in charge this year. It will not only save us from Mom's well intended, yet mediocre, cooking, but it will also provide me with a much-needed diversion.

Our little assembly should make for the perfect, Picasso family portrait; Christopher's freewheeling mom battling it out with my stogy dad, Mom trying to make polite, yet embarrassing, conversation with Christopher, Donovan being the biggest ass possible to everyone, and me sitting in a corner and having a melt down while chewing on my hair. The food better be good so that people have something to focus on, else they may start throwing it at each other.

"Mom, do you think Donovan will go totally ape if I only make a pumpkin and a caramel-pear pie and skip the apple?"

"Oh, I forgot to tell you. Donovan isn't coming."

"What?" Having Christopher in my life made me hopeful that Donovan would at least want to resume being civil.

"He said that he is too tied up at school, and we will see him for Christmas through New Year's Day."

"God! I can't believe him! How can he do this to us?" I *smack* my pencil onto the table to punctuate my disappointment.

"Lily, sometimes you get a little over dramatic."

"All right, Mom. Level with me. Your son won't be home for Thanksgiving. That makes this the first holiday we haven't all spent together. How is this not bugging you?"

Mom grabs her cup of tea and joins me at the table. She's trying to cover how much Reverse Polarity Donovan is troubling her too. "Honestly, I feel a little abandoned, but he's having a hard time in college. He's afraid of failing his finals. Also, I don't think he's doing so well on the football team and doesn't want to face your father. I can't say that I blame him."

"I'm sorry, Mom. I didn't mean to attack you like that."

Bravery covers her face like a mask. "I promise he will be home for Christmas, or else you and I will kidnap him, okay?"

"Okay, Mom. Deal."

Mom wipes the lipstick off of her cup with her thumb. "What are we having?" she asks.

"All the traditional stuff. I'm trying to jazz it up while minding The Eccles' *delicate English constitution.*" My eyes roll, and I withhold my rant about the one thing I would change about Christopher, had I the power. Why couldn't he be French? "If you can shop early Wednesday, I'll cook after work and all day Thursday. I need you to buy the wine though."

"Oh, dear. Are you sure you want me to do that? I have no idea how to choose wine."

"Don't worry, I'll figure out exactly what to buy and where to get it. I'd do it, but I lost my fake ID."

"Should I be worried that my underage daughter knows more about wine than I do?"

"Nah. It's an occupational hazard to at least know how to research this stuff. I know more about Cognac though. Blame Josette. No reaction about the fake ID, huh?"

"Are you kidding? A perfect angel would never do anything like that, which is why I'm going to search your room while you sleep."

"Cute, Mom."

ॐ

Christopher nearly bounces through the front door and shoves flowers in the faces of Mom and I. "Merry Thanksgiving!"

"It's Happy Thanksgiving, you cheeky bugger!" I say.

"Oh no, luv. You've got it all wrong. See, you Yanks say Merry Christmas while any *sane* person will tell you it's really Happy Christmas. Since you're all anticlockwise it must really be Merry Thanksgiving." Christopher kisses me firmly on the cheek and beams at Mom. "Mrs. Beckett, you've got a lovely daughter."

I groan at his ridiculous Herman's Hermit's joke that makes Mom giggle. "I can't believe you went there. Hello, Mrs. Eccles. Lovely to see you. Mom, Dad, I would like to introduce you to Grace. Mrs. Eccles, this is Lana and Edward."

"Sweetie, how many times do I need to tell you to call me Grace?" The attractive blonde looks to my parents with a brightly painted smile that has to be visible from space. "Lovely to see you. Thank you for inviting us to your little gathering."

"Our pleasure," Dad chimes in with a grin that has little pools of saliva forming in the corners of his mouth. "May I take your coat?"

"Oh, thank you." Grace removes her long, white fur coat to reveal an almost respectable length mini-skirt and tight sweater. She's a pretty lady of about sixty, with the figure of a hottie in her twenties. She must have been quite a looker at one time. Now she appears a little weathered around the edges and on the verge of trashy. Nonetheless, she's captivating.

"Please come in. Can we fix you a cocktail?" Mom asks as her wide eyes finally start to narrow. She still needs to close her mouth though.

Christopher whispers as our parents saunter off, "You should've seen what she tried to leave the house in. I practically made her put on a skirt."

"She reeks of cigarettes."

"This morning she reeked of wacky backy. I don't suppose there's any way that you and I can sneak off?"

"After all the time I spent cooking? Not a chance."

"Bugger. I just hope your mum and dad'll let me keep

seeing you after tonight."

Dinner isn't nearly as awkward as anticipated—partly due to directed conversation and partly because of the cocktails consumed before. Wisely, Christopher and I planned topics of conversation considered to be fairly safe along with noting those that are off limits. If something off limits arises, or if one of us becomes embarrassed, we're to resort to the safe list. Politics, any war, and Christopher's father are all strictly off limits while education and things both moms can bond over, like shopping and music, are safe. After dinner, if The Eccles' haven't fled screaming, we'll send the parents into the den for dessert and more imbibing.

To help us cope with the tension a game's been created called, "Who Has the Most Embarrassing Mum?" Immediately Christopher scored for Grace's outfit. He tried to get another point for her reeking of cigarettes, but I insisted my mother's perfume was also score worthy. Christopher tried to fight me on it, stating that perfume could be used to cover a stench while fags created one, but he lost the battle when he got a whiff of Dad's cologne. Though this was a game for the moms, Dad's cologne was so bad that Christopher conceded the stench war as a draw.

Another point went to Christopher for Grace constantly touching Dad. Mom scored me two points for showing my baby pictures and then talking about the rash I had when I was three that left a mark permanently on my bottom. The *So that's where it came from!* look that Christopher shot was incredulous enough for me to lose future sympathy for him. Thank God everyone had finished with dinner and was on their third cocktail.

"Speaking of marks, Christopher's father has an amazing one on his arse too. My Gawd, what an arse he had!" Grace's comment causes Christopher's eyes to morph from lively to stagnant.

"Oh, tell me about Christopher's father!" Mom's excitement sells out she's had far too many Martinis.

"Well, he was quite the catch and exactly my type when I met him—a musician, naturally. They are the worst kind to get involved with. He's quite older and started in a skiffle band. By the time I met him no one knew what skiffle was anymore. I was such a young lass. He was handsome and looked so magnificent on that stage holding his guitar and singing harmonies in a beatgroup with the other cute lads. Birds were constantly flocking around him, but it was me who had his eye."

Christopher is all kinds of embarrassed and racking up points rapidly in the evening's game. But Mom's totally entranced as she scores another point for me. "What band did his father play in? Would I have heard of them? I am a huge fan The British Invasion. I even named my son Donovan."

I smirk at Dad's flinch every time that's mentioned. How Mom ever got away with it, she'll never reveal. It has to be a zinger of a sex story.

"Probably not. They never made anything of themselves outside of England. They were called The Robert Dickson Six and had a small regional hit called "Walking Through Fire."

Grace begins to sing, and I bite my tongue. She then goes on to talk about how dashing Christopher's father looked in his mod clothes, and how she finagled herself backstage at the tender age of fourteen with the intention of shagging him. "Paul didn't know that though. I lied about my age until I was up the duff with our first son, and we had to get married. By then it was too late. Oh! You should have seen the look on his face when I told him!"

"Isn't there dessert?" Christopher announces more than inquires.

Feeling the retaliation has gone on long enough, I save him. "Come into the kitchen. You can help me."

As soon as we're out of earshot, Christopher lets me have it. "Lilyanna, we had a deal! Mum was not to speak of my father. There's no stopping her now."

"Sorry, but after that look you gave me regarding my rash mark—which my father saw you do, by the way—I figured all bets were off."

"Bollocks! This isn't funny. We need to stop her. Grab dessert and go like the clappers before she gets hysterical!"

Just as I crawl into bed, Christopher calls.

"Darling, I'm sorry about my little wobbler earlier. I don't think I warned you properly."

"Is everything all right?"

"Yes, luv. You might say we dodged a bullet though."

"What was the bullet?" I ask.

"I should've told you more about how Mum gets when she talks about me dad. She won't admit it, but she still fancies him. Whenever she talks of him there's a big chance she will throw a Benny, especially when she's on the piss. I'm dreadfully sorry if I was rude."

"It's fine. I'm sorry things got that way. Do you mean that she still loves him and can't accept the divorce?"

"Yeah. The way she explains it is if you really love someone and can't be with them it makes you a little crazy. The longer you were with them, or the closer you were, the madder you get. Anyway, she had a lovely time and said the more she knows you, the more she wants you to be the daughter she never had. She also adores your mum and wants to have tea with her."

"Is that wise?"

"It's fine. Lilyanna, your father's not too well chuffed on me, is he?" Christopher sounds disappointed with himself. From the little he has said, it seems that he does not get along well with his father much either.

"It's not you. He has bizarre ideals regarding how people should be. I suspect that's part of Donovan's problem. He's trying to live up to a standard my father has that he doesn't share."

"Bloody hell, that's naff. I guess I'll never be the son your dad wishes he had."

"Darlin', if you were, I wouldn't love you. Not one bit."

After the call I snuggle my pillow. It's not nearly as cozy as Christopher. Just as sleep drifts over me, reality hits. What did Christopher mean when he said Grace wants me to be the daughter she never had? Does he realize how that sounds? I love him, but a teenage romance with Christopher is all I signed up for. My feelings for Donovan are still unresolved, which was a big part of why I needed him home for Thanksgiving.

Is a true future with Christopher possible? It seems perfect. We both want a happy home life and a family while pursuing our careers. We share a sense of humor and really love and respect one another. When we're apart it's as if a piece of me is missing.

But I once had all those things with Donovan—and so many more. I may never get them with anyone else.

Suddenly, my life is more complex than ever.

18

While it's nice to have escaped the trenches, I'd rather be at Battlefield Work. Christopher is in Manchester for another week, and tomorrow marks not only Christmas Eve, but also the long awaited, and somewhat feared, return of Donovan.

The silence in the house gives a sense of impending doom as I prepare to make tomorrow's dessert. Usually this task is enjoyable, but I've made so many gingerbreads, fruitcakes, Bûche de Noël, Lebkuchen, and Panettone that the sight of a single Christmas cookie may induce a stroke.

Christopher's delicate statement regarding my over-doneness with Christmas fare summed it beautifully: "You're just bloody rowed out, luv."

The world stops for everyone whenever Christopher enters the bakery. I'll never forget the time he walked in and saw Jennifer at the counter, who actually said, "Hi, Chris. I'll get Lily for you."

"Thank you, but please call me Christopher," he replied.

"Oh, I'm sorry. I'm also sorry I've had a hard time with your accent. I think I have it now. You're from a place called Cockney, right?"

"No! No! No! Cockney is an accent from East London! I'm from Manchester! It's nowhere near London! Oh, Blimey!"

Everyone in the back of the shop was in hysterics as he burst through the doors and stormed to Josette. He looked like a marionette with his arms flailing and head bouncing. "Bloody hell! How is it she can understand you, but she can't understand me?"

Now he walks straight in like he's the King himself. Josette never seems to mind and has invited him to stick around, provided he washes his hands the second he comes in and wears an apron. Several times she's tricked him into working. It's always entertaining to see how long it will take for him to realize what he's doing. His dishwashing skills have improved greatly. Now he rarely breaks a thing.

His return for the New Year can't arrive fast enough. Life is so much richer with Christopher. Conversely, the thought of Donovan coming home is discomforting. But since Donovan encouraged me to push my limits, I should make something incredibly fancy and laden with cream and chocolate and tons of calories to show off my capabilities. Hopefully he won't be such an ass that I'll throw it at him.

While heading to the counter with the intent of flipping through my formula book for just the right thing, a figure lounging against the fence in the snow-covered yard forces me to shriek. The heart-stopping man in black is still and silent with eyes lowered beneath his mantle of raven hair. His chiseled features gleam magnificently in a hint of sunlight that breaks through the clouds. He waves coyly and motions for me to open the window.

The chill that blows into the warm house likely adds to the tone of my near verbal assault. "What the hell are you doing here? I thought you weren't coming until tomorrow?"

Donovan's smile is cocky, yet charming, as he flips his head to the side to remove a feather of hair from his glorious face. "Well, I didn't know what to expect, but I hoped for a better greeting than that. Mom and Dad home?"

"No. Dad's at work, and Mom's doing last minute shopping. You know how she is." Damn it! I'm jittering. How is it he still has this effect on me?

"I was counting on that." His eyes scan the yard before turning back to me. "Can you meet me at that restaurant you like in two hours? The one with the great French food."

"You mean Bel Ami? That's an hour's drive from here."

"Yeah, that's kind of the point. I thought I'd come home a day early and steal you away since we're probably not going to have much time together over the next few days. Can you meet me?" He's so cool and collected, yet a little unsure of himself. My old Donovan has returned, but I sense a second shadow to him. He's carrying a burden that no one can distinguish.

"Sure, but why don't we just go there together?"

"I have some stuff to take care of. Also, I don't want Mom and Dad to know I'm here yet. I'm staying at a motel tonight. I'll see you in a few hours."

This is odd. Donovan has been back for two minutes and already the freak show has begun.

ॐ

Just as I thought Donovan couldn't get more unreadable, the universe again proves me wrong. All appears normal on the surface: My brother asked me to lunch and wants time alone with me in a public place. There's no obvious freakishness except for the cloak and dagger game. But why didn't he call my cell phone? Everything with him is a hodgepodge of bizarre.

When I arrive at the restaurant, Donovan is already sitting outside. The way he checks his watch makes me think he's been there awhile. He sees me and stands uncomfortably. He slips his hands into his pockets. I don't think he knows how I am going to react to seeing him. However, I'm unable to control my rush of emotions. I sprint, jump onto him, wrap my legs around his waist, and lay kisses all over his face. Obviously, decorum isn't a concern.

"Geez, Lil! You almost tackled me onto the concrete! You could've cracked my head open." When he pulls his head back, his eyes have the glow my heart craves. "Thanks for breaking the ice. I had no idea how to do it."

Our conversation is anything but strained. College has been great for him, and he's finding direction in his life. His grades are less than stellar, but, considering how much he has going on with football, everything's going decently.

112

Excitement fills his eyes as he asks about my job, which Mom told him little about. I'm bursting with details—totally talking his ears off. But despite the free-flowing chatter, I'm constantly fussing with my napkin, and Donovan keeps swirling his coffee and tapping his foot.

"I can't believe Mom hasn't told you any of this," I say.

"I've been avoiding her and Dad as much as possible. I know it's going to bite me in the ass, and they'll grill me over the next few days, so that's why I wanted to steal you away today. By this time tomorrow, Mom will have me cleaning the garage. How have things been with you and Mom? Do you two talk much?"

There he goes swirling his coffee again. Just the thought of my jittery brain repeatedly watching it whirl makes me a little dizzy. "It's gotten better over the last few months," I say. "She's really trying to be my ageless friend though. It's kind of weird. Her issues with Dad are obviously still there. I can't say I confide in her, but I'm definitely not hiding things. Especially not like I'm hiding things from Dad."

"Oh God! *Be careful* with Mom, and *always* hide things from Dad! Never let them know what you're really up to."

I cringe. "They know a lot of it already. Believe me, I especially didn't want Dad to find out."

Donovan looks at me out of the corner of his squinting eyes. "What exactly are we talking about here?"

"Just some personal stuff that slipped out on Thanksgiving. Dad's never called me out on it, but I suspect he knows his daughter isn't exactly innocent."

"Lil-y ..." Donovan looks freaked, then the obvious smacks him in the face. "Wait, is this about your boyfriend? I was wondering if you were ever going to get around to talking about him."

"I really don't want to talk about this."

"Oh, why not? I can't possibly imagine why you wouldn't want to share every detail of your sex life with me of all people." His words may be sarcastic, but his body looks tense. I don't think big brother likes the implications.

"Oh, God!" My face cowers into my hands. Smugly, he waits for me to speak. "Why? Why should I tell you this?" I throw my hands in the air and bob my head. Crap! Now I'm acting like Christopher. "Blimey!"

"The one thing Mom did tell me is that he's from Manchester."

"Of course she told you that! She can't stop talking about it!" I turn my gaze to my coffee. I wish I could jump into the cup and drown. "This is too awkward."

Donovan's eyes dart around the room before he reaches across the table and grabs my hands. The gesture captures my breath and throws my head completely off track. "Look, Lily, you're my sister and, believe it or not, my best friend. I worry about you. Please, tell me how you're really doing. Let me know if you're being treated right or if you're with some loser and I need to shake some sense into you."

He drops my hands and leans back with crossed arms and a smug grin. His big brother mask has returned. Begrudgingly, I spit out only the basics; how I met Christopher, how he's a little too proud of being from Manchester, and about his parent's split.

Donovan leans forward. "Okay, Lil. Tell me the rest."

I mirror his stance. "Like what?"

"You've told me straight facts but nothing about what he's like as a person or how he treats you. So either something's wrong, or you're not opening up. Which is it?"

"I just feel awkward. I'm still very confused."

"Is this because of something he does, or because you and I had some *weirdness* in the past?"

Donovan's eye roll just got annoying again. Does he have to belittle us that way? His flippancy is turning me into a total wreck. There is no choice but to enter survival mode and let myself gush over Christopher. As soon as I start, warmth rushes through me. "He's totally adorable. The jocks can't stand him because he's this scrawny, pasty bloke with a cute accent the girls are nuts over. He's totally awkward around them, which makes the jocks even more bonkers.

The word klutzy suits him, yet he's an incredibly talented guitarist. He can turn someone's mood around with his smile, and when he's miffed he becomes animated and looks a little like a marionette." I exhale with high hopes. "Does that answer your questions?"

"No. Not even close."

"Ugh!"

"You're talking about all these girls swarming him, but you haven't said how he treats you or if you're the only girl in his life. I'm kind of seeing a big red flag here. Are you sure he's not using you along with every other female within grabbing distance?"

I can't take this anymore. I'm ripped between the amazing man that sits across from me and the one I've recently fallen over the edge for. But Donovan has asked for it. He's looking to find something bad in Christopher, and he's out of luck.

The truth flows freely while the rush of emotions that fill my heart catch me off-guard. "He treats me perfectly and always makes sure I'm looked after. I am *definitely* the only girl in his life. I know this not only because he tells me, but also because he shows me how much he loves me in everything he does. He asks for nothing yet gives me more than I can measure. Christopher is amazing, and I must be the luckiest girl in existence."

Donovan's guard has fallen, and he's gone green. Neither of us was prepared for my response. "All right, I'll stop worrying. You seem happy. Do you think he'll be in your life for long?" He raises his coffee and takes a long sip. It's just like Mom does when she's hiding in fear of an answer or attempting to be sly.

"Definitely the rest of our senior year. Things will change so much in a few months that I don't know what to think beyond now. I told Mom and Dad about pastry school." The waitress arrives and leaves our check.

"I heard! Good job on doing that and not getting killed by Dad. I knew you'd have the upper hand."

"It's so unfair to you."

"Bah! I'm used to it. Then again, I'm hiding from him today and dreading the rest of the week." Donovan pays the check with a wad of cash and stands to leave. "Hey, Lil, thanks for meeting me today. Please try not to get upset if I don't talk to you much while I'm here. I'll see you tomorrow."

I watch him walk away. That is so unlike him. Normally he would walk me to my car. I just don't get him anymore.

19

Donovan's life is like a bullet train skidding him into depression. His withdraws often occur for unknown reasons, but the day he helped Dad, he appeared broken and stripped of all pride. It was of no surprise when he disappeared after dinner without a word.

While he continues to be civil to me, he's definitely still the Donovan I no longer know. I dread how he will act tonight at Mom and Dad's New Year's Eve party. Poor Christopher. Heaven only knows what's in store for him.

I'm awake long before everyone else, so I decide now is as good of a time as any to talk to Donovan. Actually, it might be the best time. He's done a pretty good job of avoiding me, so I need to catch him while I can. Tonight is going to be stressful for us both. Not only will he meet Christopher, it's the anniversary of when everything about us changed for the worse.

I slip into Donovan's room and nudge him. "Hey, pissy pants, wake up."

He groans, and his eyes slip open. He jumps when he sees me. "What the hell are you doing?"

"Relax. Geez!" I kneel beside his bed. "I have to go to work, but I want to talk to you first. I won't ask if you're okay because obviously you're not. Is there anything I can do?"

He rolls to face me and moans, "Nah. Mom and Dad are driving me crazy, and I'm not looking forward to dealing with the influx of people tonight. I tried to get out of being here but Mom got all—" He sneers and dismissively waves a hand in the air.

"Do you mean she had kittens?" I say in my best British

117

accent, attempting levity.

"Oh, that's right. Your scrawny dreamboat comes home today." He rolls onto his back, puts the pillow over his head and mutters through it, "Honestly Lil, I'm kind of on the fence about meeting him."

I rip the pillow from his face and bounce onto his bed. Maybe I can get a smile out of him. "Oh, bloody hell. Are you puttin' me on? This ought to be the show of a lifetime for ya, gettin' a front row seat for Mum gettin' on the piss and droolin' over a scrawny lit'le English bloke like she did when she was nine. Oughtta be a downright disgustin' site!"

"Oh God. Is it really that bad? And please stop talking like that." He takes back the pillow and resumes hiding.

"It hasn't been, but Christopher keeps threatening to mess with her. I'm guessing tonight will be the night. From the tone of our last video chat, he's up to something. Oh! And his mom's coming, whom I think has a twisted little thing for Dad."

Donovan lifts the pillow. "Hey! I know what you can do for me. Go into the kitchen. Get that really nasty butcher knife and whack my head off."

I nudge him to raise his head so I can slip his pillow back where it belongs. "Seriously, would you please put forth an extra effort to be pleasant? At least to Christopher. He's already kind of freaked about meeting you after the little display I mentioned that happened with Al's brother. Bob didn't paint you in a very nice light. Unfortunately, I didn't help matters."

"What do you mean, 'put forth an extra effort to be pleasant?' Am I not always the most charming man you've ever met?"

"Quit making sarcastic remarks and being all—" I mimic his trademark blinking eye roll before leaning in and whispering, "It's just too damn sexy."

Donovan's eyes almost pop out of his head while mine quickly slam shut. We both go rigid. What the hell was I thinking? My intended joke was in no way funny. Now I'm stricken by an overwhelming sense of guilt. "Sorry, I had to get at least one in before you left." I start to flee, but I'm arrested by Donovan's touch upon my arm. He sits and pulls me down next to him. My lids go tight again. I refuse to open them and face the shame my words brought. What on earth came over me?

"Lily, look at me. I know you were messing with me but really, look at me. Just look me in the eyes, and don't think for a minute. I need a moment of honesty."

Sanity begs me to take flight and not return home until Donovan has long left, but his request is conquering. The sensation as he runs his fingers along my jaw line and calls my eyes to meet his reminds me of his true nature and brings on a yearning for the days when we were discovering our hidden desires.

We stare into each other's eyes, and the intended moment becomes a display of devotion. After my heart seizes and I surrender to what we have never leaving me, Donovan breaks our lock and falls back on the bed. "Yeah, I thought so."

"What did you see?"

"The same thing you did in me."

I escape our reality in haste, absolutely hating myself for being victimized by the emotions that rip me apart.

20

After a strained week, Christopher's charming face will be my salvation. Missing him this much was previously unimaginable. However, with Donovan here and my morning joke that lead to a daylong guilt trip, I'm a little edgy.

Donovan's been a whole new kind of ass since our morning encounter. He alters between being a vicious tiger about to strike and an abused house cat that cowers from a sudden movement. With the exception of a few minutes this morning, his guard has been raised the entire visit. But there have also been brief moments when he's intentionally slipped. He's allowed me glimpses into his true self; ones that tell me he's still in there and needs me to know.

When the doorbell rings, my nervousness caves way for excitement so intense it's almost panic. I sprint and fling open the door, ready to throw my arms around the man I cherish now more than ever. However, instead of passionately embracing Christopher, I find myself laughing at him.

"Hello, luv! Miss me?" Christopher stands with two bouquets of flowers in one hand, a guitar in the other, and a beaming grin on his face. He's wearing the most ridiculous, yet kind of sexy, clothes I've ever seen; Beatle boots, grey, drainpipe trousers, a light blue, satin poet shirt, and an ultramarine ascot that make his azure eyes burst.

"Mom, your dream date is here," I call towards the kitchen. "Oh my God! Where did you get that outfit?"

"Do you like it? I think it makes me look rather dashing," he boasts while turning and checking himself out.

"I—actually—think it makes you look kind of hot. I'm

Gobsmacked."

"Ah, I sure have missed you, pet." He kisses me sweetly before checking himself out again. "Do you really like it?"

Mom strolls into the room. Donovan, who seems to have sprouted three inches, follows her. She gushes upon seeing Christopher. "What's all the commotion—oh, my goodness! Oh, Christopher! Where did you ever get that outfit?"

Donovan's attention snaps in my direction. I can hear him think as if he is screaming. "*You have got to be kidding me!*"

"*I told you!*" I tell him back.

"I raided Dad's storage and had the tailor do a number on it. I thought it might be a lark to wear. Here you go, luvs." Christopher hands bouquets of white and red roses sprinkled with silver to Mom and me. He then turns his attention to Donovan who's trying his best not to look like he has no clue in the world what ladies see in Christopher. "Hello. Are you Lilyanna's brother?" Christopher asks while extending his hand.

"Yeah, I'm Donovan. Nice to meet you." Donovan's wall dips ever so slightly, and his discomfort clambers up my spine.

"A pleasure. Do they call you mellow yellow?"

"Oh, Christopher!" Mom gushes.

Donovan raises his eyebrows. "Quite rightly, but I prefer Sunshine Superman."

"Ah, clever one he is."

"Wow," Donovan mutters under his breath. He and Mom go back to the kitchen.

I can't help but beam at my mod treasure. "I missed you so much!"

As night falls, the house becomes crammed with my parent's conservative friends who quickly show signs of inebriation. The men are a little sedate, but the women are starting to woo it up. It's only a matter of time until one of them replaces her party crown with a lampshade.

Christopher and I shelter ourselves from the festivities unfolding around us by snuggling on the living room sofa. I'm self-conscious as hell, but Donovan wanted me to find someone special, so I'm allowing my feelings for Christopher to show honestly. Games like I played with Al are no longer an option.

"You been getting on with your brother?" Christopher asks. "I tried talking to him, but I don't think he's too well chuffed on me."

My reaction shows a bit of agitation. "Why? What'd he say to you?"

Christopher shifts his weight. "Oh, nothing really. I can tell he's very protective of you."

My eyes demand that he spill all of the details.

His tone changes to one that sounds almost boastful. "He just said you're obviously very fond of me, and he hopes I never do anything to hurt you."

"Or?"

"There was no *or* vocalized, but I believe *or I'll rip your scrawny little arms off* was implied." He makes a brushing motion with his hand and kisses my cheek. "It's nowt, luv. I happen to be very much in love with his sister, so I'd like to make a good impression. Thoughts?"

"Not a clue. Right now the two of you have pretty much nothing in common. In fact, I venture to say that you're everything he's not."

Donovan is reluctant to respond to my gesture for him to join us. The way he walks reminds me of a movie where the film has slowed. He sits next to me and reclines into the corner of the sofa before putting his feet in my lap. I feel like I'm territory that's been claimed. I'm quick to comment on his demeanor. "I don't know if I've ever seen you so bored in all my life."

He lets out a grouse. "You know how Mom and Dad's friends are. They're just as stodgy and dull as Mom and Dad."

"They did tell us we could invite people."

"I see you were as keen on inviting your friends as I was. No one wants to be trapped here."

My darling Christopher is determined to make a good impression. "Don't look now, mate, but there's been a bird watching you all night." He points to the only girl here that's about our age. She's been more interested in her book than being social.

Donovan doesn't look. Instead he keeps a close eye on Christopher. "You seem to have your fair share checking you out as well. You must be quite popular."

"Really? I never notice anyone but Lilyanna." He snuggles tighter and kisses my cheek. "Jammy sod I am."

Donovan's brows rise. His expression would be amusing, if not for the circumstances. As if the situation couldn't get more awkward for him, Grace approaches her son and requests that he grab the guitar he brought so as to entertain the ladies. When she saunters off in her ultra-tight micro mini, she commands Donovan's full and mortified attention.

Christopher rubs his hands together and jots off with gusto, preparing himself for what terrors and delights may lay ahead. I grab Donovan's hand and jump off of the sofa. "Let's get a good seat for the fireworks."

The display inside the den would be sickening if it weren't so entertaining. Every female, most of them over fifty, have their eyes on the scrawny English lad with the guitar and mod clothes. Christopher is merciless as he plays nothing but old British pop standards that mature American women would know. He's a never-ending jukebox of happy, peppy pop songs, and his audience sings and dances like star-struck teenyboppers.

"This is vile." Donovan says revolted, yet amused by the display. "Really, this is disgusting."

"This is every day of my life."

He shoots me a look like I've fully lost my mind. "Why do girls, grown women even, go crazy over this guy? I'm sorry, Lil, I just don't get it. He's so, so—"

"Scrawny? Happy? Charming? Human?"

"Yeah." Donovan looks like he feels unclean, but when he gets a good look at Mom singing and dancing he's compelled to flee. "Oh God! I'm going to get something to drink."

I'm actually enjoying the spectacle and can't fault these women one bit. Mom has always said that the happiest music came from Manchester, and the British Invasion was a time in music that will be revered and studied for centuries. Upon appreciating the sea of happy faces, I find no way to dispute her.

I join Mom for a few dances. Her smile provides a window into how she must have been at my age. To me, she is no longer the persona of a dedicated housewife or my wannabe teenage friend. Now I understand the reason for her regression: She's desperately attempting to retain a part of herself that's being stripped away. Is the stripping a byproduct of my father's ideals, the passage of time, or society's notion that in order to mature you must lose part of yourself?

Then the shimmer in Christopher's eyes captures my thoughts. This particular gleam tells of an exceptional kind of love—one that should never be reserved. He was born to play music and make people happy with his talent and charm. For him to do anything else would be a betrayal, not only to him, but also to all.

The contrast between Mom and Christopher brings forth a revelation of the constant need for honesty with myself. Without it, you become lost and feel your life is worth nothing. I suspect this sums up Donovan's problems. Still, is that enough to have driven him to hurt me so badly? One year ago tonight he shattered my heart. If he would talk to me, maybe I could find forgiveness. I hate that a part of me wants revenge. Mostly, it's how I feel I've lost the most important thing in the world that compels me to return to his side.

Donovan hands me a bottle of juice. His eyes are fixated on Christopher. "He's extremely talented," Donovan says.

"He's so precise. It's interesting, because every now and then he laughs and shows how comfortable he is, which is obvious in how he plays. But he's generally very focused, which he needs to be, because some of what he's playing is incredibly complex. But it's all so clean."

Donovan seems temporarily at peace with himself, but that changes when Christopher slips into his rendition of The Hollies' "Pay You Back With Interest." While the tone is bright, the sentiment is depressing. It tells of someone unable to spend time with the people he loves because complications claw him away, and he vows that someday he will make it up to them. The lyrics are haunting, but something in how Christopher sings them is gut wrenching. Every word rips from his soul and sends daggers into my heart.

I'm not the only one affected. Donovan is glancing down at me with watery eyes. They send a message of love, apology, and remorse. Unable to listen any longer, Donovan retreats upstairs. After a moment long enough to conceal my pursuit, I follow his tracks with a deep sense of foreboding.

Softly, I knock on his bedroom door. I fail to get a response. I call his name, and even though there is no reply, I know I need to go inside.

Just enough light creeps in from the street to illuminate Donovan sitting on his bed. His face is blanketed in tears of sorrow. The way he has his arms wrapped around his knees reminds me of a little boy. I sit next to him and touch his hand. It's quaking. What could possibly do this to a grown man? Especially one who was raised to believe that men don't express emotions, even privately.

"Donovan, you're not doing so well. Do you know that?"

"I know, Lily. I know."

"There's something very serious going on. Please let me help."

Languidly, he closes his eyes as if about to go into a trance. "The best way for you to help is to let me be alone for a while."

"No way. You're scaring me. I'm not letting you out of my sight tonight."

"Go downstairs, Lily."

"No. It's fine if you don't want to talk or if you want to ignore me again after you leave, but I'm no longer allowing you to hide from me when you're in plain sight. You don't need to say a word, but I'm staying here until you are ready to go back down."

Donovan and I reappear as Christopher hits his old school Brit pop limit. He takes his time putting his guitar into its case, as if knowing troubles are at hand. "Everything all right?" he asks while looking at the floor.

I take Christopher by the hands and stick my face into his view. "Why the avoidance?"

"I'm sorry, luv. I saw what happened earlier, and I'm concerned. Ever since I got here I've felt something is very wrong that I cannot fix. It's all over your face. I'm probably just a little sentimental tonight. Everything all right with your brother?"

No, and I still have no idea why. "He's carrying a heavier load than I can imagine, and he's not willing to talk about it. He tries to play it off, but he's a very emotional person. I'm incredibly worried about him. Can we please be sure to keep an eye on him tonight? I was really hoping to sneak off and show you how much I missed you, but I promise I'll make it up to you." The touch of my lips to his expresses my adoration more than words ever could.

"Everything's fine with us?"

I snuggle into his shoulder and surrender to his embrace. "Yes. Why would you think differently?"

His voice is serene and laced with love. "When I am here, I know how far away I am from Manchester, but when I was there, it hit me how far Manchester is from you. I often couldn't sleep, so I'd go outside and look at the stars while thinking how they were the same ones that watched over you, but they actually made you feel farther away.

Lilyanna, I think I'm deeper into this love thing than I should be."

He graces me with a kiss, leaving an imprint that will tingle throughout the night. It butchers me that this moment cannot be enjoyed for all it's worth, but my emotional tug of war continues. I risk turning off my brain and allowing my emotions to speak, unaware of what Christopher will hear. "I hope you never go away again, not even for a day. Every time I look into your eyes I feel myself getting pulled in deeper. I don't know how much farther a person can go."

"Blimey," he whispers, "I'm a lucky sod." His eyes seize my heart until I feel overwhelmed and turn away.

Christopher turns his attention to Donovan, who's across the room and having his ear talked off by the girl who's been crushing on him all night. "Who is that bird, anyway?"

"Apparently she's the daughter of one of my dad's business associates. I've never seen her before."

"Since he's occupied, sure I can't run you astray as the clock strikes for a bit of the old How's Your Father?"

"And you wonder why no one understands you!"

There's an old adage that if you want to know how someone really feels, you can sense it in their kiss. If this holds true, at the stroke of midnight I learn that Christopher's love for me may be time transcending. More and more I'm feeling the same way.

Nothing would be better than to stay by his side and continue with our passionate display, but there is unfinished business that walked into the kitchen just as the countdown began. A year ago, Donovan wronged me. As much as he is hurting, I owe it to myself to find a way to heal. Still, I need to respect the upheaval I witnessed earlier.

Donovan has kept himself occupied by restocking buckets of ice. I nudge him down the back hall where we grab coats and slip outside. There is no resistance on his part.

As he starts to put on his coat, I gently touch his hand. He stops, and his eyes rise to meet mine. I am so torn. In order for me to heal I need to chew him out for what he did. But I love him, and I want to help him through his hurt. Somehow, there has to be middle ground.

My tears begin to fall. I won't yell at him, but I will be honest. We both deserve that. So instead of screaming anger, I whisper love. "One year ago tonight, you bailed on me. I couldn't stand the thought of staying at that party another moment, and I didn't dare beg you to come get me. I also didn't want to call Mom and Dad and have to fabricate an excuse for leaving early, so I walked home in the snow. I know this is petty, but I need you to have a taste of how I felt."

I feel so guilty, but damn it, he hurt me, and his cruelty has never really stopped. Part of me wants to beat the crap out of the big, dumb jock, but God, my heart bleeds so much for him. He looks like Pandora the wounded house cat, and I really just want to pick him up and hold him.

I wipe away my tears. Donovan used to be the one to do that. Now he won't even look at me.

I can't do this anymore. I hand Donovan his coat. He drapes it on his arm and stares at it in silence. I'd give anything for him to talk to me.

"I'm sorry," I say. "I know you are hurting, but I owed it to myself to tell you that. Anyway, someday when you finally tell me everything, like you say you will, the explanation for that is at the top of the list, okay?"

He nods to the ground. "It's fine, Lil. You don't need to go easy on me. I deserve a lot worse."

"Yeah, but there is a difference between giving you a piece of my mind and being downright cruel to someone who is hurting." I touch my lips to his cheek and dare to let them linger. My love flows into the kiss as much as I can allow while respecting that a year ago he told me we were through. My heart also reminds me that there is a man I never wish to hurt just inside the door. "Happy New Year. I hope this one is better for us both."

Maybe it is my imagination, but as I turn and walk away Donovan speaks to me from within.

I love you, too.

21

In true Donovan style, on the last night of his visit, he disappears after dinner. Though I have respected his privacy, after his meltdown last night, I really need to make sure he is okay.

After driving to every coffee shop and movie theatre within miles, I find his car in a cinema lot. I pull out two wool blankets from my trunk and sit in my chilly Bug for almost an hour. If I'm lucky, I'll only catch pneumonia instead of having every cell in my body freeze. Truly this man is going to be my demise.

When he finally approaches his car, I get out of mine and accidentally scare the crap out of him. He really has gotten edgy. Donovan groans at my request to get into my car. After eyeing the surrounding lot, he then agrees without question. The silence is deafening as I drive us to the top of the hill overlooking the town.

He only slightly protests when I ask him to walk with me to a small patch whose view is unobstructed by trees. I put down a blanket folded over several times to make it thick, yet just big enough for us both to fit on, before I ask him to sit.

Donovan complies with my request.

I triple fold the other blanket and wrap it around his shoulders before asking him to spread his legs. He looks at me like I've intentionally thrown myself off of the apple cart.

My words are chosen carefully, "Don't fight me, friend. Tonight I'm in charge." I sit with my back snuggling against him and wrap the blanket around us both before continuing. "Hear me out. We are just going to sit here. We can talk about anything you want, or we can sit in silence, but you are not hiding alone tonight. And, just to be clear and remove any tension, tonight we are friends and only friends. Nothing else. All other roles, real or implied, are non-existent."

Without a fight, he pulls me close. His warm breath creates a fog over my vision. "Why do you have these blankets? Never mind, I don't want to know what they've been used for."

I reach back and bash his arm. "You aren't the only one who needs to escape and think sometimes."

"I thought your life is perfect. What are you escaping from?"

"Hello! I believe you've met my parents. Seriously, everyone needs to escape once in a while."

"Don't you have Christopher for that?"

The truth is a little painful. "I have Christopher for a lot, and sometimes it's for that, but I can't talk to him about everything. Sometimes people need to sort things out for themselves. I'm sure you understand."

Donovan's hold on me tightens. The heat of our bodies, down coats, and wool blankets is barely enough to keep us from shivering, but the warmth from his heart gives me hope for the real Donovan. We stare at the lights of the town below for a long time before he speaks. "I needed this."

"Yeah, I kind of figured."

"Lily, how is it you're always so strong and sure of things?"

"I'm strong because I decided a long time ago that I had to be, else I would wind up like Mom. I'm subservient to no one. As for being sure of things ... There are some things I'm not so sure of, but when my inner voice controls my lips I know it's right, so I don't question it."

Donovan tucks his head into my shoulder and pulls me a little closer. His tone is sincere, but his actions claim territory. "You're lucky to be in love with Christopher. He's exactly what you need right now."

"I never told you that. How do you know I'm in love

with Christopher?"

He tucks my hair behind my ear and leans in as if fearing someone may hear his confession. "You and I still know each other better than anyone. I see how you look at him. I've seen that look before."

How pathetic is this moment? "You know, Donovan, you're pretty tight-lipped, but when you do say something you really go for the gut. Still you don't admit anything, so I'm never sure if you're saying what I think you are. Is that what last night was about?"

"Last night's upset was a drop in the old bucket. But I mean it; you're both very lucky. He loves you more than you realize."

My next words are daring, but they need to be said. "I'm very much in love with Christopher, but let's face it, there's something going on here with us. Like it or not—admit it or not—it's there, it's real, and it's strong. And it's not just some passing physical thing. It's buried deep in my soul and rips at me constantly. So for now, I just take each day as it comes. Can you do just that much with me?"

Donovan sniffles. "It's how I've been living my life every day for the past year, Lil."

I turn to face him, but he looks away. "No questions, okay? In fact, let's not say another word to each other until I leave tomorrow."

I try not to sound sarcastic, because this question comes from the sadness in my heart. "You mean until you sneak out tonight like last time?"

"Yeah. No more words to me or to anyone that we were here, okay?"

I turn my sights back to the lights of the town where tomorrow my life will resume as usual. Tonight, I'll just sit here and pray for the man who needs to talk but won't. "It's a deal."

22

"I'm up a gum tree. Why are we doing this?" Christopher asks while leaning against the counter in my kitchen. With an extreme lack of coordination, he tosses a raisin into the vicinity of his mouth.

"Because it's Josette's birthday, and I want to do something nice for her." I pour Cognac over a pot of warm raisins before igniting them.

"Cor blimey! Call out the Fire Brigade! No luv, what I don't understand is why we're making her a cake when she owns an entire shop full. It seems rather silly."

"You don't understand women much, do you? Every woman wants to be treated like a queen, and everyone on the planet wants a cake on their birthday. It shows people you remember they exist and you love them. I owe Josette a lot, including meeting you over a month before all the birds in town did." Setting down the pot that has lost its flame, I kiss Christopher on the cheek. He shies his chin into his shoulder and blushes. "Had that not happened they would've gotten to you first, and I wouldn't have had a chance."

"Not bloody well likely. Those birds scare me!"

"For that I'm grateful." I touch my lips to him again before moving on to sift the flour.

"Anything special I should know about Valentine's Day in America? I fear I shall need rescuing from the Queen if I hash it."

The thought of my first real Valentine's Day invigorates me. It also freaks me out. Christopher always wants to do right by me, and lately he's been increasingly obvious about it. I'm a little skeptical as to his intentions.

133

"You don't have anything to worry about. You always take better care of me than you need to. With you, every day is Valentine's Day."

"Bloody hell. I really better outdo meself."

A week later, per Christopher's insistence, I watch out the den's back window at sunrise. Very strict orders were given that I not do anything this morning that could possibly enable me to see any human being other than the ones in my family. Why am I doing this? With Christopher there's no telling. It could be something sweet and endearing, something silly and utterly ridiculous, or all of the above: Like a brass band could invade with him marching in the lead.

After a moment, a ruckus is heard, like someone tried to come over the fence and has fallen on his bum. It's followed by a mutter of, "Bloody hell!" A cringe accompanies my chuckle, and I brace myself for whatever antics may follow.

Christopher does his best to appear as if he's casually strolling through my yard when he sees me and detours to knock on my window. Apprehensively I open it to the passer by.

"Excuse me, miss. I wouldn't happen to be the first gentleman you've seen today? Sans your father, of course."

Should I really play along? "Why yes, kind sir. Actually you are."

"Well, flukey bugger I am. Are you aware of the day?"

"I believe it's Valentine's Day." The display stymies me. Maybe that noise I heard was him cracking his skull.

"Right you are! And in case you haven't been able to tell, I'm from England—Manchester, in fact. Did you know that in England when a lady looks out her window on Valentine's Day it's believed that the first man she sees is the one that's meant for her?"

"Why, no. I had no idea." Just where is this going? For months he's made stronger attempts to convey his feelings for me, like they've become so deep he can no longer express them to his satisfaction.

"Well, you wouldn't happen to be available for dinner tonight, would you?"

"Dinner sounds lovely. I should tell you that I do have a boyfriend. I think he is from someplace called Cockney, but that's not as good as Manchester, is it?"

Christopher throws his arms in the air and my less refined love returns. "Oh, rubbish! You were doing so well!" With mock exasperation he concedes to handing me a brown, paper lunch bag. "Here you go. I made you something." Nestled in it is a box containing a very gauche looking chocolate cupcake with pink frosting and colored sprinkles. "I made it meself. Well, I had a little help from a box of mix and a can of icing, but I still made it. It might surprise you to know that I'm quite a disaster in the kitchen. I made two dozen of those buggers, and that's the only one that resembles something edible."

His face glows in hopes that I like my gift. He never fails to completely move me. "Christopher, it's truly amazing that you did this for me. It's perfect and so incredibly thoughtful. I just love it. You can tell the Queen that you won't need rescuing. Come around front. I have a little surprise for you."

I meet Christopher at the front door with the intention of pulling him inside and giving him a Valentine's greeting he'll remember for a lifetime, but he grabs me first. "Come out a moment. Step out on to the porch and follow my lead." Slipping his arms around my waist, he turns me to face the street. "Nestle your head into my shoulder. Without looking up, follow the blue car across the way. I know this sounds daft, but someone's been watching since I left the house."

By the time I process his words, the car speeds off. "I couldn't see who it was. Did you get a look at the driver?"

"All I saw was a baseball cap." Realizing the insanity of the notion, Christopher tries to lighten the mood. "I must be going batty. Do you think it's the lack of humidity?"

"Yeah, that must be it. Either that or you're bloody

bonkers!" I lightly smack his head before rustling my fingers through his hair.

"Thanks loads, luv."

"It was probably a jealous member of your fan club. Then again, maybe we need to get you into a more humid space. No one else is home and our shower can get very steamy, very quickly. Come on."

"Crikey!"

With damp hair and telltale grins plastered on our faces, we arrive at school, unable to keep our lips off of each other.

When we finally pry ourselves apart, Christopher opens his locker, and a slip of paper drifts to the ground. He seems to think nothing of it as he picks it up and glances at it. But then the grin I hoped would never leave his face fades. He hands the note to me.

If you don't really love your girlfriend like everyone thinks you do, meet me outside the gym at 3:30 P.M..

His eyes plead for mercy as he unsuccessfully tries to speak. Who would possibly do this? One member of his fan club has really lost it.

"It's fine," I say. "I know I'm the one you love."

It's not fine at all! How dare someone do this? It's all part of the childishness I despise about high school.

Over the last few months, I've seen Christopher in a lot of stressful situations. His temper has always remained even, so his anger is new to behold. "Unfortunately for her I have some place important to be, which is anywhere else in the world that my luv wants—preferably far from here!"

He slams his locker door, grabs my hand and drags me off. He always walks me to my first class, but now we are headed in a different direction. Upon reaching the door to his first class, he makes a point of putting on a show of his affection. "Meet me here after class. From now on, you will know where I spend every moment!"

23

Why is it that when life reaches cozy perfection, disasters are most likely to strike? Instead of the cuddly evening I had envisioned with Christopher, tonight is just plain uncomfortable. With the exception of the few days after his shadowy groupie left him an enticing note and he was annoyed, he's been slightly uncomfortable since New Year's Eve. I don't know if the problem lies with me, events back home, or struggles with his evolving emotions. Whatever it is, I have the overwhelming feeling it's something over which I'd rather stay in the dark.

Often it seems he is about to finally confess his woes but words fail him. Just like now, his speech always begins the same way: "Lilyanna, do you remember on New Year's Eve when I came back from Manchester and got all sentimental at your house? There's something I really need to tell you, although maybe you figured it out that night and that's why you left."

Christopher's pained expression foretells that a big bomb is about to go off. If his pattern holds, the next thing he'll do is say how much he loves me, then get choked up and start stroking my ring finger.

"I don't know if you realize how much I truly love you. I think I love you more than I should at this point in my life."

So far he's right on cue, meaning he will next divert the subject. Except it doesn't look like he is going to this time. My heart goes into my throat. Either he's about to burst out with something wretched, or he'll soon be on one knee. I'm praying for a third option.

"When I was in Manchester, as good as it was to be home, I missed you terribly. I also did something that was

137

maybe stupid. I couldn't blame you if you hated me for not telling you, but without my knowing, Dad arranged an audition with the Queen's Academy of Music. He sort of threw it at me when I landed, and the audition was the next day. My performance was horrid. Logically, there was no way they'd accept me, but I found out today they did. Full scholarship and everything."

The devastating news to come is already strangling me. All I can do is watch my world crumble.

"I always planned to go to Queen's Academy and now that I can, I don't want to because I'd have to leave you. Thing is that I really don't like living here. You're the only good thing this country holds for me. I've been here almost a year, and I'm still on the outside. I don't understand people here, and they certainly don't get me."

"What about your mom?" I can scarcely get out the words for the forming tears.

"Funny thing. Dad and Mum seem to be working things out, and he wants her to come home. If I go I know Mum will too. She won't stay here alone. I'm afraid that if I don't Mum may not go back, and they'll never work this out. It'll destroy her. You see how she's been. She's normally not like this at all. I feel it all rests on me. I can't possibly turn on her.

"Lilyanna, I'm sorry I didn't tell you sooner. I honestly didn't think they'd take me, nor could I face the possibility that they would. I really buggered it. Dad has a lot of influence. I'm certain he bought my way in. I don't want to go this way, but if I had time to prepare they would have accepted me, so I'm torn."

My understanding of the horrific strains of being torn does little to lessen my sorrow. There have been times it seemed that Christopher was sent to save me from a forbidden world into which I should never venture, but now it's as though the angels have betrayed me. I want to beg him to tell me this is all a bad joke, but his expression screams that this is as real as it gets. How could he possibly keep this from me?

Feeling buried under layers of truth and guilt, my words burst forth. He may need to hear them as much as I do. "I don't know if I would have done it differently myself. Sometimes people need to keep things private while they figure out what to do. I've most certainly had my share of experiences being torn—but oh God, Christopher, this is completely devastating."

He pulls up my chin so he can squarely face my eyes that are filled with heartbreak. "Lilyanna, I'm going to tell you something incredibly important, and I need you to understand every word exactly how I mean it. I have to return home. I'm leaving in June, and if you decide to come with, I'd be the happiest bloke on earth. I won't ask because that would be as unfair to you as it would be to me if you asked me to stay. I want to do right by you. I even thought about proposing, but we both know that would be a mistake. My parents got married very young for a rushed reason, and their lives have been a mess. Please know that the sentiment is there though. If you come with me, I am certain we'd marry in time, but I can't make the same errors. Do you understand?"

Words dart out of my mouth from a source so foreign I don't even recognize my own voice. "If I think that going is a realistic option, then we'll talk about living arrangements and all that?"

Christopher seems taken by surprise. He's not the only one.

"If you seriously consider it then yes, I'd be open to any arrangement you're interested in." He takes both my hands in his and eagerly kisses them. He's obviously excited about the possibility of being home and being with me. Christopher always makes me feel like I have the power to make his dreams come true.

Upon arriving home, the gravity of the situation sinks in. I've been so engulfed in my attempts to forget what disturbs me and enjoying my blessings, that I forgot my world will soon change and decisions are required. Now my options are far more complex than anticipated.

I've genuinely fallen in love with Christopher, and the thought of saying goodbye sends shards of glass into my heart. It's far different than when Donovan left. I needed distance and knew I'd see him again. Christopher, however, may be about to leave my life forever. That may seem overly dramatic, but how often do long distance relationships work? Donovan can't even be bothered to drive an hour and a half to come home for Thanksgiving dinner.

The vastness of my love for Christopher has always been a bit of an enigma. I've forced myself to dodge the reality of my emotions for him because they're essentially the same as those I feel for Donovan. So either I am truly in love with them both, a thought which my mind can't process, or not with either, which my heart knows not to be true. Either way, there is no more hiding. I love Christopher far deeper than I ever imagined possible.

Though my resolution is known in my heart, I need to never look back and question if the situation was properly examined. My sanest approach is to list all of the items I need to consider before reaching my decision and possibly braving the courage to beg Dad to pay for school abroad.

1. Do I love Christopher enough to marry him?
2. Where is the closest school worth attending?
3. Am I willing to leave my friends and family?
4. England, do I want to be there?
5.

Including the final point is ridiculous. Why should I think about Donovan if he's not considering me in his decisions? I don't even know his challenges. The glaring fact that he's my brother never crosses my mind anymore. To my heart, he's a lost love that won't come back yet doesn't have the nerve to go away.

5. Donovan

24

Christopher comments while looking at the movie theatre's marquee, "I can't believe there are twenty-five bloody films here and not a single one worth seeing. American cinema is in a sad state."

"Let's force ourselves to pick something. If we don't, I'm going to start crying all over again," I reply while snuggling closer.

"Sure, luv. Enjoy what we've got for tomorrow never knows. Let's start ruling them out, shall we? I insist it be funny, or what you Yanks think is funny."

"You mean like how you Brits think your food is good?"

"Ouch! You hit me right in the bread sack with that one." He giggles and tickles my waist. "Play nice."

"Okay. Nothing romantic. Nothing sad. How about a kid's film?"

"Like a cartoon? Sounds bloody awful. All right then! We'll sit in the back and make a laugh of it."

Christopher was right. The movie was indeed bloody awful, and the worse it got, the more we heckled. We were obnoxious enough, but when Christopher exclaimed "Blow me!" rather loudly—forgetting the phrase has a completely different connotation in America—I reacted by accidentally spraying the water in my mouth all over the back of the family in front of us. The ridiculousness of our actions, along with the humor we found in being ejected from the theatre, was exactly what I needed. Or maybe it was exactly what I didn't need. This would be so much easier if life with Christopher didn't make me so carefree.

After the movie, Christopher drags me to the only fish and chips place near town. As we approach the restaurant, he grabs my arm and pulls me around the back. Every chance he gets he does something goofy to make me smile, as if proving how happy I'd be with him. With a giggle, he pins me to the wall and kisses me, giggles again, and follows with another kiss.

"Why are you giggling? Are you on the piss?" I chuckle and playfully push him away.

"Look at you being all British! It suits you." Again he giggles.

"Why are you giggling?"

"Because you're going to laugh at what I say next." Like a spy on a covert mission he cases the area. He then touches his lips to my ear, as if revealing a delectable secret. "Bonk me quick."

I snort a laugh.

"Shh. Bonk me quick before someone comes."

I shoot him a look that implies he's insane.

"You know I'm joking. Well, half-joking."

"Well, that's a bloody crime then, eh? Drop 'em!" I demand while turning the tables and pinning him to the brick wall. I undo his belt and a look of intrigue mixed with panic hits his face. Unsure of what I'll do next, I go for his zipper. With the mood I'm in, I'm leaning toward lifting my skirt and going for it. Just as the zipper comes down, and I'm about to cave to my whims, a soft noise from around the corner distracts me. "Did you hear that?"

"Will you keep going if I say no?" The noise repeats. "Bloody hell! I'd better get you in. Remember what you were doing for later."

Inside the restaurant my taunting continues. "How do you like the chips?" I ask with a snicker. I already know the answer won't be favorable.

"Sweet Bloody Nora, they're awful!"

"Then why did you want to come here?"

Christopher turns his gaze downward. "Ulterior motive."

"And what might that be?"

"I'm hoping to get you to like British food so as to up

me chances."

"So you took me to a place that serves *bad* British food?"

"You Yanks like this stuff, so I figured even if it's bad, then me chances were upped."

"First, I don't like British food." Christopher predictably reacts with clownish disdain in a dramatic display of hand gestures. "I know. I'm sorry to offend you, let alone the Queen, but this Yank has to be honest. The food is not a deal breaker. It doesn't help but ... Anyway, did you know the owners of this place are British?"

"Blimey! They must be from Liverpool." He throws a crumpled napkin on the table. "Wait. Are you toying with me?" he asks with a sternly pointed finger.

"No, really. They're East Enders."

"Do you mean from a place called Cockney?" His bobbing head makes me laugh so hard my sides hurt. I finally catch my breath when he starts again. "I can't believe you don't like me food."

"It's not yours I don't like, it's England's."

Christopher puts his elbow on the table with his chin in hand. The same expression his face held the night before when he wanted to ask me to move but couldn't bring himself to do it washes over him. He eyes the room in search of a diversion. "Isn't that a friend of yours over there? She looks familiar."

I've devised a more inciting digression. "Sooooo, it's seven-fifty now and I have to be home by ten. If you finish those chips fast enough, the bonk won't have to be quick."

Christopher's jaw drops in mid chew. My look tells I'm totally serious. Under the table, my unadorned foot slides along the inside of his leg. Comically he starts cramming chips into his mouth. I grab his keys and start to leave while declaring, "Not fast enough! Don't make me start without you!"

"Only if I get to watch," he yells as he sprints to open the door for me.

"That's a possibility."

After our date, I look at the stars outside my window while remembering Christopher's words regarding his realization of how far apart we were over Christmas. I'm lost like that now, and he's less than a mile down the road. The thought of him moving without me seems insufferable.

List item number one: Do I love Christopher enough to marry him? Simply, yes. When I'm with him I know no worries. He always provides for me, just as I want to do for him. I can definitely envision all that goes with marriage like having kids and dealing with adult problems with him. Christopher would be an amazing father and a faithful husband with whom I feel we could love and respect each other through anything. While nothing is certain, the answer to this one is easy.

When I think of my friends and family, staying in The States appears to give me a better opportunity to see people more often, but there's no guarantee. Often people lose touch when they move to the next county. Conversely, if I don't go, this is likely the end of Christopher and me.

I put a check next to item one and denote that I could indeed eventually marry Christopher. I then write "six of one, half a dozen of the other" next to number three, regarding leaving friends and family. As far as the people in my life are concerned, it all comes down to Christopher and Donovan—the latter of which I wish I could ignore.

∞

The ride to school is unusually quiet. Christopher is far from being his characteristically happy self. My thoughts revert to last night, and I wonder if I said or did something that could have put him in this mood. With the exception of the tension we are under, it was a perfect evening that left me almost begging him to carry me off to anywhere his heart desired. But now my charming knight is hurting, and I've no idea how to rescue him. As he begins to get out of the car, I touch his hand and he stops.

"Why the cold shoulder?" I'm unable to conceal the misery on my face.

"I still feel guilty for not telling you. I really balls-upped. I wish I could go back to before that audition."

"And what? Not do it? That's ridiculous."

"Lilyanna, I have massively screwed-up, to use your wording, in several ways. I had a bugger of an audition and didn't tell you because I failed. Then I got accepted though I didn't earn it. So I bodged everything right from the start, and now I've hurt you and destroyed us. It's bloody ridiculous!"

He storms out of the car, slams the door, and charges off without me. Men! At least this one told me why he's broody.

After the morning passes without word from him, I decide to take matters into my own hands. Christopher normally greets me at lunch with a respectful peck on the cheek, but after his wobbly this morning, that's no longer an option. When he meets me at my locker, I pin him to it and give him a kiss that makes half the people in the hall stop and whistle.

"I'm feeling rather Randy. Ready for a little of the old How's Your Father?" I ask it a tad too loudly, thus causing Christopher to turn Lobsterback red.

"Well, that's a good way to call me an arse, isn't it? You should be smacking me head against the wall and turning it into a pulp. Instead you're nice to me. I don't deserve you."

"Yeah, I know. Come on. Let's get out of here. I need some serious cuddle time."

He bows to me, grandly. "Anything for Milady."

He takes my hand and leads me to the parking lot. Upon reaching the car, Christopher snatches my keys and opens my door before kissing me. "I missed you last night. I've been such an arse today. I'm sorry. Please forgive me."

I'm about to tell him that in a few moments he can make it up to me but I get distracted. In the distance, a girl plays with her cell phone. Is she taking pictures?

Once she's detected, the blonde girl quickly jumps into a blue car and speeds off. Is she stalking Christopher? For what sick reason is she taking pictures of him kissing another woman? Does she have a wall of them with my head X'ed out?

Without a word as to the reason, I get Christopher out of there.

25

The metaphoric 5-ton weight dangling over my bed, representing the question I arguably should have addressed first, wakes me from my sleep. Item number two: Where is the best pastry school near Manchester that is the right place for me?

I grab my laptop on a mission to choose a premiere school that is as close to Christopher as possible and hope they have a scholarship program for foreign students. I'm bewildered when I find only one culinary school in all of Manchester. Are there really no pastry schools? I continuously widen my search until something appropriate appears in London.

Is London even a possibility? It doesn't take long to learn that—at best—it's a two hour and thirty minute train ride each way. It's longer by car. This equates to five hours commuting on the train alone! Fare is between fifty and one hundred pounds *each way*. If I could convince Dad to let me go to another country, while paying for school and living expenses, to be with a man he doesn't like, the commute is so great that my only option is to live in London and see Christopher on the weekends.

This can't possibly be true! I throw on yesterday's clothes and bolt for the door.

It's still dark out when I arrive at the bakery. My entering through the back door practically scares the life out of Josette. The flick of her spatula makes a big, chocolate splash on the wall behind her. I grab a rag and wipe away the blotch that looks oddly like Connecticut. "I'm so sorry to drop in like this. I really need a friend, and you're the best person for the job."

Josette looks at me through eyes filled with concern. "Of course, Lily. I would be happy to help you. Pull up a chair, and I'll grab us some coffee."

I take a seat by the back door. My fingers tap anxiously on the table. Josette brings me coffee and a freshly baked Pan Au Chocolat. It's sad that I've no appetite. Coffee will only add to my agitation, but the warmth of the cup in my hands aids in centering my focus.

I gather myself, and then tell Josette the reason for my intrusion. "I have a decision to make that will have a big impact on my future. I don't need to put my career one hundred percent first, but I can't screw up. I need your advice strictly from a professional standpoint. Please don't hold anything back. My personal feelings are not important."

Her eyes lock on mine. "I understand."

I aim my voice at sounding as mature as it did the day I met Josette. "Christopher is moving back to Manchester, and I want to go with him. I can't find any pastry schools near him that are on the level that I'm committed to attend. The closest one is in London. I would have to live there and commute to him on the weekends. I'm very uncertain if that is where I should go to school. Can you give me any guidance?"

Josette drops her head before giving me a long and sympathetic look. My heart sags in acceptance that the reply will not be favorable.

"Lily, per your request, I am going to be very blunt. There are fine schools in London, but given your ability and desires, I recommend a true culinary arts program that combines targeted business skills with the study of your craft while earning a degree. It would be one of the strongest moves you could ever make. What you need is an AA or bachelor's degree from the pastry division of the Culinary Academy in mid-state New York.

"Think about it, Lily. To do anything less would mean going to pastry school and college at the same time. It would be exhausting, and you wouldn't get the right education. If you live in London, you would rarely see Christopher. Would you be happy? I don't think your father would allow you to jump on a plane, come home, and start over. You haven't told your parents about this yet, have you?"

Josette's truthful words are like being in the path of a plummeting cactus. As hard as I try to be professional and stay emotionally detached, my heart is shattered. "Oh, Josette, I want to go with him so badly. It's just so—"

The banging of garbage cans outside abruptly cuts my thoughts. That was no rat or stray cat. A human caused that noise, and I'm being followed. I bolt outside and see a blonde girl get into a blue car and speed off. This time I know exactly who it is. Her name is Cheryl, or, as Christopher came to name her on New Year's Eve, Donovan's Bird.

ℴ

Forget the jokes about denial being a river in Egypt. Denial is a river running through my body that science confuses with my arteries.

"Where should we start with our research? You name it, and I'll surf on it," Sally says while reclining on her bed with her supportive face on. It's not at all to be confused with her supportive-because-you-are-right face.

I plop down on the end of her bed. I already sound resigned. "You don't think I should do this, do you?"

"Remember what you told me this morning? 'It doesn't matter what anyone thinks. Mine is the only opinion that counts.' "

"Just start by telling me what you know. Anything at all." I bury my head in the bed and brace for bad news while Sally reminisces over the cumulative weeks she's spent in England.

"I think food would be your biggest issue. They have the basic fast food, which you don't eat. People like to eat in pubs, and those are like the pubs we have here. Supposedly they're better there, but that was lost on me. There are all kinds of restaurants in London. Oh! And they eat a lot of curry. The afternoon tea thing is kind of fun." Sally seems to have unearthed a treasure. "You'd really like that. It's similar to high tea here with the scones and all. Hey! We should go to a tearoom for fun! We could take Christopher and listen to him complain about how the Yanks screw it up. Oops. Sorry, Lily. I meant—"

I raise my head just enough to smile and roll my eyes. "You meant exactly what I was thinking. Let's stop talking about food. If there's anything I'd change about Christopher, it's his palate. Good Lord, no wonder why that guy's so skinny! He probably doesn't eat much because his food has no flavor."

"Lily, I'm really glad to hear some realism in your voice. Honestly, I think Christopher is amazing, but you considering moving is—"

"Absurd? Bats in the belfry? Institution worthy? Full on Van Gough? I know, but I need to keep going. Tell me something I'd like."

Sally gets a gleam in her eyes. "I saw some *really* cute boys there."

"Not helpful."

"The transportation system is great. I loved the tube. It will take you anywhere in London quickly."

"Hey, Sally, you know me pretty well. Do you think I'd like it there?"

"I think you'd enjoy London, but honestly, it's so far away from Manchester that—"

"That unless I really want to live in London it's not worth it? And unless the perfect school magically appears in Manchester I'm crazy?"

Sally sets her laptop aside. "Lily, why are you doing this? You know England is not the best decision. I know you love Christopher, but can't you just join him after going to the right school instead of killing yourself while doing the wrong thing?"

I do love Christopher, but how can I possibly tell Sally that my entire tizzy is because my relationship with Donovan needs resolving. I can't promise Christopher that if I stay here I'll wait for him, just like he can't promise he'd still want me once I got my head together.

26

I'm long overdue in reevaluating my feelings for Donovan and know the outcome will shape my life. There are other reasons not to go to England, but my internal conflict regarding a possible geographical relocation goes beyond my deep love for Christopher.

I have forced myself mute in hopes of avoiding this inevitable moment. It's time to accept my emotions without fear of any of the dark places they may take me. Only then can I truly let Christopher go.

Pulling the handle on the dresser drawer, I feel an ancient tomb is creaking open. A picture of Donovan is revealed. It's the real Donovan, before Dad imposed ideals upon him. Memories of him being a happy and loving person warm my being, fill my eyes with tears, and bring forth the truth.

"I don't want to leave you behind, but maybe I should. It's possible that I do have a choice, albeit not an ideal one. I don't want this reality. I love Christopher so incredibly much that this is ripping me apart, but the truth is that I can't go because I love you just as much in the same way and in so many others. If I didn't, I'd ask Christopher to wait for me and then commit to joining him after school ends, but I refuse to string him along."

Accepting my situation makes the reality of whom I love hit on a whole new level. I used to be able to look at my love for Donovan with defiance, but now my twisted reality is altering my future in discernible ways. Society's hand smacks my face and causes all hell to break loose in my brain.

As my mind reels at my contorted fate, I need a face to talk to—not to listen, but to use as a focal point. I search the posters on my walls, but there is no face that tugs at my inner voice. Wisps of irrationality begin seeping into the air, and they need quelling.

Instinctively I flee downstairs, grab a stack of Mom's records, and bring them to my room. As I riffle though them, several become ornaments for my dressers and shelves while others are flung aside. Their faces are insignificant.

"Chad & Jeremy – no. Beatles – no. Billy J Kramer – yes. Mindbenders – yes. Small Faces – no. Herman's Hermits – yes. The Monkees – sort of, skip it. Chestermen – yes. Hollies – yes. Peter & Gordon – no. Crap! How do I know this ridiculous stuff? Damn it, Mom!" I scream for the empty house to hear.

As my meltdown increases, some of Manchester's best stare at me. This must be like Mom's room over forty years before.

While pacing and yelling in tortured frustration, my tears fall harder than ever. I'm losing it and am unable to control the pleading words that jettison forth.

"Tell me! One of you, tell me why my life is like this? Can anyone? Is there anyone on this earth that can explain my life to me? Yes, I know you can't answer me, but work with me here!"

An unknown face grabs my attention like an old friend. My blazing rant momentarily shifts to a slow, soul eroding sorrow. It's like he's reaching out to me, telling me I'm entitled to this moment. I find myself pleading to the unknown guardian of my sanity.

"Why can't I go with Christopher? I *want* to go with him. I certainly love him enough. It would be such a bad decision, but it would also be such a good one. I could escape all my problems and move on with a beautiful man who truly loves me. Why can't we just fly off together and leave this mess behind?"

I turn to the picture of Donovan, and resentment fills my voice. "I could escape you. You are one of the things keeping me here. Damn it! What will it take for me to be free of you? Will it ever be possible?"

Looking back to the stranger, I seek divine comfort. "If he could stay, then maybe things could be different. But when it comes right down to it, he could stay just like I could leave. Maybe we both have things to accomplish that require us to be apart."

My scream at Donovan's image is filled with so much treble that my throat vibrates. "Unfair! Un—fucking—fair! See! It's not so hard to admit something and face up to it, and it doesn't even need to take years to do!"

Frenzy masters me as I burst out the front door into the cold, dark night. I'm scarcely able to see. Now if only I could stop feeling.

27

"Graham Nash and Peter Noone!"

"What, luv?" I've blindsided Christopher. He was sitting on a bench and playing guitar under the stars when I stormed up from out of nowhere, still overpowered by delirium. I must look hideous. My face is a mess of dried and fresh tears, and my arms are red and burning from scratching them.

"Graham Nash and Peter Noone!"

"The singers?"

"No, the bloody bicyclists! Graham Nash and Peter Noone! Damn it! Even Davy Jones!" My foot stomps in childlike frustration.

"Okay, luv. The singers. I get it." He draws near me, guarded, as if approaching a mental patient. He speaks as gently as he possibly can. "Now, stop throwing a wobbly and tell what's going on."

"Why can't you be like them? They did it."

"Do what, luv? What like them?"

"They were from Manchester. They moved to America and stayed. Why can't you?"

"Oh, luv." He tries to hold me, but I nearly shove the poor guy away.

"No! I get to speak! If you get to leave then I get to speak!"

I struggle to seize the last possible straw, though I know that even if it were in reach it would be a huge mistake to snatch. "I'm sorry. I am so, so sorry. Graham Nash and Peter Noone are both from Manchester and moved to The States. Maybe you're just in the wrong place. Maybe we should try living somewhere else. There are great music and pastry schools in big cities all over the country. Let's just try some other place. If it doesn't work, then you go back home."

He dares to take a step closer while still speaking as if I'm about to break. "What's so wrong with Manchester that you'll go someplace else and not there?"

"The nearest school that is even close to offering what I need is in London. Do you know how far away London is from Manchester? I'd commute over five hours a day just to be with you. Believe me, I really considered it. But there's no way I can do that. Even if I physically could without falling over dead from exhaustion, I could never afford it. I'd have to live in London, and could only see you on weekends, if we are lucky."

"Oh, luv. Come here." He sits me down and wraps his arms around me before continuing with a voice echoed with sniffles. "I'd no idea you were trying so hard. I hoped, but I barely dared."

"I know you can't stay, but I need to have it out with you and tell you all the things that are killing me inside." Finally I exhale. "Graham Nash ... Graham Nash left the Hollies, his friends, and his family to come to California. Within a few days they formed Crosby, Stills, & Nash. Soon they were playing Woodstock. Why can't you be like him?"

"Lilyanna, I can't do that. I already left and even though I was dragged away, I'm the one who can put everything back together. So much is riding on this. I've no choice but to go." Misery fills his downcast eyes as he continues, "Allan Clarke, Tony Hicks, and Bobby Elliot."

I peer at him quizzically.

With a huff and a drop of his shoulders, he repeats himself. "Allan Clarke, Tony Hicks, and Bobby Elliot!"

"The other guys from the Hollies?"

Christopher seems to be on the verge of his own little wobbly. "Yes, the *other* guys from the Hollies. It was more than Graham that gave them their burst, you know. The harmonies originated with Graham and Allan, and then they added in Tony to round out the bottom, which is one of the things that gave them their signature sound. Look a little closer to Tony's playing, and you'll find it's quite unique. Add in Bobby's fantastic drumming, rotate a bass player, and you have a smash resonance that folks revere for yonks."

"I don't get where you're going with this."

Christopher regains composure and starts over. "Allan Clarke, Tony Hicks, and Bobby Elliot all *stayed* in England — *keeping the band together* — and giving them some of their most successful hits. Do you understand now?"

I lay my head on his shoulder, and the tears flow for both of us. "I wish you could be more like Graham."

"Just as I wish you could."

"I know you're doing the right thing."

"So are you, my luv. So are you."

28

Languidly I play with a French fry, drawing it slowly through the ketchup and staring at the trench left behind in the thickness. This is exactly why Christopher and I rarely put ourselves in situations where talking is pretty much the only thing to do. Tonight the emotional weight is too heavy, and we're crumbling.

Christopher breaks the awkward silence with a lack of enthusiasm that reflects the opposite of his usual, animated self. "You know, luv. This not talking about what's on our minds isn't helping. You haven't even told me if you've settled on a school, and it's daft I'm afraid to ask. I'm sure you have it all figured out, but if you've skived off, I may need to give you a good verbal lashing."

I drop the cold fry in disgust. The act ignites a fire under me. "You know what really sucks? I know exactly what I need, and that's perfect, right? Thing is, I could have what is technically a better opportunity that I may be squandering. But I don't want it. How wrong is that?"

"What's the opportunity, and why don't you want it?" Christopher dips a fry in ketchup. I wait for him to eat it in anticipation of his impending reaction. Suddenly he looks like he has eaten a lemon. "Bloody hell, that's revolting! How do you Yanks eat like this?" Pushing the fries aside, he regains his focus on me. "Sorry. Carry on."

"When I decided to go to pastry school I planned to do the standard, thirteen hundred hour program, work while taking a few college courses, then save enough money to open my own shop. I don't need to be a famous pastry chef, and frankly, I don't even know that I'd want it. I want to be exactly like Josette; have my own shop, make the things I

158

want to make, and also have a life away from it. I don't want to be some celebrity with a reality show. It'd be nice to be known and respected, but on a reasonable scale. You know?"

"I know exactly. But why the little wobbly?" Christopher is trying to appear chipper with his hands uncharacteristically in his lap. It's pathetically cute.

My hands jettison into the air before I plop them down on the table in a mini-rant. "With my grades I qualify for a fantastic program at the top pastry school in the country. I could earn a bachelor's degree, and then get a job doing pretty much anything in the industry. It sounds great, but I don't want to spend years of my life in school. I *hate* going to school! Pastry school is different. It's primarily hands on doing something that I love, but to mix it with that type of studying I honestly think would ruin it for me. I *want* to get to work. Am I crazy? Does this make sense, or should I have someone lock me up before I hurt myself?"

"It's not crazy. If you really know what you want, and have valid reason as to why, that's what you should do."

I sit back and examine Christopher with a quizzical eye.

"What, luv?" he asks, sipping his soda and fidgeting.

"What are you not telling me?"

"Whatever do you mean?"

"You're holding back something. Spill it."

Christopher searches the room for a distraction.

"Spill it!" I insist.

Christopher throws up his hands and plops them onto the table. He grazes a wad of ketchup, creating a tiny splatter that goes unnoticed to him in his tizzy. "You know I want to move, right? Like, I really want to go home."

Finally he's returned to the same planet I'm on. "Boy, do I ever!"

"Well, I do want to go to Queen's Academy, but there's a little more to it. I fear asking meself if I even should go, given the circumstances. Truth is, I have to go somewhere. Well, I guess I don't *have* to, but I'd be whacked not to."

Christopher gazes at the splatter and shakes his head as if he's in betrayal of himself. "Blimey! I'm prickly talking about it, but remember how I said me dad has power? He's not exactly short on quid either. He set up funds for us lads when he dies, but I have to be at least eighteen and go to uni to get it. I could go to any uni, and since I came here that's what I'd planned to do. But with needing to go home and fix me family, and the door to a place like Queen's Academy opening, I couldn't bloody well say no. But it doesn't change the fact that it all feels mucked up."

"Wow. You never talk about your father. That's the most I've ever heard, and yet you've still said nothing."

"Well, Dad and I don't exactly see each other. We get on all right, but we're like chalk and cheese. I'm a huge disappointment to him. He can't even stand how I talk, which is barmy because all his old mates speak exactly the same way." Christopher shakes off his angst over his father's disappointment and moves on. "But anyway, if you know what you really want, then that's what you should do. If you don't take advantage of opportunity because of your personal needs, that's one thing. But if it's because of laziness, that's bloody well not right."

"I'm not lazy. I just need something more active. I have to be true to me."

It takes a moment to process all that Christopher has said. There's so much more to both of us than the other ever imagined. Just as I'm about to try to comfort him, Donovan's Bird appears in the corner of my eye. The girl has her hair up and sunglasses on, but it's definitely her.

Upon the meeting of our eyes, she ducks into the restroom. She's not very bright to corner herself like that. It's confrontation time.

"Excuse me a moment." My lips caress Christopher's before I walk off and slip into the restroom. A decade seems to pass before the bird flies out of the stall. When she sees me she looks like someone set off the fire alarm.

"Hello, Cheryl. That is your name, right? Cheryl?" It's

hard to sound friendly and casual while wanting to take the life right out of her.

"Uh, yeah. You're Donovan's sister, right?" Cheryl fumbles to open her purse and search for something.

"Yes, Donovan's sister, Christopher's girlfriend, six of one. You were at my parent's New Year's Eve party, right?"

"Yeah, I was there." Cheryl's fidgety as she puts on bright orange lipstick that clashes with her red sweater. She looks like she's afraid I'll attack. I can't say I won't.

"I thought I'd seen you someplace; like there, the movies, driving past my house, and behind my work *ridiculously early in the morning*. We sure seem to be in the same places a lot. I'd really appreciate it if you'd stop following us, and I'd appreciate it even more if you wouldn't take pictures. I don't know what kind of fascination you have with Christopher, but it needs to end now."

"Oh, please! Why would I have any interest in Christopher when I have a man like Donovan?"

Yeah, that's where I thought this might be going. "How long have you been seeing my brother?"

Cheryl looks positively radiant! "He's been mine since New Year's Eve. Well, I haven't actually *seen* him since then," she says with a huff, "but he adores everything about me."

Wow! For a girl who seems so awkward she sure has a high sense of self-worth—too much so for Donovan. He likes confidence, but self-absorbed is a major turnoff. What happened to the shy girl who wouldn't socialize on New Year's Eve?

"I've been concerned about my brother," I say. "We used to talk all the time, but lately he's been distant. How is he? What do you talk about?"

"He tells me all the time how blistering hot I am. During the rare times he's not, we talk about all kinds of things. Like college and football—stuff like that."

So that's what he is baiting the trap with. I can't see Mr. Hearts and Flowers saying those things to someone unless they were way into the hot monkey sex stage. There's no way he's interested in this girl. "Does he ever mention me?"

"Yeah, all the freakin' time! He asks about you a lot."

"Is that why you're following me? So you'll have something to talk about? I'd think you would spend your time seeing him. Is he not accepting visitors now?"

"Excuse me? I'm not stalking you to get to your brother, if that is what you're asking. He's afraid his precious baby sister is going to get hurt, so he asked me to keep an eye on you. Seems like the way into his pants is through you."

I'm a—I'm not really sure where to go with this, but she certainly has my attention with her choice of words. "So, instead of you spending time with him, he asked you to leave Christopher notes, take pictures, and eavesdrop on my conversations because he wants to be sure I'm safe. Is that right?"

She's fidgeting with her purse and scratching her arms. My counter attack is getting through. "So?"

Time to make my move. "Cheryl, please don't take what I'm about to say personally, but stay away from Christopher, me, and my family. *Never* speak to Donovan again."

"Yeah, right!"

My voice becomes sad and dire for what I know is the reality of what I'm saying. Donovan has really lost it. How dare he use someone for his twisted little games? "Cheryl, please listen to me. Donovan is not well. Step back a moment, and ask yourself if this makes sense. Has he made even the slightest effort to see you? My brother is a hopeless romantic. Has he sent you flowers, cards, notes—anything at all? If not, he's using you. All women deserve much better, and he will never give you more than he already has. For your own safety, promise me you'll never contact him again."

"Donovan wouldn't hurt me."

"Hasn't he abused you already? Try calling him and make a date for this weekend. Offer to drive to him so he has fewer excuses. Wait. Let me guess. You've tried that already and failed. You have tried that every week since you met him, which was about five months ago. Five months is a long time for a man who claims he adores you to avoid opportunities to see you."

Finally I get through and convince a heartbroken Cheryl to delete the pictures on her phone, but not before she emails me one of Christopher kissing me sweetly. It's how I always want to remember him. When I get home, I print three copies; one for my room, one for Christopher, and the third I sign in silver pen, "Thinking of you." The next morning, I find Donovan's address and mail him the picture in an envelope with no return address.

29

It took a day of Mom and I shopping in Providence, but I finally found the perfect prom dress—a strapless floor-length gown with cascading ruffles in a rich violet fabric that illuminates with hints of pinks and blues. We lucked out in finding a pair of deep silver-grey heels adorned with little flower-shaped rhinestone clusters. The stunning ensemble screams royalty so much that Mom tried to buy me a gaudy tiara. Instead I talked her into a modest faux diamond pendant, matching earrings, and a mani-pedi for the same price. Thank God!

Though Christopher should be here at any moment, I've been ready for hours. I began my preparations as the clock struck two. Since I only curled my hair and doted over make-up, the whole process took about fifty-five minutes, which means I have had over three hours to pace.

My blood pressure crests as Dad insists on answering the door when the bell rings. After all, this is the big night when daughters come home drunk and pregnant, so of course he wants to scare the tuxedo pants *on* to Christopher. I'm surprised he is not wielding Crazy Glue and threatening strangulation with Christopher's bow tie. But Dad has been surprisingly easy on him since the announcement that Christopher is returning to England, and I have scored a sizeable scholarship to the Culinary Academy in mid-state New York. In fact, Dad is so happy that he's paying for a boarding upgrade so I can have a tiny little place all to myself. Yep, being the daughter pays off!

Christopher surprises me not only with a lovely wrist corsage of little white roses and violet ribbon, but also a matching bouquet for my nightstand along with some pink roses for Mom. But the real shocker lies outside my front door in the form of a white limousine. I had expected to cram this dress into Grace's Mini Cooper, but never would I have dared to dream this.

"Christopher, how did you afford—?"

"A little gift from me mates back home. It sort of showed up at the house as I was leaving. The note said they wanted to make our last big night together special."

My tongue seems to forget how to swallow at Christopher's words. Other than a few stolen moments we will have between now and graduation, this is just about it for us. At least we will go out in style.

I'm caught off guard when we arrive at an upscale restaurant in Providence. For the past ten months our haunts have been respectable but budget priced, and we have mostly shared in the expenses. Apparently this is another gift from the folks back home. I wish I knew more about Christopher's life in England, but he has always been reserved—as if in guard of his two worlds.

My evening of regality continues when we arrive at the Providence Biltmore where our prom, along with that of two other high schools, is taking place. As we walk up the stairs in the grand foyer to the gold-filigree and glass elevator, I take a moment to drink in the gilded ceiling that flourishes above me. Surely I am in a castle and my prince has never looked more dashing. The ascent to the Grand Ballroom on top of the eighteen-floor building provides a lovely view of my kingdom.

All my life I have dreamed of this day. I had envisioned the school gym illuminated by twinkling lights and gold stars hanging from the ceiling that transformed it as if by magic into a miniature wonderland, much like my mother described her prom. But I'm lucky to attend one of the modern proms of today, one where the class has held bake sales and car washes for years to escape our small town and ascend into heaven.

The entrance into the ballroom sweeps me off of the

floral carpet as I soak in the arched windows boasting magnificent drapes of maroon that drip into perfect folds. Crowning the glory is a ceiling of rosettes that descend flowers from heaven.

Christopher and I dance the night away in each other's arms, all but ignoring the presence of others. During this rite of passage into adulthood, high school fades away and the enigmatic future unfolds ahead.

As the romantic melody ends and the *thump* of dance music begins, Christopher escorts me into the elevator.

"Where are we going?"

"To find a place where we can have a moment alone. I have something for you."

In our exploration of the hotel we discover an empty lounge with a roaring fire burning in a marble fireplace adorned with golden urns filled with flowers of red and white. Curling up together on a sofa, we take a moment to indulge in the ambiance and enjoy our privacy.

"Have I told you how gorgeous you look tonight? You have always been the most striking woman I've ever laid eyes on. I didn't think it possible for you to be more beautiful than you normally are, but tonight you've proved me wrong."

He reaches into his pocket and removes a small box. My heart nearly goes into my throat. He said he wouldn't propose, but this certainly looks like it contains a ring.

From inside he brings forth a gold ring that sports a single pearl, my birthstone, surrounded by diamond baguettes. "Lilyanna I—it's taken everything I have not to ask you to stay with me. Though I've no idea what it is, I've always sensed you have unfinished business to attend to. But once it's done, I hope you'll find your way back to me. I saw this, and it reminded me of the necklace you wore on our first date. I hope it will always remind you of the ring I really want to give you. Maybe someday ..."

My heart is destroyed all over again as I watch tears unashamedly pour down his cheeks.

"I love you, Lilyanna Beckett. Now and always."

"Oh, Christopher. I love you, too."

ॐ

On my eighteenth birthday, Christopher sends a baker's dozen of sterling roses with a beautiful card explaining how their unique color tearfully reminded him of my eyes. He also calls my video chat to sing a song he's written that tells of how much he loves and misses me. The entire time he sounds cheerful, but his body language sells him out. It couldn't be more obvious how much he hates losing me.

The same day I receive a bouquet of eighteen white roses with an anonymous card reading, "Thinking of You." At least Donovan is being his usual ass of a self. I hadn't expected to hear from him after my little stunt with the photo, but here he is acknowledging his stupidity. Knowing him the way I do, the card might as well say he's sorry and that he loves me.

Now, ready or not, I find myself grabbing my bags and walking out the front door of my parent's house. I'm off to my new home hundreds of miles away in mid-state New York. In some ways I wish it were further—like in another country. In other ways I'm relieved that I can drive home or to Donovan in a few hours. Either way—I'm moving forward.

30

"Lily? Are you all right? What's wrong?"

I stand in my hole of a student apartment, musing over how sad the situation is. Donovan sounds completely shocked by my phone call. My self-governed living gives renewed independence to my spirit. With that comes the resolution to get my best friend back—though I have no idea how to go about it.

"I'm fine," I assure Donovan. "I guess a little astonishment is in order since this is the first time either of us has called since you moved out."

"Wow! It's really great to hear from you!"

"You sound like you're in a good mood. Did I catch you doing something you shouldn't?" A wink tics as if he could see it. What the hell am I doing, and how the crap do I stop?

"I wish. Same old boring day for me here. How's school?"

"It hasn't started. A few days of freedom remain so I'm trying to get settled. I've done so much already that it makes my head kind of hurt." I remove a half-unpacked box from the sofa just purchased at a garage sale and plop myself down. I instantly regret it. It's so hard that my butt seems to smack onto the frame. But there's no reason for complaints. I'm technically in a one-bedroom apartment, though it is really a glorified studio with a nook for a bedroom. The neighborhood is fine, but the inside of this thin-walled building must be reminiscent of the housing projects.

"That's what you get for graduating high school and moving a few weeks later. Why didn't you wait for fall?"

The truthful answer is a little hard to swallow. "I couldn't stand being home anymore. Since there was no reason to stay, I slipped into a last minute start of what is technically the spring semester." My butt struggles to find a comfortable position. No wonder the guy was selling this sofa so cheaply.

"Yeah, how is *Christopher*?" Donovan says the name cautiously, like it's a demon burning his tongue.

"Christopher might as well be on another planet. He seems good, but he tries to be cheerful even when he's crumbling. His troubles are not always clear."

"That's hard to believe since you can read me like a book."

"That's because you're my soul mate." The words do not come lightly, nor are they regretted. It's time we got our friendship back and either permanently hide from our emotions or face them.

"What was it you said last time I saw you? How I don't say much, but sometimes I really throw out zingers? Pot, I would like you to meet the kettle."

"Well, I was trying to figure out how to start this part of the conversation, but my frequent inability to filter emotions obviously has paid off for once. Donovan, how are you really? You freaked the crap out of me on New Year's Eve. I've almost called you so many times, but I'm really trying to respect your wishes. Now that we've both escaped the house I hoped it might be easier for you to talk."

His sigh stammers. The attempt at an answer is a small step forward from the common question dodging. "I'm all right, Lil. Just all right though. Struggling is still pretty commonplace, and every day is harder than it should be. It would be so much easier if just once in a while I could be someone else."

"What's wrong with being you?" The question sinks my heart. The answer will likely have a similar effect. How can I possibly ream him for what he did to Cheryl with this subject matter already at hand?

"My life is very complicated and has been for the last year and a half. It just got a little easier but not much. I can't talk about—"

"Is this the thing you promise you'll tell me someday?"

For once he makes no attempt to cover his frustration with anger. "Yes. Just the option doesn't exist now. I really wish I weren't me. It'll change someday. I'll make sure of it. But right now ... Right now I'm screwed."

"Donovan, if you can't talk about your problems, maybe you should try writing them. That way you might feel as if you've talked about them."

"Actually, Lil, that's another can of worms."

"Well, if you need me, I'm less than two hours away. And you know you can always call or even write. Just please stop being so distant. I hope this doesn't complicate things, but I really miss you."

"Thanks, Lil. I miss you too. Maybe I'll send you a note or something."

ಐ

School's inaugural day thrills my mind, exhausts my body, and brings grumbles to my belly. As much as I have always had an odd affinity for it, the thought of touching anything with bread as a component is nauseating. Too much of my day was spent in a classroom discussing its history, culinary evolution, and cultural diversity. Voices in my head screamed, "Who the hell cares! Let's just make some!" My head is also a little achy just thinking about the homework for my culinary math class. Culinary math is akin to practical algebra, making me wonder why I wasted time in trig.

Josette passed on the best advice in the world when she talked me into a year-round, twenty-one month AA program with the option to stay on for my bachelor's degree. It excites me to think that in less than two years I'll be free to do anything or go anywhere in the world, without obligations.

With all of the changes occurring prioritizing food has failed me. How did *that* happen? Three-day-old Chinese take-out that was triumphantly unpalatable when it was fresh is my only option.

"Yuck!"

My reaction to the first bite inspires memories of Christopher and his disdain for non-British food. His rant over this dreadful slop would be nothing short of comically terse.

God, what is it with me? Two days ago talking to Donovan worked me into foolhardy yearning, and now I'm daydreaming of Christopher. Both make my heart feel like pasta dough that has passed through an extruder.

The pathetic meal in my hands is exchanged for today's mail. Among the usual junk for the current resident resides a suspect letter addressed to me from someone named Alex with a mailbox in Connecticut. That's odd. The only person I know in Connecticut is Donovan.

Darling Kate,

It was so good to hear from you today after not being with you since the beginning of the New Year. I have missed you terribly, and my heart aches for not having seen you. Please write if you miss me too. Maybe I can have the courage to tell you things in writing that I never could in conversation.

All my love,

Alex

Who the hell are Kate and Alex? The whole thing is in Donavan's handwriting. What the crap is he up to now? Has he fully lost his mind?

After an evening of switching my attention between homework and the camouflaged correspondence, that has somehow managed not to give me the heebee-jeebies, its meaning is deciphered. In our last conversation Donovan wished he could be someone else. How much he meant it is a little troubling. The handwriting appears like that of a sane man, but the contents don't sound like Donovan. Instead, the names and characters are derived from a movie we saw years ago about two people in love who are forced apart.

The once cryptic letter now floods me with intense emotions too long suppressed. Sane or demented, Donovan is finally reaching out across a dark chasm and expressing his feelings. The gesture should not go unreturned. Then again, is it really Donovan to whom I'd be confessing or some dissociative identity?

The following day the haunting question still tugs until a sign appears as if from heaven.

While in the campus bookstore, a *thunk* hits my feet as I pass a glass stand covered in frivolous knickknacks that this penny-pinching student would normally ignore. Bending over to retrieve the attacker, my eyes lock on the white roses that adorn the stationary that threw itself at me. Maybe the angels didn't betray me with Christopher; they're bringing me back to Donovan.

Once back home, my mind replaces the faded paint on my apartment walls with rose filled trellises, the scratched wood of the kitchen table with wrought iron, and the stale air with a perfumed breeze. The words begin their flow the moment my hand engages the pen. This time they will be brief, but if the confessions continue, my heart will eventually tell Donovan all it holds.

Dearest Alex,

How much I have missed you. I am still settling in a new home, and while I try to fill it with my love for you, it still feels cold and empty. I long for the days when you were near; when all I needed to do was reach into the darkness and you would be my light. You mentioned that you ache to see me. Do I dare hope that someday you will become my light again?
All my love,
Kate

31

Two months into my new life and the passion that school brings proves the career path on which my feet tread is the right one. Even while sweating it out in a stuffy kitchen in the middle of one of the hottest summers on record, my smile cannot be detached. Something about baking bread comforts my soul like a heated blanket comforts my body on a frigid night.

Thoughts of Donovan, both fanciful and lascivious, have returned. Each note Kate and Alex exchange becomes more heartfelt, more meaningful, more loving, and more admitting. Anticipation always enrobes me when a letter from Alex is due. If Donovan isn't sane in our distorted reality, then I'm not either.

But it's all fantasy—just as it's always been—and you can't put your arms around it.

Irrationally, feelings of infidelity toward Christopher bedevil me. While neither ever said we were through it was very much implied. He's long overdue in returning email, which may be a sign that he has moved on. Truthfully, I need to move on with a social life based in reality, not one that involves swapping love letters as a fictional character with another invented being who's really my emotionally challenged brother.

Success is an earnest goal, but somehow every date unearths disaster. My wrestling belt for being the World Titanicweight Champion of the Cataclysmic Date Division should arrive any day now. As soon as even minor potential exists, all goes to hell.

First there was Nick, a cute guy who works in the school cafeteria. Everything was great until Nick was upfront about his jealousy issues. When he learned Christopher is still on my friends list, he flipped out like the entire U.S. Olympic Swim Team shared my bed. Upon discovering Nick's inability to understand the difference between the United Kingdom and the Wild Kingdom, I pondered setting him up with Jennifer.

Enter Troy, who treated me very gentlemanly despite his leather-clad bad-boy look that I found enticingly hot. However, every time he kissed me, he giggled. This was charming when he kissed me goodnight after the first date and slightly amusing the second date. But when we started making out on the third date, it was time to find someone else.

Then Howard became the crowning champion in the loser competition. He made Al look like Prince Catch-of-a-Lifetime. After an elegant dinner, I was confused when Howard's next event of choice was to see the movie *Cinderella*. Once seated, he left for popcorn. About ten minutes later I noticed him sitting a few rows over and kissing another girl. Perverse curiosity kept me glued to my seat until he returned. Wasting little time, he made a very forward advance on my chest, which only succeeded in him getting his thumb bent back nearly to his wrist. Howard then yanked me out of my seat and marched me over to his other date, claiming he'd found them a feisty one for the evening. After my knee met his dangling think sacks, I sprinted from the theatre with a fury.

Later I learned the movie was not the version intended for children.

Needless to say, my social life sucks. Upon conceding that every romantic situation in my life is, and forever shall be, hopeless, come October, Kate receives a very eye-opening letter.

My Lovely Kate,

My apologies for the delay in writing. School has begun and I find myself short on time. However, please do not take this as me no longer

desiring you. Since we have begun our letters I find myself loving you more than ever, which I honestly did not think possible. I have never really said that to you before. I do love you. I hope someday to have the courage to say it into your eyes. Please have faith in my words. I do plan to make it all up to you someday.
All My Love,
Alex

It's a return to the short and sweet letter, yet it says so much more than all of the others combined. Suddenly the madness makes sense. He may be hiding, but the real Donovan definitely still exists. Something in him is changing, for he's finally told me that he loves me. Or at least Alex loves Kate, which is the closest Donovan has come to being honest about his feelings in years. After losing Christopher I have three bad experiences only for it all to be followed by a confession of love; clearly Donovan and I are being pushed together.

My Darling Alex,
Please do not ever feel I could lose faith in you, your words, or your love for me. No, you had never told me of your love before, and in reading of it I find myself fulfilled. Whenever you think of me, imagine me in your arms telling you that I love you, truly and unconditionally.
Forever,
Kate

32

This year, Thanksgiving has lost every bit of its charm. My arrival home features an overtly welcoming mother, who is going mad in a quiet house, and a stuffy father, who will never change his ways. Donovan is either stuck at school or making excuses not to come home, which goes undiscovered until my arrival. Kate makes a mental note to chew out Alex for acting like Donovan.

The quiet of the house holds vigil to the panic felt one year ago when Christopher announced Grace wanted me to be the daughter she never had. Where is the man who was so upset over leaving that he wanted to propose and whisk me away? He spent months confessing his love and getting 'all sentimental' only to say, "Cheerio, luv. Be seeing you. Or not."

Looking down at the ring Christopher gave me, I realize the time may have come to lock it away where it will go unremembered until I'm old and gray. At least if it is left at my parent's house it can be retrieved over Christmas break, if I feel so inclined. I ponder doing just that and my video chat rings. The timing is bewildering. Then again, maybe it's Alex calling for Kate. Wouldn't that be a lark? If that's the case, I'm running off to Africa to live among the lions and changing my identity.

"Merry Thanksgiving! Mum just came in and showed me the calendar. She insisted I call immediately and thank you again on her behalf for your hospitality last year. I think she misses you."

Dear God, is Grace psychic? "Oh, so this little resurfacing is because she twisted your arm and not because you actually want to talk to me." Midway through the sentence my skin prickles at how harsh the words sound, but it's too late. Christopher turns his eyes downward.

"No, luv. I'm sorry if it sounded that way."

I rest my elbow on the desk with my chin in hand. Christopher's image makes my soul ache. "Christopher, I'm so sorry. I didn't mean it that way. I just really still miss you. Why have you disappeared?"

"Can I just say that being here is not all it's cracked up to be and leave it at that? Really, luv, it's fantastic to see you. I wouldn't have called if I didn't want to."

"I just wish you wanted to a little more."

"Lilyanna, I always want to talk to you. Tell me all the wonderful things I've missed."

The miles have taken their toll. At least Grace is still pulling for us. With her, hope springs eternal when it comes to love. Grace appears to be the only one who won't accept what Christopher and I can't state. Whether or not we want it, our relationship is experiencing death throws.

Upon returning home I expect to find a letter from Alex, but a note is still long overdue.

Dearest Alex,

We have been apart physically, mentally, and geographically for so long that my heart questions if my feelings for you are still true. I have hidden too long. I have pretended too long. I need proof that our love is not imaginary and that our passion is based on devotion and not simply yearning. Reality must be on the horizon so that I can move forward with my life, even if it means leaving you behind forever. Soon we shall see each other again. Might you have a moment to share with me so I can discern my true feelings?

Yours always?

Kate

If Donovan can't respect this, I have to halt everything and never think of him again even if every aspect of our relationship is forever abandoned. My masquerade mask just leapt into the trash.

33

The *clink* of my pencil hitting the desk signals the completion of my last exam before Winter Break. The timbre also notes the conclusion of the sixth month of my twenty-one month program. I'm all set to leave first thing in the morning to spend Christmas with my family. However, what could be the best present already arrived when Kate finally received her latest letter from Alex.

My Lovely Lady,

I find great excitement in knowing I shall be with you again soon. My only hope is to have a few moments where we can enjoy each other's company fully, and I can alleviate your fears. My true wish though, is that we could somehow escape the clutches of others and run off alone. If I could see you privately, even if only long enough to share a brief moment, my heart shall be fulfilled.

With longing thoughts,

Alex

Is this really it? After two years of denial is Donovan truly ready to fess up?

The next day I arrive home to find a grumpy Dad, a reserved Mom, and a bitchy Donovan. The initial welcome had been pleasant. When Donovan greeted me at the door he received the hug of a lifetime accompanied by a lingering kiss on his cheek. The moment was heart captivating.

Mom ran from the kitchen to lock her arms around me while boasting how much she misses me. Dad even bothered to leave the den—book and pipe still in hand—and give me a kiss on the cheek. But now it is five minutes later and Dad's resumed reading, Mom's back cooking,

Donovan's off brooding, and wispy clouds of tension float through the air.

"All right, what'd you do?" I ask while standing in Donovan's bedroom doorway. "You got home like an hour ago and disaster has already struck. Are you going to tell me what's going on, or is that another answer for someday?" Exasperation blankets my face. It sure didn't take long for the fairy tale to fracture.

"Bob, tell us what the lady has won!"

"Fine. Are you at least glad to see me?"

"Hey, you're the one who stormed in here without saying hello. I was just lying here, waiting for you to grace me. Aren't you like royalty now that you bonked an English—*man*?"

"Boy, you really are jealous of him. I see you for the first time in a year, and within seconds you're harping on my ex-boyfriend who is thousands of miles away, and whom I'll probably never see again."

Donovan's tone overturns. He sits up and motions for me to shut the door. Suddenly he sounds rather sheepish. "Is he really out of your life for good?"

"Didn't your spy tell you? I know she overheard enough to give you all of the information you need."

"I think someone intercepted her before I received my final report." Donovan's palm flies forward before my head finishes snapping at him. He sounds as ashamed as he should. "Apologizing to her is top of my hit list this week. I've no idea how I can make it up to her, but I have to figure something out."

It's still unfathomable he used someone like that. At least he seems truly regretful. I plop myself on the foot of his bed with my knees hugged close to my body. The subject makes me doubtful it's safe to be in the same state as him. "Donovan, why did you do it? If you wanted information, why didn't you ask? You know I'd tell you anything."

"Hey, Lil. Tell you what. I'll do my best to be nice to everyone this week if you promise to stop asking questions I can't answer right now."

"So in other words, I should leave you the hell alone. Okay. See you next holiday—*if* you show up."

His touch upon my sleeve grants me the excuse to halt. I've no desire to leave, nor do I wish to fight. I'm just so damn mad at him for how he's acted the last two years that how to handle this is beyond me. My hand itches to slap him.

"I'm going to apologize to Cheryl first thing Friday morning, *if* she'll see me. How about I take you to lunch after for that alone time? Same place as before? One o'clock?"

Though his eyes are filled with the same expression of love he's almost acted on so many times, the high level of my annoyance won't be quelled. "Sure. Bring Cheryl two bouquets of flowers because I'm sure she'll throw the first one at you. Hopefully it will have thorns. And show a lot of remorse. I mean *a lot!* Also, don't be surprised if the sight of you freaks her out. I kind of let it slip that you're crazy and might be dangerous."

"Yeah, I kind of figured."

He regretfully shakes his head as my anger continues to flow. "Hey, it was the least I could do after how much havoc she caused. Christopher had to be constantly sheltered from your drama."

"She got in deeper than I ever expected. I never thought it would get so bad or that she'd be so transparent." He looks up and sighs. "Do you ever talk to him? Do you regret not going to England?"

My heart sinks. "I talk to him occasionally, but he's gone. We both did the right thing, but I'd be lying if I didn't say that I miss him all the time."

Donovan takes my hand. "Maybe now is a bad time for you to make relationship decisions."

"You know, when you left I missed you too. I still do. If I waited until a time when I didn't miss someone I love before getting into a relationship, I'd likely die an old maid."

ॐ

"How is it I'm so stupid? How could I think, even for a second, that I could've gotten away with that in the first place? And how was I dumb enough not to realize that *both* her Krav Maga trained brothers would be home for Winter Break?"

Donovan gets absolutely no sympathy from me. He sits across the restaurant table while sporting a huge black eye. He had this coming—although the timing is really a downer since this is supposed to be our first date. We've spent the last few days in the blissful awkwardness of being around each other but not being able to be together. Now we're finally somewhat alone in a crowded restaurant, and he looks like a character out of a bad fifties monster film.

Donovan has a lot of things that he deserves. Although he's long past his due for many good ones, this one is just as necessary.

"Do you have to look like you're enjoying this?" he says, wincing.

"No, but why lie?" Admittedly his bloating, Technicolor eye does bring me some satisfaction, though the rest of him has me concerned. "How are your ribs?"

"Painful!" He squirms while trying to adjust so sitting doesn't send stabbing pain through him. "This isn't turning out to be the romantic lunch I'd hoped for. I'm really trying to make things right in my life starting this week."

I motion for his hands and he gives them to me without reservation. The electricity of his touch still has the power to jumpstart my heart. "Does this mean I'm seeing the return of Donovan and the disappearance of Alex?"

"How freaked out are you by that?"

"Quite a bit at first, but I remembered what you said about needing to be someone else and frankly, it came at a time when maybe I needed that too. I do have to admit that it has been really enjoyable. Just how truthful is he?"

"Very."

"I think Alex is amazing, but I'd rather have Donovan."

"So would I but in less pain. Can we never talk about that weirdness again? Actually, let's not talk about anyone else existing at all. This is a lot for me already. I'm feeling pretty courageous, and I don't want to blow it."

"Anything you want." He's not the only one with courage. My heart dares to look at him the way it did two years ago, back when we were about to face our emotions and cast aside society's intrusive opinions. Just like then, I am restlessly in need of some affection. "Maybe we should leave. We've been here twenty minutes, and we've yet to see our waitress. I can think of better ways to spend the little time we have." Many, *many* ways!

His voice turns timid. "Lily, I'm trying to do this right. You deserve someone who will take you someplace decent and do nice things for you. Just enjoy it."

God how this man touches my heart. "Have I told you how much I love the real you?"

"On second thought maybe we should get out of here."

Finally our waitress appears. "Hey, Lily! I haven't seen you in ages!" At the sight of Jennifer, Donovan quickly drops my hands with a pain-filled wince.

I should've seen this one coming. Josette is related to the owners here, and therefore, so is Jennifer. Josette must have finally canned her and shipped her off to work for her other kinsfolk.

Jennifer turns to Donovan, obviously expecting to see Christopher. "Hey—Oh, hi Donovan." In true Jennifer style she returns her sites to me. "What happened to that guy from Ireland?"

Donovan's gone white. It could be the mental shock that just hit his system, or his injuries are far worse than they appear. Either way he's got me freaked. He's been brave long enough. It's past time we postpone the date and head for the hospital.

ℬ

Jennifer's unwelcome appearance was worth her weight in gold. Thank God we arrived at the hospital when we did. Donovan has three fractured ribs and was in danger of a partial collapse of lung tissue. Not only is he still in physical pain, but also the shock of running into someone we knew under the given circumstances has freaked him out and sent him plunging downward emotionally.

My persona of the devoted nurse has been everything but enticing role play. Donovan's been brooding in bed ever since we returned home and has nearly banished me from his room. Although we seem at peace, all we rebuilt may have crashed and burned.

As midnight chimes life into the morning of my departure, I slip into his room in hopes that we can at least leave all this where we were upon our arrival last week. It's risky though. Can we survive being plummeted back to square one?

I slip onto the bed and tuck my head into his shoulder. His aroma is more appetizing than anything I've ever cooked.

"Lily," he whispers, sounding like he wants to yell at me. "What do you think you're doing?"

"I'm spending a final moment with you while Mom and Dad snore. Are you all right?"

"Do I look all right?"

"We both know that's not what I'm talking about. Before we ran into Jennifer there was a wonderful man back in my life. Seeing her was awkward, but it was really nothing." What's he doing on his back? That's not what the doctor ordered. "Hey, you need to lie on your side. It'll help your breathing." Carefully I help him roll over to face me. His tone softens upon his gaze on my sincere expression of devotion.

"Nothing? How can you say it was nothing? We were holding hands in public and got caught."

Staring into his eyes like a molten-hearted puppy, my hand slides up his arm and through his raven locks. My leg curls to touch his. If he's going to revert, it won't be without enamored protest. "No, we were talking in public exactly like we've done many times. In fact, last year we were in that same restaurant, and you thought nothing of holding my hand then. The only difference was your intentions, which no one could see but you. I would still like to know more about them."

There's no question in his mind as to my desires. They make him inwardly vulnerable though he struggles to be outwardly unyielding. As he returns my embrace, pulling me so close that our lips feel like butterflies fluttering against each other, he begins to cave to our overwhelming emotions. "Your skin is so smooth I can't tell where your night gown ends and it begins."

I entwine myself with him, and our hearts are pulled in deeper, yet with shuddered breath, he tenderly begs me to stop. "Lily, please don't do this. We can't go down this road."

He presses his body into mine and the rhythm of his blood overwhelms me. Memories of the time Christopher told me he was falling bathe my mind. They confirm that now my feelings for Donovan must come forth in hopes they will make him just as defenseless as Christopher made me.

As my lips begin to share the emotions in my soul, my mind hears the sound of shattering glass. Donovan snaps at me with words that leave my heart as empty as a robbed tomb. "Go away! You've totally lost your mind! Do you think we will ever be able to get away with it even for a second? You need to leave—*now!*"

And that's exactly what I do. I've had it with this ass.

I flee the room, and the tears start falling against my will. He's not worth them!

No, but what we've lost is.

34

"Come on, Christopher. Answer."

Calling Christopher is risky given my fragility after last night's episode with Donovan. I need my old love to be happy to see me and not leave me feeling like I'm attending yet another funeral for love lost.

Finally he answers. "Hello, luv! Nice to finally engage you again. All right? Did you have a Happy Christmas?"

He's rather jovial. Hopefully it's because of me and not due to someone else on his mind.

I'm seriously mental. I can't have him, and I can't have Donovan, so why am I wasting time clinging to them both?

"Yes, everyone's as normal as ever which is not saying much good. Hey, you owe me emails. I was beginning to think I would never talk to you again. What have you been up to?"

"Nothing special really, just this, that, and the other. Well, actually just this and that. The other seems to elude me." He places his hand on his chin and circles to watch a nonexistent object fly by. I laugh. "Oh, blimey! I suppose you think my misery is a riot."

There's the man I love—arms flailing, head bobbing. The absence of seeing it in person makes my chest cave. "Would you mind terribly if I told you I'm relieved?"

Sheepishly he gazes at me while toying with his finger on the desk. "Do you mean that after all this time you might miss me just a little?"

The truth springs forth from my gut without permission. "Christopher, not a day goes by that I don't consider dropping everything and heading off to the airport."

"Just can't let go of this dashing creature, eh?" While

mocking straightening a necktie, he flashes his famous grin before getting serious. "Really, Lilyanna, how'd I ever get so lucky? I never deserved you. I want to carry on, but it hasn't been easy. I still love you, you know? But really, what choice do we have now?"

"Well, Graham, if you ever want to meet me in California, drop me a line. You never know what I'll say. And for what it's worth, I still love you too. No matter what happens I don't ever see that changing."

With watery eyes, we finish the call. It pains me to admit that we each need to move on. God knows I'm trying.

My attention turns to the ring he gave me. Again I start to remove it—but it's time to accept that won't happen. Truthfully, I adore it. It's become more than a gift from my ex. It's a reminder that I'm a survivor. For that reason alone I wouldn't dare break its bond with my skin. So in the spirit of survival, with one free day before school resumes there are but as many goals. It's time to formally tell Donovan to piss off!

∽

Today is the day. Today I move on once and for all—from Donovan, from Alex, from the madness.

It's time to revamp my life again. The last time that urge overcame me I went out for a nice cup of coffee and a Pain Au Chocolat. That single action led to a fantastic job, getting into the best pastry school in the country, a true friend and mentor in Josette, and meeting my beloved Christopher. Can lightning strike twice?

Driving towards a supposedly great coffee shop in Poughkeepsie my objective is to have breakfast while deciding how to tell Donovan to shove it up his ass. It's long past time to take out the trash and make room in my heart.

But can the door ever be slammed shut on Donovan and our complexities?

The question causes my mind to wander, jettisoning me past my intended exit by several miles. Donovan's dorm is now only an hour and a half away. The fewer the miles between us, the more rapid my pulse, and the faster I race toward him.

My tires squeak and the car bounces as it hits the driveway to Donovan's dorm. Alex writes from a P.O. Box, so Donovan has no idea that Kate knows how to find him. This should scare the crap out of him!

A frat-boy jock responds to my pounding on the door while Donovan lies on the sofa. He's long past the danger zone but still on the recovery end of dealing with his fractured ribs. Storming past the oversized jock, I grab Donovan's collar and yank.

"Lily!" The freaked out expression on his face is priceless. You could stick a football in that mouth.

"Shut up and come with me, or I'm going to create a scene that will really make you sick."

His eyes widen and his legs obediently follow. He respects my demand that he get into the car while fearing to say a word. I take him to an empty park, and we trek through the snow to a bench. The fire in me flares so much that my breathing turns to huffs, and I fly into an unwavering rage.

"Talk!" I scream, pushing him onto a bench. "Talk to me before I break the rest of your ribs! Tell me why I lost my best friend, and why you twice led me on only to dump me! You were at the restaurant being all sweet and charming and talking about doing things the right way. Then you turned on me!"

"We almost got caught!"

"We weren't doing anything nor were we going to there! Do you think I'm stupid? Why do you keep starting and stopping? You do know you're toying with me, right?"

My hands fly up in disgust. "Of course you know. I'm so stupid! This is what you did to Cheryl. You take girls who have feelings for you and play insensitive little games and make them all crazy. Is this how you get your kicks? Do you think it's easy dealing with my emotions? I'm just as confused and concerned as you are. Maybe even more so because your lack of acceptance forced me to go on with my life, and I found someone wonderful that I've now lost. So first I lost you, then I lost him, and now I've lost you again. Why do you turn on me like this? You used to be the greatest guy in the world. You always treated girls with respect. Everyone admired you for that! What the hell happened to you?"

"You're right," he says so quietly his words are almost inaudible. He's a shrunken man sitting with his head down in shame. "This is totally unfair. I didn't mean to hurt you. Both times I had very good intentions. Both times it took a lot to get the courage to approach you that way, but for God's sake, people say what you and I feel is wrong."

The tighter my fists clench, the greater the volume of my voice. "People? It's *our* relationship. Don't you think that's something *you and I* should talk about? Tell me exactly how *you* feel and if *you* think it's wrong. You're entitled to your opinion. But to dismiss us without talking to me is callus. At least tell me what you're feeling. What? Can't? Why not? Afraid it will become real? Afraid you won't be able to walk away from the truth? If it's so wrong, then walking away should be easy. Besides, you've never told me how you feel, so when it comes right down to it, *I don't know what the hell you're thinking!* And what the crap is the deal with Alex and Kate?"

"Alex and Kate can have the relationship we never can."

"That's a huge crock of crap! How can two, non-existent people have a real relationship? Can you put your arms around a fictional character? I sure can't, and if you think you can, then you need professional help! Seriously, if you don't like who you are, then turn yourself into who you want to be and stop hurting people!"

"It's not that easy," he says. "I'm not like Christopher. I can't just flutter through life being comfortable in my awkwardness."

Now he's really crossed the line! I lunge forward and scream in his face. The treble makes him wince. "Never, *ever* say his name again! I had to hide the truth about your little spy because I didn't want him to think I was related to a *crazy person!* Besides, he's out of my life, and I don't want to talk about him anymore." My last words cause me to choke and turn away.

"Lily, I'm so—"

My body spins to face him. "Do *not* say that you're sorry! Do *not* try to comfort me! Your days of doing that are over. The only thing you should do is tell me the truth, but you won't do that. Until you do, *you can go to hell!"*

Our rollercoaster ride is over, and his shadowed eyes show he knows it. I drive off in a fury, leaving Donovan to wallow in the snow. The moment gives me both the exhalation of liberation and the cutting pain of profound despair.

Thirty minutes after abandoning Donovan I'm completely lost, disoriented, and suffering from food depravation as my Bug zooms down the highway. The next road sign reads New Britain. It's not only far from amusing, but I'm totally going the wrong way. Maybe the universe is telling me to drive straight into the Atlantic and head for England.

My grumbling stomach propels me to continue forward in search of food and directions, but all the up-coming towns have British names. After the showdown with Donovan, the last thing I need is to pine over Christopher.

Since turning around means passing the exit for Donovan's dorm, I'll have to resist returning to where I left him and running him over. I'd better eat—fast.

With my blood sugar crashing, sucking it up by going to the nearest drive thru in East Berlin and attempting to find something resembling food seems my only option. The cashier looks at me in horror, which morphs into sympathy. She hands me damp napkins. Crap! The yanked rearview mirror reflects my entire face streaked and smudged from mascara running as a result of crying. The pedal has now reached the floorboard while pushing the speedometer of my limits!

My feet storm to the makeup counter in the nearest shopping mall. Dramatically, I smack down the credit card Dad gave me for emergencies, flail my arms, and plead, "Fix me!"

A few pampering hours later the world beholds my new face, accompanied by two new outfits, and the best attitude I've had in months. Next on my list is that nice meal Donovan previously promised without concern over the stability of the company.

My phenomenal dinner cost Dad a paltry $77.52. On whimsy, I skip the coffee with dessert and head for the cafe that was on my morning's destination list. At nearly ten at night the place is packed with students from Vassar. I sit at the only table available and focus on the trash novel in my purse and the steaming cup of luscious brew before me.

"Oh, man! There's not enough coffee in the world!" a voice from the next table moans.

The utterance is followed by the loud *thunk* of a head hitting the tabletop and a small wince. My chuckle halts when my eyes feast upon the source of the voice. He's absolutely beautiful! Shoulder length dark brown, wavy hair, a few well-placed birthmarks on his cheeks, soft, young, yet manly features, and the slightest upturn to his nose. When he opens his eyes to see who's laughing, their deep hazel-brown has an unfair advantage over my hormones. He's gorgeous! My God, how had he gone unnoticed?

"Bad night?" I ask.

"School started today, and I'm already creamed. I'm so screwed," he says, again smacking his head on the table.

"If school just restarted, how are you already screwed?"

"I'm pre-med."

"Ah! An overachiever. I get it now."

He sits upright and rubs his hand over his lovely face

before resting his chin in it and staring straight ahead at the wall. "I'm in over my head. I'm taking too many classes." Shaking his head, he blinks his eyes as if removing the haze of a dream.

"Hey, here's a news flash. You can probably drop one, and it'll be fine."

He seems to never have thought of the obvious, but then jiggles the notion from his mind. "Nah. It's far more fun to torture myself. Besides, if I play my cards right, I only have a year and a half left—else I might be here forever."

"I doubt that. Need some help?" I ask, surprised at my calm demeanor in the sight of heaven.

"Yeah, mental!"

"Seriously, I used to help my brother all the time. We came up with a great system. Wanna try?"

An hour later Julian walks me to my car. I drive off with a phone number and a study date with a gorgeous guy who's warned me that he doesn't have time for a social life. If the only way to spend time with one of the most handsome men on the planet is while studying, I may turn into a genius.

35

"I don't want to go home for spring break. I don't want to go home for spring break." The declaration is repeated in hopes that when my eyes open, the calendar will read one week later, and I'll be safe.

Sitting across from me at the table in my apartment, Julian peers from behind his Behavioral Sciences book and blasts his super nova smile. "Then why do it?"

"I don't want to go home for spring break. I don't want to go home for spring break."

"Lily. Don't go then."

My hands pop up in surrender. "You're right. I shouldn't go!"

He smiles and shakes his head. He does that a lot with me. "I never said that. But if you don't want to go, then why are you going?"

"Uuugh! My Mom is making a big deal over it and keeps talking about how great it's going to be with us all together. The thing is, it's *never* great when we're all together. The last time my family had a normal moment with all of us in the same room was at least three years ago."

"Seriously, Lily."

"I *am* serious. If I weren't serious I would've said it had been a *jillion* years ago! I don't want to go home for spring break. I should just stay here with you, and maybe then we can finally have some serious time alone." My gaze is coy, yet quite sinful, as I bat my lashes.

"Sorry. I have finals that week. I'm not even going to have time to slip in while you sleep. You're on your own."

My head plummets back in melodramatic disgust. Julian returns his attention to the book while still chuckling at my antics. The exchange pretty much sums up the months of our affair. Julian spends way too much time studying. Any hopes for a normal relationship are on hold until after his internship, and he hasn't even begun medical school.

Julian possesses a character that illuminates the night. He's also completely gorgeous and beautifully well built under his baggy layers of clothes. At six foot four, he towers over everyone not only in stature but also intelligence; yet he never makes anyone feel inferior. Volumes could be written on his greatness. Law almost won out over medical school because he believes that as much as there is suffering there is also injustice, and that we wouldn't need as many doctors if human rights were upheld around the world. It's a view I'd never considered and reflects one of his adore-worthy aspects: He feels compelled to change the world for the better.

While Julian often finds some semblance of time for me it requires effort. Often he appears just long enough to bring dinner and help with the dishes before leaving to study. Sometimes he'll slip in late at night, and the only evidence he's been here is when I wake to find the other side of the bed disturbed and a note attached to the mirror. Weeks can pass without any real time with Julian, and it's almost fine because he constantly finds little ways to show he cares. Life with Julian is pleasantly uncomplicated, making going home that much more difficult.

As I walk up the steps of my parent's home, my brain takes a moment to prepare for whatever it may find inside. My last contact with Donovan was when I told him to go screw himself and abandoned him in the park. Now we will spend four days under the same roof. I tried to make it less. It was supposed to be more. A lot of creative excuses were generated to make it only four days.

Mom practically attacks me before my feet get over the threshold. "I'm so glad to see you! This is going to be so much fun! It is going to be the perfect week!"

Am I in the right house? "Mom, either you know

something I don't, or Dad's been slipping you some little yellow pills."

"Oh, don't be ridiculous! I need you to help me get ready before Donovan gets here. I can't wait to meet Marcia!"

"Who's Marcia?"

"Don't tell me Donovan didn't tell you? He's bringing home his girlfriend for us to meet. I don't think she knows this yet, but he plans to marry her as soon as they graduate. Oh! I'm just so excited! Isn't this wonderful? I just wish you could have brought Julian. How is he? Oh! And have you talked to Christopher lately? Donovan says you still speak to him."

Dear God, please help me. Please help poor Marcia. This is not going to be pretty.

❧

Marcia is beautiful, smart, and talented, so what she sees in the current incarnation of Donovan absolutely baffles me. Cheryl had been the victim of his charms, but she was awkward and probably didn't get much attention. Marcia is definitely the type of woman with options. If she has self-esteem issues, she's crazy.

But this relationship is sensible because Donovan is acting his true self towards her, not the swamp monster that's possessed him the last few years. He seems genuine when he talks about how great Marcia is and how in love they are. However, since his glow towards her is usually followed with a smug look towards me, his intentions are questionable.

The kicker is the disturbing fact that Marcia is my doppelganger. We both have long, wavy brown hair, trim curves, are about the same height and weight, and have similar eyes, though Marcia's are blue and mine are grey-violet. It's creepy! We both love to cook, hate crappy food, and have similar taste in music. We even watch the same TV shows. Either we're cosmic twins or Marcia's a plant that's been fed copious amounts of information.

After two days of dealing with Donovan's constant pompousness, the time has arrived to dig towards the bottom of this madness.

Marcia has accepted my invitation to a girl's night at the movies. As we put on our jackets to leave, Donovan motions me into the den. His biting tone matches the grip he has on my arm and is accented by threatening eyes. "Just what do you think you're doing?"

"I'm taking Marcia to a movie. Rumor has it she might become my sister-in-law, so I should get to know her."

"Lil, I mean it. Don't screw this up!"

"I would *never* do that to you. Despite my apprehensions regarding your character, I'm taking this situation earnestly. Are you serious about my twin or is this a game?"

"Your twin?" Suddenly the wind of truth smacks like a door whipping into a wall. Donovan rattles his head to replace reality with denial. I escape his grip and resume leaving.

"You girls going out?" Mom asks. "I think it's wonderful how well you get along."

Dad jumps in with the winning words of the night. "Of course they get along. With the way they look and act alike, I'd swear they were sisters. Lana, are you sure there's not something you want to tell me?"

Neurotica caresses Donovan. Checkmate!

36

"Wow! You look fantastic." Julian stumbles out of bed and wipes the sleep from his eyes. "What's the occasion?"

I stroll to him while wearing a lovely pink frock. My neck cranes to kiss the gorgeous half-naked Adonis. My face gleams like lamp on a post. "I am going to a tea party to welcome my future sister-in-law to the family."

"Wait. What? Is this the same brother who, over Spring Break, brought home a girl that he just met?"

"He's the only brother I have. Kiss, please." My angelic demeanor is maintained and he satisfies my desires. I'm going to keep a positive attitude if it kills me.

"Tell me this is at least the same girl you showed me the picture of. The one I said looks like you."

"Yes. More kisses please." I close my eyes and only have to wait a brief moment for my request to be fulfilled. I get the added bonus of a smile as radiant as a uranium mine—which quickly drops.

"Don't you think it's a little weird that he's engaged already? I mean, didn't he meet her like two months after you and I met?"

I stroll to the dresser to finish my primping. "Well, they actually get to see each other—unlike another couple I know."

Julian slips his arms around me from behind. Even while wearing heels my head barely reaches his shoulders. "Lily, I'm serious. Doesn't it seem a little sudden?"

My head falls back. "Oh God, yes! What the hell is he thinking?" I throw myself backward onto the bed. Melodrama is my best friend. "He's obviously lost his mind. They aren't planning on getting married until they graduate in over two years, so why get engaged now? Why not wait until he's known her a reasonable amount of time, like say, a year, which is still too soon in my book."

Julian slides onto the bed and curls next to me. "Glad to hear you say that."

"Promise me something?"

"Anything." He kisses me then visibly rethinks his previous words. "Maybe anything."

"If I kill him, you'll bail me out of jail?"

ℬ

Spending the last few weeks blocking the ridiculousness of Donovan and Marcia out of my mind hasn't been too difficult. Actually, anything concerning Donovan has been much easier since abandoning him in the park. The happy memory never gets old! But the closer I get to the tearoom, the more I squirm. The whole situation makes me feel like I'm buried in worms.

Donovan isn't serious about Marcia. Had he brought home a girl who wasn't my duplicate, and if he didn't snicker in my direction like a five-year-old every time he kissed her, then I could take him seriously. However, this is just a joke, and poor Marcia deserves better.

The stress-induced drive brings out the lead in my foot, and I arrive at the tearoom ahead of the crowd. Our private area is lined in elegant Victorian paintings and boasts a window overlooking a small valley. The pink roses that adorn the table fill the space with a lovely aroma and are the perfect complement to the tea set, which is a heavenly shade of blue.

"Christopher," I utter. The cups are almost the same hue as his playful eyes. Being out for tea, such a British thing to do, is bad enough, but to have something that reminds me so blatantly of Christopher is a little much right now with all of the commotion over Donovan's engagement. The forming pools of water are blinked away just as Mom comes in.

"Oh, it's just perfect!" Mom clutches her hands together like a stereotypical early nineteen sixties TV mom, which is appropriate since her puffy dress, tiny hat, pearls, and white gloves make her look like Donna Reed. "Isn't it perfect, Lily?"

"It's delightful, Mom. Marcia will love it." The expanse of blue teacups brings about regret for not attempting to talk Dad into allowing an international relocation.

Mom's excitement cuts short my cerebral sojourn across the pond. "Oh, there she is!" Marcia stands in the doorway. Her pink dress complements mine. "Oh, Marcia! That dress is so cute on you. Come here and let me hug you."

As I look to Marcia to apologize on Mom's behalf for her gushy behavior, my grin crashes. Today we seem to be twins in discomfort.

"Thank you, Lana," Marcia says. "Lily, can I talk to you for a minute?" Marcia sees the guests flooding through the door and yanks me into the restroom. She wears a look of dread. "I have to get out of here." Her sights turn to the window, and she attempts to open it.

"Whoa, Marcia. My family's crazy but they're not that bad! Relax. It's going to be fine."

"You don't understand. I can't marry Donovan."

My feet stammer back as I pretend to be surprised. I put down the toilet seat and sit. An attempt is made to not make it sound like I know Donovan has done something really stupid, but the obvious is hard to cover. "All right, what did Donovan do?"

Marcia's moist eyes cave to heavy sobs. "I don't know what I did. I told him I was nervous about meeting so many people and how I looked forward to seeing you. I commented how funny it is that you and I are so alike, and how lucky he is to have you as a sister and parents that are supportive because mine aren't. Then he just went crazy."

"Crazy how?" If he touched her, he better hope the police drive faster than I do.

"He started screaming that I don't know what I'm talking about, and his family doesn't really love and support him. That there's only one person who ever understood or believed in him, and when he lost that, he lost everything. Now no one knows who he really is—not even himself. Then he grabbed his keys. He yelled at me not to stop him, but I didn't listen and kept pulling at him, and he kept yelling at me to stop. I begged and pulled and finally he yanked his arm away. I thought he was going to come after me, but he stopped and punched the wall so hard he broke the plaster."

My hand covers my gasping mouth. The astonishment isn't over Donovan's actions as much as how my abandonment has affected him and others as well. I was only trying to protect myself. "Marcia, I'm—I'm so sorry."

Marcia braces herself on the sink and stares down it as if some kind of explanation must be in the drain. "He sat on the floor, crying. He kept saying he'd never done anything like that before. Was he lying? Do you know of him doing this kind of thing?"

Never.

My head slowly shakes as I speak. "He used to be the gentlest person imaginable. I've no idea what happened to him. He won't talk to me." I remove a paper towel from the dispenser, dampen it, and hand it to Marcia. She begins to touch up her makeup. "You said you were tugging at him. Were you really doing that? Are you sure you're remembering that right, or are you projecting some of the blame onto yourself?"

Marcia stares at my reflection. "I panicked. I've never felt like he really loved me. Sometimes it's like he wants me to be someone else. I just got insecure, like if he left, I'd never see him again. Stupid, huh?"

Not at all. Part of me feels the same way every time we say goodbye.

"I need to get out of here. Please thank your mother, and tell her the engagement is off."

37

The chiming of my video chat halts my morning departure. Who could possibly be calling? My parents are likely still asleep at six o'clock.

But that's in The States. In Manchester it's eleven!

"Hello, luv! Happy Birthday!" The most charming face I still have ever seen beams at me with blue eyes that pierce through the monitor and into my heart. Once I set my sights on Christopher, my bum can't stop bouncing in its seat.

"Thank you! It is now." Without a thought, my lips hit the screen and smack him one on the cheek. He shies as if he were really here.

"Cor Blimey! I wasn't expecting a greeting like that!"

"And I wasn't expecting to hear from you. It's been yonks!"

"Well, stone the crows! I suppose it has. You look exceptionally radiant. Why the big ear to ear?" He makes a swoop with his finger to trace my smile.

"We haven't spoken in so long that I thought you forgot about me. I'm so glad you haven't. I've been wanting to call you for the longest time."

"Well, why didn't you?" His head bounces as he asks. Seeing Christopher's animation again warms my heart.

My hands fly into the air. "Why didn't you?"

"Long, sad story." He plops his elbow on the desk with chin in hand.

My tone gets weighted. I place my hand on the monitor and start toying with it. "You know, it's all right if you've moved on. It would be hard to hear, but—well, if you have, don't tell me—but don't make that a reason for not talking to me. I miss you terribly."

"Oh, luv. I miss you too. What's that you're doing to your monitor?"

"I'm trying to stroke the hair from your face so I can see you better. Silly, huh?"

"It's darling."

"From now on we talk at least once a month, okay? No matter where life takes us." I kiss my fingertips and reach them towards him.

He returns the gesture and virtually places his hand against mine. "It's more than okay."

"I went to tea a few weeks ago. They had cups that were the same color as your eyes, and I started tearing."

I can feel his heart grip across the miles, just like mine. "I can't believe you still think of me," he says, sounding choked up. "I think of you all the time, but I never expect you to think of me."

"I can't imagine ever stopping."

38

Usually when Julian wakes in the middle of the night he can manage to slip out without even one of the old floorboards creaking. However, now that it's a rare time when he can sleep in, he's up early and making all kinds of racket.

"Are you all right?" I can barely wake myself to ask.

"Yeah. Whatever you do, don't go outside."

"Okay," I mutter as he slips out the door.

Just as slumber is about to resume, Julian's voice rings through the window. "Who the hell do you think you are?"

I spring out of bed and throw the curtains aside. "Oh no! No! No! No! No! No!" I tear out the door, down the hallway, and outside, and then try to break up the two men dueling it out by forcing myself between them. "Stop! Stop fighting!"

"No way, Lily," Julian says. "This guy was sneaking around and looking in your window." A half-dressed Julian lunges at the determined man who doesn't have a prayer against Julian's stature. Julian hits Donovan so hard he must see black as he stumbles.

"Julian, stop hitting my brother!"

He pulls his next punch. "Your brother?" Julian asks. He looks disgusted. "Donovan?"

"Yes, you Neanderthal."

Donovan stares at the blood he's wiped off his jaw as Julian tries to introduce himself properly. "Man, I'm really sorry. I just saw some guy sneaking around and was worried for Lily. Hi, I'm Julian. Nice to meet you." Julian extends his hand but timidly returns it to the pocket of his jeans when Donovan glares at it like it's an alien life form.

While heading for the entrance to the apartment building

202

Donovan baulks, "Nice greeting. Are you going to invite me in or do I just do that myself?" He turns back and eyes me standing outside in a tank top and boy-shorts, or what is basically my underwear. Half of his lips curl. "Cute outfit."

I feel on display as we walk back to my apartment. Upon reaching the living room, my desire to excuse myself in search of less revealing garments is neglected for fear the boys will start going at it again. Both look at each other like caged tigers that want to claim territory.

"To what do I owe this charming visit that comes completely unannounced?" I ask.

Donovan plops on the sofa, puts his feet up on the coffee table, and reclines back. "The main door was locked, and your cell phone's off. I needed to talk to you right away, so I was trying to figure out which apartment was yours. I thought I was sly, but your guard dog sniffed me out."

"Cut the crap!" I tell him. "Why are you here?"

Donovan straightens his back and removes his feet from the table. "Mom sent me. We need to talk."

Julian heads off to the bedroom. "Let me get Lily a robe, then I'll give you two some privacy."

Donovan and I have yet to take our eyes off of each other, as if with any movement an explosive will blow. I release a huff of anger, and I can't help but feel I need to get over it quickly. I sense a lump in Donovan's throat.

Julian returns and helps me put the robe on. "I'll be in the bedroom if you need me." His words are directed at me, but Donovan holds his beastly glare.

Donovan motions for me to sit next to him, and I hesitantly oblige—keeping distance and facing him while hugging my knees. This is no charming little visit to plan a family summer vacation.

"They think Dad had a stroke last night. He's in critical care. They have no idea what caused it or what'll happen next. I'm on my way home for a few days. You should join me."

౫

For two days I pace in the hospital's waiting room. Mom's sorrow is unwavering, and I feel utterly useless. Dad is barely conscious, and my relentless efforts to comfort Mom bare no fruit. As far as Donovan goes, I just want to embrace him and make amends, but my arms can't seem to open.

The news on Dad is slow coming from doctors lacking in bedside manner, and they all speak in tongues. My only act of usefulness was calling for reinforcement. Upon Julian's arrival I introduce him to my sobbing mother who stands to hug him in gratitude. "Thank you so much for coming. It's very sweet of you to drive all those hours to help us."

"It's no problem, Mrs. Beckett," Julian replies. He and Donovan acknowledge each other with polite nods. Peace is at hand. "Mrs. Beckett, I need you to introduce me to the people at the nurse's station. Then I'll see what I can find out."

Mom takes his arm as they walk off. The sight is breathtakingly sad.

Resigning myself to sitting next to Donovan, we stare at our crying mother with Julian attempting to comfort her. "What, no crack?" I ask.

"It's just not the time nor the place." His respect for the situation is short-lived. "Since you put it out there, damn he's tall. How does that work out for you?" Cocked eyebrows accompany his dirty grin.

I can't help but snicker. "You're unbelievable!"

"Got you to smile." He winks and squeezes my hand. Other than when he grabbed my arm during Spring Break, it's the first physical contact we've had since I pushed him onto the bench the day I told him to go to hell.

The doctor arrives and takes Julian to see Dad. In gentlemanly fashion, Donovan relinquishes his seat to Mom. He's been even harder to read these past days. The source of his agitation is more than Dad's distress. It's also something far deeper than my presence or that of Julian.

Several minutes pass before Julian emerges and pulls a chair next to Mom and me. He looks like the bearer of bad news.

Before he begins, Julian scoots his chair a little closer to Mom, like they're old friends and he's lending support. If there's one thing Julian doesn't need training in, it's bedside manner.

"The CT showed bleeding from a brain tumor. They just got the rushed MRI result back, which let them get a better look at the problem. There's not only the issue of the tumor, but it appears Mr. Beckett has experienced mini-strokes for the past year, so there's a lot of weak tissue." Julian pauses and takes Mom's and my hands. He then looks to Donovan in support of his plight before addressing Mom as tenderly as possible. "There is a mass of tumors. They have no way of telling without a biopsy, but the MRI detected a classic pattern for High-grade Glioma, which is cancerous. Mrs. Beckett, your husband was probably having symptoms for a long time. Did he never express anything to you?"

"Nothing," Mom says through sobs. "Occasionally he would mention a headache, and recently his stomach had been bothering him, but he never made anything of it. He's very proud and feels that real men do not complain."

"That's very unfortunate," Julian says. "Please know that with his lack of communication, there was no way you could have known there was a greater problem." Julian looks to Donovan and then me. His deep swallow warns us to brace ourselves. His attention returns to Mom. "Mrs. Beckett, I'm sorry, but they do not feel an operation would be a safe option for your husband. The doctors believe that the risks far outweigh the benefits."

Mom can barely speak as she continues looking at Julian's massive hand holding hers. "Do you agree with them?"

"The doctors seem to know what they are talking about. I'm far from being a doctor and know very little about the brain. What I can do though is, with your clearance, take a copy of the test results to the doctors at Vassar and get their opinions. Would you like me to do that?"

Mom nods and wipes away tears. "You are very kind. I guess that is my only hope."

ॐ

Dad's prognosis is grave. Every doctor to whom Julian shows the test results agrees that the situation is complicated, and any attempt at surgery will likely result in Dad's demise. While Mom is repeatedly told Dad has only a few months to live, Julian gently warns me that, per his information, the estimate is very optimistic.

My heart tells me I'm devastated, but my mind is so busy holding it together for Mom and tending to her that my sorrow is placed on hold. Someday it's going to unleash, and I pity anyone around me when it does.

Most of Dad's days are spent at home, but there are periods when hospital stays are unavoidable. These times always hold added tension, partly because of the situation and partly because the doctors are terrible at communicating in a way Mom can understand. It adds to her sense of denial.

In an effort to help me retain my sanity, Julian valiantly takes time away from his free Fourth of July weekend to help. The situation is surprisingly peaceful on the surface, but if you dare to look beneath, you'd better be armed.

While setting some lemonade on the patio table, I observe Donovan and Julian silently shooting each other intimidating looks. Lucky me gets to stop the battle of testosterone before it rages.

"All right. Now what? Weren't you two going to release all that stress while playing catch?" My hands sit on my hips, mocking the two men determined to start World War III.

Donovan looks like a five year-old accusing a bully. "He started it."

"Oh, please!" I say. "What are you two bickering about?"

Silence.

My entire body caves in surrender. "Are you just not telling me, or did you forget how it started?"

More silence. Looks of confusion reverberate.

"Oh, you've got to be kidding me! You guys really can't remember how it started?"

They look at each other blankly before Julian also regresses. "He called me Sasquatch!"

Donovan throws up his hands and storms off. My laughter is almost insuppressible, but the childishness of the display makes me too astounded to release it.

"What the hell is it with that guy?" Julian asks. "He has got to be the cockiest bastard I've ever met. Don't you think he's a little odd? I mean, what kind of guy sneaks around his sister's apartment, spying on her?"

"Obviously the one who wants to get his ass kicked."

"Lily! I don't think you're seeing what's going on here. Have you taken a good look at how he treats you? You two bicker and snap at each other all the time. There's something not right with him."

"What are you talking about?" I ask, although I'm well aware. It's obvious that Julian sees it too. The fact that he's freaking me out is a little hard to disguise right now.

"He looks at you unnaturally, like you're some lost love or something. He just turned on me in a heartbeat and got all territorial. When I asked if he was challenging me, he said the threatening one is your ex-boyfriend. What the hell is that about?"

Damn it! While it's admittedly nice to have some reassurance that this is not all in my head, Julian's totally on to Donovan. Thank God Mom is still at the hospital and Donovan is out of earshot. God only knows what kind of trauma this would cause, especially now. Julian is hitting too close to reality, and he needs to be heaved away from it before he sees my end.

"What? Christopher? Threatening? Oh, that's just hysterical!" And it is very amusing when thought of in the physical sense, but Donovan nailed it: When it comes to my affection truer words cannot be found. Christopher is a threat to any man I'll ever give the time of day. Just hearing his name tugs at my heartstrings.

"Wait. Is that the one in Manchester? All the way across the Atlantic?"

"Finally someone knows where Manchester is!" My relief in Julian knowing the obvious seems to frustrate him even more. "Seriously, we both know you could crush Donovan with one hand, therefore you could pick up Christopher with two fingers and fling him to Pluto."

My words seem to go unregistered. Julian still looks annoyed. Looking as directly into his eyes as possible, I take his hands in mine and speak in earnest. "*I hear you.* I'm sure it seems weird, but you don't have any siblings. Donovan sees his baby sister out in the real world, and he's worried. He knows I'm capable of taking care of myself, but that doesn't change how he feels he should be looking out for me, especially with what's happening with our dad. Add the fact that I have a man he doesn't know practically living part time under my roof, and well, maybe you can see where he's coming from."

Finally Julian starts to buy it. He slides his arms around my waist. "You'd think he'd try to get to know me instead of acting like I'm some kind of threat. He seems like a jealous bastard. I don't like how he treats you."

My hand playfully runs down Julian's chest to his abdomen, commanding his attention be distracted. "Well, I'm sure he is. Have you looked in a mirror lately?"

"Huh?"

"It just bewilders me how you have absolutely no clue how gorgeous you are. Every guy should be jealous of you."

He kisses me, and with his resulting smile, I feel I've dodged a bullet.

39

Upon opening the home page of an online newspaper, the headline sends a jab through my heart: *Music Mogul Paul Eccles Dies.*

Manchester: Paul Eccles, the veteran music mogul who propelled songs from a vastly talented stable of young writers to the top of the pop charts for the last 47 years, died last night of sudden heart failure. He was 71.

My shoulders drop at the weight of the news. Is that Christopher's father? Christopher rarely speaks of him. If not for Grace always pining over her beloved Paul, I wouldn't even know his name. The bottom of the article holds the answer.

Eccles is survived by his wife of 43 years, Grace, and their five sons, Paul Jr., Richard, David, Robert, and Christopher.

A whirlpool of emotions sucks me under. My poor Christopher. It's eleven o'clock in Manchester—not too late to try his video chat. It rings a long time before he answers.

"Hi, luv," he says. The bags under his eyes and his gravely voice answer my question before I can ask it.

"I just read the news. How are you?"

"Oh," he says languidly. "I'm not so bad but Mum's a wreck. The lads all escaped the house to get away from her, but I couldn't leave her alone. She's destroyed. How did you hear? Oh, I guess that's silly to ask. It's probably in all the papers."

"I wasn't sure the article was about your father until it mentioned you and your mom. You never told me who your father was."

"It didn't seem important. When people know you're the son of someone famous they treat you differently. I knew you wouldn't, but I've had a lot of unearned privilege because of my father. When I was in America no one knew any of it. I got to be me and not me dad's son."

"Is there anything I can do?" With a kiss on my fingers my hand reaches toward his image.

"No, luv. You're already doing it. You called at exactly the right moment. You never fail me." He reaches out as if to grab my hand.

Sharply he turns his attention to Grace's voice wearily calling out, "Christopher, there's a man downstairs that needs something signed. Can you help?"

"Sure, Mum." His stare drags back to the screen. "Mum is under strict orders not to sign or do anything. We've already had a swindler at the door."

"Can I talk to her?"

"You sure you want to?"

"Yes. I really do." My eyes water merely thinking about Grace, a woman who has just lost a man she's loved for almost fifty years. Her undying love for Paul is both an inspiration and a source of fear.

Grace sits at Christopher's desk; looking about as bad as a woman who's spent a day crying over the loss of the only man she ever loved is entitled. "Lilyanna, darling," she sobs. "It's so good to see you. How I wish you were here."

My own tears stream with hers. My attempt to hold it together for Grace's sake is futile. The more her sadness is seen the more it is absorbed. "Grace, I'm so, so sorry. I know you loved Paul very deeply. I will never forget all the times you told me how much you missed him and all the wonderful stories you had. You were so lucky to have each other."

Grace pulls the tissue away from her eyes. "Thank you, dear. I'm so glad that you and Christopher still speak. It gives me hope for him. I worry so much for my son."

My limbs weaken at the increase of sorrow filling her eyes. Maybe this is why Christopher has been so distant.

"He's such a stubborn lad, just like Paul. School has him

miserable, and he can't keep up. He locks himself away, and studies his books and tries to play things that are above him on instruments he doesn't enjoy, and it rarely works out. Oh, why didn't Paul let Christopher fail that audition? Christopher never should've gotten into that school. Now he feels he has something to prove, but everything he touches falls apart.

"He should have stayed with you. He should have done what Paul and I did and stood by each other. Maybe if we had waited longer to marry we wouldn't have had so many problems, but I wouldn't trade a single one for anything. Every time we yelled we still loved each other. I wouldn't even trade moving away for a year because in the end I got to come home, and it was better than it had been in ages. He was the love of my life. Actually, he was so much more than that. He was also my soul mate. I'll see him again. Soul mates never really leave each other, do they? Oh, somebody please tell me I'll see him again."

Nothing else in the world exists as I lock on Grace's words. In her grieving, Grace answered so many of my questions, not only about Christopher's life but also my own. Christopher hasn't been reaching out to me not because he no longer cares, but because he's failing at something that was a part of the reason why he left me behind.

But that is not all I learn. Through Grace's words something critical that has been overlooked for years is finally assimilated and incontrovertibly simplifies the complex relationships that plague me. I've always thought that a soul mate and the love of your life are the same person, but that's not necessarily true. Donovan is my soul mate. On the deepest of all levels I know we have traveled together before, and we will travel together again. This time there was the unfortunate circumstance of landing in the body of what would be his sister, a body that is taboo. It's a cruel and evil twist of fate.

Doom is not upon me after all. The love of my life can

still be had; maybe it's Donovan, maybe it's Christopher. I know it's not Julian. Maybe it's someone still unknown to me. How can you know who holds the crown when there's still so much in front of you?

ॐ

Donovan finds me sitting on the floor outside his apartment, reading a romance novel. His rolling eyes convey he is in no mood to fight. Slowly I raise my hand while holding a white bookmark. I give him a sheepish peer. "Truce?"

"Are you sure? I know you still have a lot you want to say, especially after our last run-in."

"Yeah, but I don't want to fight about it. I don't want to fight with you ever again. Can we talk? Can *I* talk? You just have to listen."

He groans, sounding reluctant. "Yeah, come on in. No one else should be home for a few hours."

Donovan throws his books on the coffee table before plopping down on the sofa and putting his feet up on it. He then crosses his legs and arms as if a human in his proximity will cause an allergic reaction. Regardless, I sit close to him, pull on his arm, and wrap it around my shoulder. Though he looks as if he fears I have the bubonic plague, my head dares to rests on his shoulder.

"Just for a moment, please be the Donovan I spent the first sixteen years of my life with. Can we please go back to a time when you and I were friends who relied on each other? When we'd watch movies together and I'd bury my head in your shoulder while you protected me from the scary monsters both on the screen and in my life? I want to be five again when curling up next to my big brother was considered cute. We never questioned anything. We were just ourselves, and it was perfect. Can I please, please be five again even if only for this moment?"

He concedes and pulls me closer. "I wish it were that simple. But yeah, if we need to ignore things anyway, we might as well do it comfortably, at least for this moment."

"Sometimes I feel if we did it all the time then the other stuff would just fade away, and we would go back to being friends and never consider anything else."

"Maybe you're right. Nothing else is working, so we might as well try it this way. But just when we're alone, and let's not let that happen very often, okay? Just in case."

"Definitely okay." My head relaxes into his shoulder. I almost feel five again. "I broke up with Julian."

"Why?"

"I'm not in love with him."

"Yeah. I could tell."

40

Dad's condition has taken a dramatic turn for the worse. This hospital stay will be his last. It could be hours, it could be days, but the hope of another week is out of the question.

Last night Christopher inquired about my mental state. My ability to answer was replaced by a vacant stare. Like a large vat of discarded contents, digging through the muck is the only way to see what really sits inside. It might be best left undisturbed.

My cell phone has practically been chained to me in anticipation of the inevitable moment. The dreaded call comes while tempering chocolate in a Confectionary Arts class. My edginess causes me to drop the spatula and spray warm chocolate all over myself. Removing the brown mess seems trivial compared to the need to get to the hospital.

"Lily." Donovan stands in the hospital lobby as I sprint past. He catches me and his eyes reflect that the unadulterated, 24-carat Donovan has returned. "Hey, take a breath. You all right?"

Pants come out as I nod, "Yeah. Oh God. Am I too late?"

"No, you still have plenty of time." Taking both of my hands in his, his eyes lock into mine. "It's not pretty in there. He lost the last of his sight this morning. He's heavily drugged and flips back and forth between sleeping and rambling. Just be ready for anything. He's been saying some odd stuff."

Donovan hasn't made a single crack about the calamitous fashion statement of my chocolate encrusted uniform and scraggy hair falling from its clip. Judging from his tone there is no doubt this will be the last time we see our father alive.

Heartache victimizes me, and I fall into Donovan's arms where the comfort I have needed for so long is finally found.

The room where Mom stands watch over her dying husband reeks of antiseptic. The dim lights are somehow glaring. Haze fogs my vision as it locks on the man in the hospital bed attached to all the tubes. I'm told he's my father, but he's hard to recognize. Dad is always strong and sturdy, while this man is frail, broken to the core, and experiencing a horrific end that no one deserves.

"Edward, Lily is here," Mom says. Her red eyes stay focused on her husband. "She's standing next to you with Donovan."

Dad attempts a grin as uncharacteristic tears roll down the sides of his face and onto the pillow. "Lily, my darling girl, give me your hands. I was just telling your mother how very proud I am of you. You have turned out to be such a beautiful and smart woman. You have always followed your head, even when your heart tried to get in the way. Somehow you did it without losing your love and passion. I hope you never change."

"I won't change, Daddy. I promise."

"I believe you, dear. When a Beckett makes a promise, he keeps it."

My eyes turn to Donovan. He grants me a subtle nod of assurance that he will keep his promise as well.

Dad continues. "There were so many things I wanted to do in life, but I never did them. I always wanted to work with my hands, but I was foolish. I wanted to be a carpenter. It was honest work, but my father wanted me to be a businessman. Now it's too late."

"Why didn't you do it, Daddy? Why didn't you become a carpenter?"

His only response is silence.

Mom speaks on his behalf. "It was easier to turn off his desires than to try to fight his father or admit to himself the things he wanted to do." She takes an emotion-filled breath before vacating the room. "I need some air."

"Son, you still there?"

"Yes, Dad." Donovan walks to the other side of the bed and adds his hands to mine and Dad's. Somehow my fragile rollercoaster of a man has found the stability of an army.

"Son, don't be stupid like I was. I had all these things I wanted to do and never did them. It's too late now. I never got to drive across the country. I never got to build any of the things I wanted to. I worked too hard, and there were too many times I came home in the middle of the night, and your mom was asleep. I never even got to tell her I love her."

They say final confessions bring out deep-seated personalities, but this man does not sound anything like the Edward Beckett that spent years berating his son. If this is a dimension of his true self that he allowed to be lost, then my real father is unknown to me.

"You've got to do the things you want while you can and not wait until retirement or whenever you think the right time is to act. You need to constantly move forward and appreciate every day. I've been so wrong with you Donovan. I've tried to turn you into something you're not because that is what I let my father do to me. Now that it's too late I see what a mistake I made. I told you so many things that you were doing wrong, but I was the one who was incorrect. Go do what you want to do, and love whom you want to love, and tell them every day. Promise me that in time you'll forgive me. Please son, please forgiv-iv-ive me."

Although Dad is the one with the deathbed confession, the waves of emotion that flood me emanate from Donovan. He seems true to himself at this moment, which makes it all the more arcane when he visibly speaks in silence a response unreflective of his character.

"Never."

ॐ

Donovan and I amble—arm in arm, my head tucked in his

shoulder–down the bright and noisy hospital hallway. My eyes beg him to tell me the thoughts spiraling inside me are wrong. "Dad's the reason?"

His words capture my being. "No, my love, he was just the catalyst."

He unspools my hair from the clip that has barely done its job holding my tattered locks. He seems to marvel as it drifts to my shoulders. "You should wash your face. There's so much mascara streaked on it that I can barely see the chocolate anymore." Scraping some of the dried chocolate off my cheek with his finger, he licks it and shoots me a cunning smile in an attempt to brighten my darkened feelings. "Go on. I'll be right here."

In the mirror of the restroom, an empty and confused girl stares at me, saying there is something to be processed. Is it Dad's words, Donovan's reaction, or the fact that I'll never see my father alive again the reason for the trauma? The swirl in my brain that causes my hands to grip the sink and steady myself isn't brought on by physical illness.

Donovan supports my body as well as my soul as we leave the hospital.

At the home of our parents, we huddle on the sofa. The room is so quiet it seems sacrilegious to speak above a whisper. Donovan breaks the silence with the tender words I've longed to hear. "Just so you know, you can ask me anything now. One of my reasons for silence is almost gone and, while there are others, I just don't see the need to not be honest with you anymore."

"Do you promise that anything we don't discuss tonight we can talk about tomorrow morning, no matter what?"

"Yes. Then, or at any other time. I promise." With compassion that has not surfaced in years, he brushes the hair away from my cheek and fondles it through his fingers.

The pain of the day succumbs to the hurt endured in his past. Despite all that has happened there is only one thing my spirit needs to know—the only thing that can help me move forward.

"Do you love me? I mean—Do you *really* love me? Not as your sister. Not as your friend. Do you *love* me?"

"Yes. Do you remember when I gave you that silly necklace and the note about you making me fall? I meant it."

"So this entire time you have always loved me?"

"For months before you tackled me. It was just then I knew you felt it too."

His calling embrace entices me closer. My arm slides around the back of his neck. I toy with his raven locks while my heart dares to succumb to his hold. We've been here before, and we'll never be here again if this ends like all those other times. "If you knew for so long, then why all the games?"

"Are you ready for me to start from the beginning? It's going to be a long night, because I'm going to tell you every last detail of everything that happened and everyone involved."

The pain reverberating in his eyes gives me the courage to dare believe truth is upon us. Since he has yet to retreat I grow bolder, touching my lips to his but lingering in apprehension. "No. I don't want to talk about the past. Tonight I want to move forward. You're telling me that you've loved me for years, yet you've never showed it. Tonight I need you to start showing me."

His palm touches my cheek as his thumb skims across the tips of my eyelashes, my heart not quite beating. My gaze becomes transfixed on the beauty of his lips. As he touches them to mine, a soft gasp escapes me before I completely surrender to his affection—my entire body tingling with a cool fever. His tender passion reveals he has awaited this kiss for years and now fears he only has a moment to make up for what felt like an eternity of yearning.

Concern over his reaction baits my breath when he pulls away. Donovan's eyes are like soft blue waves that want to wrap themselves around me and never dissipate while the curve of his lips shimmer. Never will I be able to return to the way I have seen him in any incarnation before, for now I know his true reality.

Fearing he is an apparition, my fingertips touch his lips just as he whispers, "I truly love you, and I will never let you hurt again."

41

"I have waited years to hear you finally say what you feel, and it's exactly what I hoped and prayed for. Donovan, I want this. I love and cherish everything about you, but I'm so afraid you'll run again."

At last Donovan completes his surrender to our reality. "There is no more running," he says. "I have admitted my feelings to myself for years, and not telling you was killing me inside. Now that I have, everything else has melted into nothing. The very core of my being loves you. It's taking every bit of restraint to stop me from carrying you up those stairs and making love to you, but you need to know that what I feel isn't about that. It was never about that. It would have been so much easier if it was."

"I know. It's always been in your eyes. Every time we've been close I've felt it racing through you. But truthfully, those words are just as necessary as the need for you to show me you are willing to act on all the wonderful things you feel." I rise from the sofa and extend my hand to him. This is the moment that will make or break us. It's time we finally express our feelings the way that two people in love unashamedly should.

Donovan takes my hand. As I turn to lead him up the stairs he stops and guides me into his embrace. A gentle fire roars in the depths of his eyes as he caresses my face—the honesty of the moment outwardly moving his emotions to new depths. He sweeps me off my feet and into his arms. I curl into his hold and feel the love emanating from his pounding heart. Staring into my eyes with unabashed desire, he carries me up the stairs, pausing as he reaches the top. "Which room would you prefer?" he asks.

"Yours. I always dreamed of going into your room at night and slipping into bed with you. Some nights I just wanted to hold you and tell you I love you, but there were other times my thoughts were not as honorable."

"Mine it is then. And from now on you can do those things any time you like. I hope you'll do them all, honorable or not."

He lays me on his bed as if I am a fallen idol, resuming my place on his mantle of worship. With a breathtaking kiss that sends tingles through my body, I wrap my legs around him, pressing my hips against his and feeling the growing bulge in his tight jeans. My thoughts slip out of control. Part of me wants to appreciate every nuance of every caress while the anticipation of feeling him inside me is too great to endure. My yearning begs me to retain the poetry of the moment, but the years of pent up tension send my hands feverishly under his snug T-shirt. I nearly rip it off while pulling it over his head.

I reach for his belt and begin unbuckling. His pants are scarcely unzipped before my hand dives inside them to feel his firm erection. The touch brings us hesitation as he runs his fingers through my chocolate brown locks and continues his confession of love with his eyes. The actions ground my fury while halting my breath.

Donovan removes the chocolate-stained jacket of my uniform to reveal a pink tank top underneath. His lips taunt my neck before he peels off my shirt and bra, sliding his hands over my breasts, kissing them with eternal devotion. I become lost in the moment, unable to think of anything other than the love emanating from Donovan's lips that travel through my nipples and into my soul. It's so beautiful, so pure, and so honest that it washes away years of pain.

Donovan's kisses begin their trail down my navel as his hands linger behind, slowing following along until they reach the waistband of my pants and slide them down. Brushing his hands over the lovely curves of my hips, his kisses continue downward. He frees himself of his pants, and I feel denied of my rights. Never will I allow him to do that again.

As his muscular body glides along mine, electricity charges through me. Our lips meet one last time before his soul commands my eyes with his own.

Lily, are you absolutely sure?

My fingers lay on his heart as if swearing an oath. *Donovan, there are no words to express how sure of us I am.*

No longer a victim to hesitation, he merges with me. With a shuddered gasp, my head rolls back in ecstasy. I'm overwhelmed by the feelings of love and longing, but my emotions are quickly overcome by passion. It begins with memories of all the times I wanted to hold him and express my love with words before advancing to when I often wondered what it would be like to make love to him and how he would feel inside me.

He is bigger, harder, and more tantalizing than I ever dreamed. His thrusts are passionate and unrushed, making me tighten around him quickly. My eyes can't decide what they want to revel in more; his thrusting hips, his tight and toned torso, or his chiseled face. But one look into his devoted eyes, and I find my true point of pleasure. They are the eyes of my best friend, my lover, my soul mate, and the man I love so deeply it pains my soul. It is there that my heart and gaze cannot leave until he brings me the greatest physical pleasure of all.

Collapsing into his embrace, true peace immerses me. At last my heart can beat next to his as the heavens always intended.

42

Donovan whispers into my ear. "Hold me all night. Wake me with gentle kisses and caresses in the morning."

"What are you saying?" As morning's glow greets me, I stir to find myself blissfully in the arms of my soul mate.

"I'm quoting you. That is what you asked of me years ago when I took you home from that stupid dance. Now I'm finally honoring that request along with any other desire you may have."

"I can't believe you remembered. I want to wake up like this every morning."

"Dear God, me too. But let's not do it here. Mom has got to come home sometime."

After all we have been through we are finally about to put the past behind us. With any luck, after some awkward conversations regarding Donovan's demons, we will finally be as we have always desired.

As I bounce into the kitchen, my beloved awaits me with coffee and a gushy kiss that turns my blood into warm honey. Just as my heart feels it's about to ooze onto the floor, a car pulls into the driveway. Without haste I grab the trash novel out of my purse and sit with Donovan at the kitchen table. Tears begin to form at the impending word of our father's demise.

Donovan kisses my forehead. "I know. Brace yourself."

When Mom comes through the door I try to give her a comforting hug. Donovan does his best to be distant and broody while reading on his laptop.

"Mom, is—is he all right?" I ask.

"He was brave until the bitter end, but he is at peace now." Mom grabs a cup of coffee and sits across from

Donovan and me. After staring at her cup in silence, she runs her eyes back and forth over us. The act makes my skin crawl. "It's finally happened, hasn't it?"

Mom is sternly accusing Donovan of something he's keenly aware of. His eyes maintain their focus on his laptop as he speaks. "Yes, Mom. It has." He shoots his arm around me, pressing my head into his shoulder. I feel he is guarding me. He squeezes my hand in warning just as Mom jumps out of her seat and explodes.

"How dare you!"

I'm jolted at Mom's scathing tone and words that are aimed directly at Donovan—cold words that gust from a trembling voice.

"How could you do this? How could you take advantage of her? For years I tried to prevent this. For years I kept you two apart. Do you have any idea what you put your father and me through? Do you have any idea how much money it cost? How much of a strain it was on him to put you through treatment let alone the pressure on me having to lie to him all those years about what the treatment was for? And now, now you disgrace him, and you do it in our own home! How nice of you to wait until he was dead! You are the lowest form of life, preying on your own, innocent sister!"

Donovan is cool in light of Mom's accusations. It's the only thing calming my alarm. "Donovan, what the hell is going on?"

He shelters me again, protecting me from the lion that resembles our mother. "It's all right. I knew this might happen. I should have insisted we talk last night."

"Talk about what?" I ask, feeling wrapped in distrust. At whom the distrust is aimed I am uncertain.

Donovan stands and places his hand on my back to lend comfort. Shards of ice fall from his words as he addresses me while glaring at our mother. "Remember when you asked me if Dad was the reason I had hidden my feelings and lashed out all those years? Dad was the catalyst, but Mom was the Nazi warden who tried to have me beaten into submission."

"How dare you!" she screams. "You stop right this instant. Leave this house and my daughter alone."

Donovan holds his ground. "Do you really think Lily doesn't have a say in this? Why don't you finally let her speak? For years you assumed I was the evil son who wanted to rape his little sister, but what you never realized was not only do I truly love her, but she loves me too.

The fingers on Donovan's hand that still resides on my back grip my shirt. His matter-of-fact plea for compassion sounds like a controlled hiss. "I have spent years, and years, pushing my feelings aside and forcing her to do the same while hurting her over and over because you tried to convince me I was an evil and perverted deviant. You killed me inside with that. Do you have any idea how it feels to be in love with someone and constantly be forced to abuse them? To not be able to show them how much you love them even though every bit of your being pushes you towards them?

"I have protected her from the truth all this time. I kept my word to you and never said anything until last night when Dad basically spilled the beans anyway. Now this poor, wonderful woman is hearing all these accusations and has no idea what the hell we're talking about. I'm hurting her all over again. I'm not going to do that anymore. The Donovan you tried to slaughter survived, and I'm telling you loudly and clearly that I am in love with Lily, and she is in love with me, and we are not going to run from it anymore!"

Mom stands like a pillar of strength with her fists clenched at her sides, feeling anger to the point of panting as she wails at me, "Is this true?"

My stare feels like a repressed primal scream—the reality driving a stake through my newfound happiness.

"Just tell her the truth, Lil. There are no secrets anymore. At least there won't be soon. We all know you're bad at filtering stuff when you get emotional, so start talking and tell her how you feel about me."

Mom's words tear at me again. "Well, Lily? How do you feel about *your brother?*"

The words I've forced under for years finally surface. "I—I'm in love with him. I have been for years. He's my soul mate."

Donovan shoots Mom a smug grin before going to the living room and removing something from his duffle bag. Mom is beside herself with emotion. "This is absurd! Are you sure you know the difference between love and in love?"

"Of course I do! You just don't want to hear it."

Donovan returns carrying three books, which he hands to me. "Here, these are yours."

"What are they?"

Donovan locks a vicious glare on Mom as he responds to my inquiry. "They are the journals I wrote so that someday you could learn the complete truth and nothing would be forgotten. They start on that horrible New Year's Eve when Dad wanted to send me to conversion therapy. Since I never brought any girls home, he thought I was gay. But Mom figured out that I was in love with you. No, actually she assumed I wanted to fuck and use you. So when Dad insanely sent me to therapy for one thing, Mom arranged that the apostolic treatment be for something else.

"All those times that I was angry, or depressed, or hiding was because Mom and those barbaric bastards kept telling me I was abnormal and downright disgusting. At first I got into fights to cover the marks from where they abused me. But eventually I started to believe them, and that's when I really got violent and did stupid things like use Cheryl and later tried to marry Marcia because you kept moving on, and I kept getting stuck.

"You were always able to express your feelings and I couldn't for fear if we got caught, Mom would expose me to Dad, and then all hell would really break loose. She threatened to cut us both off so we couldn't go to school, and if I dared try to see you while you were a minor, she would have me arrested for sexual assault. She also broke into your room and checked the email on your laptop to make sure we weren't in contact. Oh, and Mom monitored all my cell phone records, so I couldn't call you. Shall I go on, Mother dear?"

"I think you've said quite enough!"

"What I haven't said Lily can read for herself. She has been the indirect victim of your abuse for years, and it's time someone leveled with her. She deserves that. Oh, and by the way, last week I got Dad to sign over our college funds, so all your power is gone. You can no longer force my silence with threats of ruining Lily's future."

Donovan's words put me in a cryogenic state. My racing heart and inability to swallow only add to the concern over my weakened knees. I stare at the journals, and my voice quakes. "You—You always promised you'd tell, but I never imagined. Dear God. I never imagined.

My sights turn to Mom. "It's true, isn't it? You made him turn into a terrible person who hurt so many people. Why didn't you talk to me?" The rage of devastation overcomes me. I explode and lunge toward Mom. Donovan throws his arms around me from behind, restraining me with an embrace. His actions ground my feet but make my words all the more powerful.

"How could you be so incredibly cruel to your own son? How could you do this to me? All those times I trusted and confided in you. All those times I tried to help you when you were hurting because of Dad."

Mom starts to interject, but my anger cuts her off before she can form the first word. "No! You don't get to stop me. You have silenced me for too long without my knowledge, and now it's my turn! It's been years—*years* that I've suffered, and cried, and hurt. You pretended to be my friend and asked me leading questions about my personal life to find out if anything was going on. I didn't see it then, but it's clear now. You have completely betrayed me. You knew I was hurting! All those times you heard me crying because I needed Donovan, and he wasn't there for me. It made me hurt even more because I thought he hated me, and you knew! You knew the truth, or at least you assumed you did, and you never bothered to ask me. How could you be so cruel to your own children?"

Breaking Donovan's restraint, I flee to his room while clinging to the journals, and almost wishing the devastating truth never surfaced. Mom's final words chime like death bells.

"Grab your things and get out of my life. Don't either of you dare set foot in this town again or disgrace what was once your family name. And don't blacken our family further by ever visiting your father's grave. Knowing you, I can only imagine you'll dance on it."

43

"Donovan, this is sweet, but if you wanted a weekend alone, why did you drive for hours to get me and then two more to take me to a hotel? Why didn't we just stay at my place and take advantage of the extra time?" Not to mention save some money. Since he got Dad to sign over our college funds, he's gone a little crazy.

"Get a load of you. We've officially been dating for one month, and already you're rehearsing to be the nagging wife." His lips adorn me with their sweetness. "Hmm. I like the sound of that."

"The wife part, or the nagging part?"

"Cute, Lil. Anyway, your place is too far away."

"Too far away from where?"

Giving me his patented blinking eye roll, a look that again sends my heart to the stars, he spins me around to face the window. "Come on, Lil. We're four blocks away from ..."

"Hey, you owe me lunch at my favorite restaurant!"

His chuckle is enlivening. "Will you settle for dinner instead? I promise to throw in a romantic moonlit night where I tell you over and over again how lovely you are and how very much I love you. We have so many bad memories that it's time we started making fantastic ones."

"I love how romantic you are." The buttons on his shirt are all too tempting not to toy with. "How long until our reservation?"

"About three hours." He guides me onto the bed, and his kisses grace my hand before meandering up my arm. Surely currents are generated as my entire being sizzles with each touch.

"Hmm. That should give us just enough time to enjoy

what I brought in my suitcase."

"Sounds dangerous. What did you bring?" he purrs, working on my neck, coasting his way towards nibbling on my ear.

"Your new favorite outfit."

The adoration stops just long enough for him to shoot me a grin rivaling that of the Cheshire Cat before resuming his breathtaking advances. "Save it for later. I don't want to wait for you to change."

Peeling away my sweater, he reveres in my femininity with his kisses and nibbles that inch their way down to my navel. Gliding his cool hands down my body, he utters sounds of arousal. My jeans seem to melt away as his mouth continues its downward progress, causing me to gasp.

With my fingers desperately in need of something to grip, my hand slides under the pillows. Discovering a small box diverts my attention from the heaven descending on me. "Hey. What the—?"

Donovan is displeased by my distraction. Then a dorky grin washes over him, and he slides up to face me. "I didn't think you'd find that until tonight. Open it."

With a lump in my throat, I raise the lid to discover a pair of half-carat, diamond earrings. "They're beautiful!"

The touch of his hand raises my chin, changing my view from the gems to his even more dazzling eyes. "Not nearly as much as you. It's time I gave you real jewelry. I know you've always wanted diamonds and everyone buys your birthstone. I'm determined you will get all the things you truly want."

ജ

Life is finally coming together. The amount of control and security that have captured me is nothing short of cozy. Never have any of the aspects of my and Donovan's multiple relationships been better. During his Winter Break he will transfer to Syracuse for a fresh start. In preparation, he's spent a lot of time reconnecting with his old friends and teammates to learn where they are and, most importantly, where they aren't. I can't wait to move in with him. These weekend drives don't leave us enough time together. Then again, we could never have enough time together. He's just perfect. He's all I ever wanted. All I ever dreamed.

Our futures are mapped out. After Donovan graduates I'll find my perfect job far away from anyone we know, and we'll live as husband and wife. It's surprising the amount of couples I've found on the Internet who have done exactly that. Once we found people willing to talk, it was simple to accept the changes we need to make. Considering how our family went to hell, we are all too happy to create new backgrounds.

But all is not perfect in Lilyville. Far from it—for now exists a problem so complex and unsolvable that it places a smothering damper on our blissful happiness, now and forever. There's no way we'll ever resolve it to our satisfaction, and Donovan knows me too well to accept that I'm fine with that. He's right. My core feels gutted. But with Donovan it's not just hurting him, it's tearing at his soul.

"You're being cheated out of something you've always wanted to be with me," he says while sitting across from me at the table in my apartment. Can't he let this die? My brave face won't last much longer.

"The last time I checked we were in this together. Besides, I can leave this relationship at any time, and I've no intention of ever doing so. I love you. End of subject."

"Lily, I know how important this is to you. You made career choices because you want a good home life, which includes kids. You shouldn't get so caught up in me that you lose sight of who you really are. Besides, have you even considered that if you get your business going and then people find out about us and run us out of town, you'll lose everything?"

"Please. One thing at a time. If we have kids, there is nearly a thirty percent chance of birth defects. Although those odds are close to those of a woman over forty, it is a risk we agree we are not willing to take. We might be able to get away with adopting or finding a sperm donor, but either way we'd still have a wreath in the family tree. I know the world is getting more liberal, but I just don't see a time within the next few hundred years that our relationship is going to be socially acceptable and the situation fair to our children."

Donovan rises from the chair. His lashes shadow his sight, but it is not the physical world that he wishes to avoid. "Lily, that's not my point."

"I know. I'm just trying to dodge what you're getting at. You're upset because you think these are more ways you are hurting me and maybe I'm better off with someone else."

"Oh, Lily. Knock it off."

I approach and wrap my arms around his waist. "You're still the incredible person I always knew you to be."

Undeserved guilt seems to plague Donovan at every turn. There are times when I feel he is still struggling to fight demons. Believing that things are suddenly perfect with him may be too magical. "It's more than that," he says. "Because you were a minor, those freaks likened me to a child molester and said I should never be around kids or meet my nieces and nephews. So either I hurt you by being with you or by not even being your friend once you do have kids with someone else. I can't stand the thought of either."

"That's absurd. For years I've seen you around kids. You've always been gentle and amazing. It's wrong enough that people we will never meet judge us based on the circumstance of being related, but to have some freak put crazy ideas in your head when you've done nothing wrong is inexcusable."

Donovan forces a snicker. "You know, they also said I could cause permanent damage to you as you are the younger and weaker sibling. They didn't like it at all when I laughed and said they obviously didn't know how strong-willed and capable you are."

My hands on his cheeks force him to look at me. "Those people have no idea who we are or what we feel. They have no right to judge either of us. Please don't let this conversation start you sliding backward. We have come so far so quickly, and every now and then you start to slip. Keep fighting, okay?"

"But it does hurt you, doesn't it?"

I've maintained my cool, but now the reality of what I'll miss hits like a steam engine. "Yes, it cuts like a knife, but it's my decision, too."

44

It's been an extremely long week, and my only desire is to put on some comfy pajamas and lie in bed while watching mindless TV. Homework can wait, and if Donovan makes it over, the only way he'll get lucky is if I don't snore in his ear.

My cell phone rings as I pull into my parking space. Upon answering it, regret is mine.

"Hi, Lily. It's Marcia."

"Wow. Marcia. It's been ages. How are you?" And why on earth are you calling?

"I'm great. I'm really sorry for what happened when I last saw you. I've known I need to apologize, but it's been hard for me to think about what was going on then."

"Well, it wasn't appreciated, but if I had to face a bunch of strangers under those circumstances, I'd want to run too."

Silence hangs in the air while Marcia's tension transmits through the phone. It adds to my apprehension. Finally, she continues. "I really don't know where to start. I'm sorry about your dad. He was very nice to me, and I'll never forget that."

"Thank you. How did you hear?"

"I have a class with Donovan. I'd been ignoring him for obvious reasons, but I overheard him talking about it, so I approached him. He asked me to lunch, saying he only wanted to apologize, and that he felt guilty about what happened. He took me to this nice little place and we talked and, well, he kind of scared me."

"Scared you how?"

Her lagging sigh is laced with guilt. "It was only partially true when I said I was panicking that he'd leave for good because I was insecure. He'd always been a little moody, but after we spent time at your parent's house it was worse. Then we had that fight, and there was something in his tone that screamed if I let him out the door, he'd kill himself. I know that sounds crazy, but he kept saying how he was damaged and—"

What? I knew it was bad but—"Marcia! Why the hell did you wait so long to tell me?"

"I—I figured I was the problem—or it was in my head. But when we had lunch today, everything was fine until he suddenly got remorseful and said he hurts everyone. Lily, I'm really scared for him."

A vice, akin to the one that grabbed my throat months ago upon learning the truth about Donovan's past, grips me. Rushing through the front door, I pull out Donovan's journals that I abandoned over a month before, not wanting to relive all those bad times when things are now so perfect. I race through the pages like it's a flipbook until I find the entry Donovan wrote the night Marcia left.

Lily I'm the stupist idiot on the universe. I thought if I moved on would be ok buts not true. Tried to love someone. Dinot realize she was like you until everyone laughed. Everyone thinks I'm a joke. I tried to love her anyway but she thinks I someone that am not and noone should love me never anyway. I can't find my keys. None knows what I am anymore. My big fear is that they all know now. Maybe I left them in the car. Can't live with people think I'm evil. I have to prove to you am not. How do I when you hate me and I should only be hated?

The journal feels like a cursed artifact in testament to Donovan's fragility. Am I reading the ramblings of a mad person who's truly gone over the edge?

"My God. I had no idea."

"You totally called that one. That movie sucked." Donovan states the obvious. Together we lie on my wonky sofa with me scrunched up practically on top of him.

Raising my head to gloat is irresistible. "I told you! When are you going to learn that I'm always right?"

"You know, you're right about that too. As of this very moment I'm agreeing that you're always right."

"Yeah, like I believe that."

"I'm serious, Lil. You've been right about everything regarding us from day one. From now on I'm always listening to you." His lips grace mine as if punctuating his statement. "Always."

"Can I take advantage of this moment?" Pulling myself up, I attempt to sit, despite his legs being in the way.

"You can always take advantage of me. Oh, wait. You're serious?"

Very. And I ensure the gravity of my tone reflects it.

"Donovan, it's time we talk about what's in your journals."

My resilient man sinks into the sofa and casts his eyes aside. I surge on while sharing my concerns over his words of self-deprecation and journal entries reflecting times when he was in danger of the destruction of himself and others. Donovan's writings feel like a journey through hell, and his personality vividly twists and spirals with each entry.

"Why don't we go through every section and talk about all the things people told you were bad. You and I can decide together if they were. Then we can put this mess behind us."

"I don't want to talk about me anymore!" His words

jump with a childlike snap while his eyes appear to bear witness to the hounds of hell.

"Darling, it's fine. I just want to be sure you are all right." I reach to touch his arm, but he cowers like an abused animal that wants to bolt for the door. His eyes are locked on me, fully dilated. His face is flush of all color and character. He's unresponsive, and his every muscle tenses to press him into the corner of the sofa as if I'm about to attack. I can only imagine what will happen if I attempt to touch him again.

I anticipated a bad reaction but not one such as this. "I'm sorry," I say. "Let's watch something else. Okay?" Moving with caution, I put some Looney Tunes in the DVD player. "It's been ages since we watched cartoons together. Remember how they always made us laugh?"

I return to the sofa and take care to sit far enough away to give Donovan space. My mind races with the possibilities of what can happen. I make note of my options from calling 911 to the best way to wrestle away a knife should he grab one. After about twenty minutes, he stops the DVD, tosses the remote onto the coffee table and stares at it. Sanity creeps over his face as he brings forth words that smear my heart and reveal only a portion of his inner turmoil.

"I am *not* evil. I am not a victimizer or a child molester. I'm just someone who can't help who he fell in love with. I can choose to avoid a forbidden relationship, but I really don't see why I can't be with the person I love because others don't understand. Maybe they are disgusted because their sibling is someone they could never fall for simply because of who they each are as people. But we could have truly been the one and only person ever in each other's lives—no searching, no lonely nights, no sleeping around. We were denied it over a cruel twist of fate beyond our control.

"Never in all of eternity would I ask to fall in love with someone who could cause people to blindly hate us or to lose everyone I'm close to and drive them to revulsion.

Mom discovered my feelings, and she destroyed me through evangelical wing nuts that verbally and physically abused me. They said I was hell-bound for my thoughts and would take you with me if I laid a finger on you. Then if either of us touched another, we would take them down too. Their eternal damnation would be my fault.

"Those people got under my skin more than I realized. I'm sorry. Not only for today, but for every moment of pain I've ever caused you."

What kind of response can I possibly give? It's clear that the repeated destruction of my spirit ripped at him far more than it did me. With the damage that has been done, he may be in need of more help than I can give. But his hurt does not erase my portion of the pain of our past, meaning both of us need my words to reach our ears.

With a touch to his chin I raise his eyes to mine. There is no other way to express myself than with but a gentle kiss and a single word.

"Forgiven."

Through his tears, he looks at me as if a more beautiful word never existed.

Just when it didn't seem possible, my love for him is deeper than ever. His victimizers have failed in a fiery blaze, accomplishing nothing but sending a defeated message of hate. "Those people lied to you about so many things. You are not a horrible person. As much as I knew we'd work, I never dreamed we could be so happy. Don't ever let anyone get to you with lies again."

∞

"Hey there, luv. Have you been hiding from me? I've been trying to reach you for yonks. I'd all but given up on hearing from you again."

I sit in front of my monitor, hugging my knees and with eyes diverted. There is so much to tell Christopher; how I miss him, how I love him and always will, how despite all of that, I am now permanently off the market. Every one of them is painful, unapproachable, and necessary. "Christopher, please don't ever say that again. Let's never say we're afraid the other is going away and accept that we will always be close and always love each other no matter what happens. It'll just be easier on us both."

Christopher possesses the same cautious look he did when I spouted off about Graham Nash and told him we had to part. At least this time I'm calm, albeit vacant.

"I'm sorry, luv. It's just I always hate how I've lost you." His hand drops onto his desk, and he turns away. His verbal restraint is a relief. Without it, this call would be so much harder. He taps his fingers on his desk as if pondering a dilemma before looking to me with concern over my silence and dimmed eyes. "Darling, are you all right? Do you need to tell me something?" His hand extends toward me.

"Christo—Christopher, it's Donovan."

"Donovan? I thought the two of you were getting on since your father died. Don't tell me you're at it again."

"No, it's not that. We get along perfectly. Better than ever." The attention my eyes give to my knees shelters them from view. "In fact, he's transferring schools, and we're getting an apartment together. Having him back in my life is better than I ever could've imagined."

"Then what's the trouble?"

My gaze returns to him, and I see his still outstretched hand. I can't bring myself to reciprocate. "I don't know how to say this." I take a deep breath and brace myself as the truth I must fully face burst from my lips. "Donovan may be mentally unstable, and I don't know what to do."

"Lilyanna, you're serious, aren't you?"

I'm beyond serious, but the words won't come as I stare at Christopher's image.

"Darling, are you in danger? Is he hurting you?"

I shake my head and grab for air. "No. I'm fine. He'd never touch me or anyone else. My only concern is for him. Christopher, something is dreadfully wrong. It's a long story, but I finally learned why he turned into such a terrible person. I'm trying to help him, but there is only so much I can do."

"You need to get him professional help. You can't take this on yourself."

"I'm trying, but the abuse he suffered was at the hands of people who called themselves therapists. After what happened to him he doesn't trust anyone. Only me."

"Then we need a plan in case the right time ever presents itself. Come on, luv. I'll help you."

46

"God, Lil. It smells amazing in here. What're ya cooking?" Donovan walks into my hole of a kitchen and wraps his arms around me. I give him a kiss so filled with hunger you'd think he'd just returned home from war.

"The most amazing Christmas Eve dinner ever, *just* for you."

"Ummm. Keep kissing me like that and we may never get around to eating it."

With my heart singing, I turn to resume my task of removing the strings from green beans. "Normally I wouldn't complain, but I've spent all day cooking. It's really hard to plan a feast for two without having leftovers for a month."

"Yeah, I can't believe I'm saying this, but after Thanksgiving, I really hope there's no turkey in this place."

"Wow! Who are you? Yeah trust me, none at all. I couldn't even bring myself to cook a duck for fear if we ate any more bird we'd sprout wings and fly away."

He nuzzles his face into my neck and starts nibbling goose bumps onto my body. The act makes my cheek nuzzle his. "Ah, are you cooking a ham just for me?" he mumbles.

"And that brings us to being what we eat."

"Cute, Lil." He goes in for one last peck on the cheek before abandoning me for the sofa. "Since you don't need my help I think I'll get caught up on a little TV."

"It was very sweet of you to offer though." Thank God he didn't try to help. The only ones worse in a kitchen than him are Dad and Christopher. Good Lord!

My nightmarish memories of Christopher wielding a knife in an attempt to help me carve a Thanksgiving turkey

241

are interrupted as a soft knock comes from the front door.

"Hey, are we expecting anyone?" Donovan asks.

"Maybe Santa's coming early with our haul," I say while running in from the kitchen.

"Yeah, what did you ask for that he had to come this early and bring it through the front door?"

Stopping him just shy of turning the knob, my eyes sparkle into his. "I didn't ask for a thing. Christmas came very early for me this year, and I've no need for anything else." My words are accentuated with a kiss.

Donovan reveals that behind our door is one of the most threatening people to ever cross his path. He looks frostier than the snow outside our window at the sight of our deceitful mother. With reservation, I welcome her in. Donovan drags me into the kitchen. His fire has returned. "Are you crazy?"

"Obviously! Let's just hear her out. She's in our territory and there's no reason to cater to her. Remember all the attitude you had when you told her off? Bringing back a little of that right now might not be so bad. Just don't cower."

"Me? Cower?" My cocky man baulks at the notion.

The traitor seems anxious to run. Donovan leans against the wall with the requested attitude coming into view. Silently I scream for him to join me on the sofa. His rolling eyes seem to be his brain's cue to trigger annoyance as he obliges and sits with me as a barrier between him and Mom. Allowing her near Donovan is risky with how fragile he's been. Prayers are quickly sent to heaven that asking for her help wasn't a mistake. Hopefully her inability to face us is an indicator of timidity.

"I came to apologize to you both, but mostly to you, Donovan. Taking over your every move and emotion was callous. I stand by trying to change your feelings toward Lily, but it should have been approached differently. You both deserved real help with a trusted professional instead of barbarians who tortured Donovan. Deep down I knew how you felt about each other, and my not admitting it was cowardly. I did everything a parent isn't supposed to do, starting with not listening. That was the biggest mistake of my life, and all of us will always suffer for it. I am truly, truly sorry."

For the first time since her arrival, Mom musters her courage and fully faces her son. "Donovan, I take full responsibility for all you went through. You have every right to despise me, and I know that you do. You never deserved such treatment. A gentle and loving person like you should never be forced to become his opposite because of someone else's biases. Parents are supposed to nurture their children and shape them into good people. I completely failed you."

Before we can respond she heads for the door—fearing we may say all of the things we are entitled to. "I should leave now. I don't want to ruin your night." We politely follow. The love she shows pains her, but at least it is there. "Are you two really happy together? Is this what you truly want?"

Donovan speaks without hesitation. "Yes, Mom. She's exactly as I thought. I love her more than I ever thought was possible."

I'm astounded not by Donovan's sentiment, but by his public vocalization of truth. His brain is starting to gather the pieces of a dropped puzzle that has fallen down a long stairway and reassemble them.

"Well, Merry Christmas to you both. I genuinely do hope you are happy."

Donovan has no parting words for our mother. I accompany her to the car. Once there she pauses, wanting to hug her daughter but obviously afraid. It's best she keeps her distance. Her damage to Donovan may be permanent, and her betrayal will always torment me. But her brief appearance was for Donovan's benefit, so any bit of hurt I feel is worth anything he gains.

Through eyes soaked in tears of remorse she leaves me with words that destroy me all over again. With all that has happened they may be the last words I'll ever let myself hear from her.

"Thank you for trusting me to do this. God knows I don't deserve anyone's faith. Take care of yourself, dear, and take care of my boy."

47

"Oh. My. Gawd! I can't believe this place! Is this Richie Cunningham's old room?" My eyes float over 'Donovan's bedroom' in disbelief at the football posters embellishing the walls and trophies adorning the dresser. It's so cheesy and so unlike Donovan. "This is incredible. It looks like some clean-cut boy's room from the nineteen fifties. I thought our living situation was to be convincing. This is so not a bedroom you, or any other man your age, would have."

His arms drop to his sides. "I had to decorate it some way. I left the good room as 'your room.' You can do anything you want, and I'll have to tolerate all your pink flowers and girly things, so be nice to me."

Donovan looks miffed, and he should. He's been working his butt off, trying to cram everything into this tiny two-bedroom apartment that's in a building that would have been new to our great grandparents. My teasing is a little inappropriate, but why stop when I'm having so much fun?

"Oh! I know. Not Richie Cunningham. What was his name? The older brother that was into sports. Chuck! This looks like it should belong to Chuck Cunningham. Remember how Dad always said they dumped the wrong brother and should've gotten rid of the wussy one?"

"Stop it, Lil," he says while blinking his eyes at me in annoyance. It makes me crank up the dial on the perkiness meter.

"It's just so … peachy! Oh, D-boy, look at how cute you are, all annoyed and stuff!" I pat his cheek before one glance at the bed makes me change my tone. "That looks totally uncomfortable."

"That's because it's not really a bed," he says, raising a

finger to it. "It's one of those things that is both a bad bed and a terrible sofa. See, you jest but I actually thought this out." He walks to the desk and demonstrates how wings fold up from underneath. "The bed rolls up and the desk doubles in size so there is room enough to study, not that a snooty graduate like you needs to. But I thought you might like the option."

"That's very thoughtful. No wonder why I love you." I slip my arms around his waist. My gleam is one that would normally make him throw me onto any bed, sofa, or chair, regardless of its comfort level.

"Oh, hey. You need to sign this stuff." He attempts to hand me some papers off of the desk, but I'm far too busy kissing his neck. "I added you to the lease, and this is the signature card for my bank accounts. Since you're managing the finances you should be able to move stuff around as you need to."

Damn right I'm in charge of the finances. He's terrible with money, and I have a master plan that—with my new job—we'll only touch our savings for his education. I have high hopes that when he's done we'll have enough left to put a down payment on a condo so we can have a happy little home. Our future is set, we just have to be sure not to screw up.

"Kiss now, talk later," I say with a shortness of breath. Donovan carelessly throws the papers into the air and obliges. Grabbing his face, my tongue dances with his before we plunge onto the bed. "Ouch! This actually is worse than it looks!" A crowbar is needed to pry Donovan off of me. "Come on, let me up."

His nibbles on my ear send tingles up my spine. "Deal with it."

My resistance stops long enough for him to let his guard down so I can force him onto his back. "Only if you're on the bottom."

His eyes of a caged animal set free reveal what kind of ideas surround him. He pulls my head towards his lips and kisses me feverishly before abruptly stopping. "You're right. This bed sucks. Let's finish getting ours set up."

"Yeah, I thought so. Wuss. It was nice of those guys to help us get it up the stairs. Who were they again?" I ask as I rise.

"Just two guys from downstairs. The skinny one thinks you're hot." Donovan winks and purses his lips together. "Ooh."

"Really?" My face contorts like it's just had a run-in with a bitter lemon.

"What? I thought you like them scrawny."

My eyes scathe, and I depart for the real bedroom. I've yet to tell Christopher all the things I should, and it gets harder every day. Since learning my concerns over Donovan, he's brought himself back into my life. Christopher checks on me constantly and helps me finds bits of courage to talk to Donovan regarding getting professional help. He deserves some semblance of honesty. Hopefully it won't kill what we have.

I kneel on the floor, and assembling the bed frame becomes my new focal point. Donovan infiltrates the room in hot pursuit of me. "Oh, come on, Lil. You know I encourage you to talk to him."

"Which is really weird, because you're the jealous type. Why are you fine with me talking to a man whom I almost ran off with?" I wave a screwdriver at him and motion for help.

"He's one of the few true friends you have. Besides, he's a great guy who is three thousand, three hundred, forty-six air miles away, and I could easily take him out just by—" He flicks a hand in the air and bats his eyes.

"Three thous—" Wonderment propels my shaking head. "I just love how modest you are. So does this mean I can talk to Julian?"

"Oh God, no! That guy's a freak!"

"Who? The Greek god whose body is mouthwateringly handsome and perfect in every way? The one who could playfully crush you with one hand?" The look I shoot him is intimidating, yet somewhat dirty.

"Oh, so that *was* it. I kind of figured." Donovan tries to look cocky, but to my delight, he's squirming. The can of worms he opened is starting to ooze.

After releasing a longing sigh my taunting continues. "Honestly, sometimes I did lay back and think of England."

It takes Donovan a moment for the full meaning of the joke to sink in. He looks like he ate mold. "Oh God, Lil! Really? Don't tell me that Manchurian lover was any good!"

"Mancunian," I correct while standing to abandon the bed frame.

"Mancunian? Really? Okay, still there's no way I'm believing that."

"Riiiiight. You look a little green. How insecure do you feel now?"

"Okay, seriously!"

"Christopher is a very talented guitarist and certainly knows how to use his hands." With a *smack*, the screwdriver lands in Donovan's palm. "The bed needs screwing. Think you can handle that?"

ॐ

At seven in the morning, the hushed sound of the front door closing awakes me. I discover a heart-warming note taped to the coffee pot.

Go back to sleep. Breakfast in bed at 8:30. A wonderful day of me treating you like the lovely lady you are to follow. I love you!

Truly, this part of my life is perfect. Donovan constantly amazes me with unlimited love, tenderness, and notes of affection. Notes from him follow me everywhere. Right now the milk in the fridge worships me, and the cheese wants us to elope to Mexico.

I ponder making coffee anyway, and then my video chat rings.

"Happy Valentine's Day! Did I wake you? I was afraid

you might be at work, and I'd missed you."

"Happy Valentine's Day, Christopher. No, I was there late last night and have today off. I was just getting up to make some coffee when you rang. I must look a fright."

"You look very lovely. I'm not tearing you away from anything, am I?" Christopher seems uneasy regarding my impending response.

"No, I'm completely alone. Yours is the first face I've seen today."

When we finish our chat, I crawl back into bed musing over Christopher's uncanny timing. Initially when he was the first man I saw on Valentine's Day he'd left nothing to chance. This time, however, his timing is impeccable. He managed it last year, too. Is the universe toying with me, or is there some great cosmic force refusing to give up hope on us?

As promised, Donovan returns with breakfast in bed from one of my favorite restaurants. Adorning the tray are a single white rose and a little red box.

"I wanted to make you breakfast, but I figured all I would accomplish is setting off the fire alarm. Besides, you're a little intimidating to cook for."

"So I've been told. I can count the times someone has attempted to make me something edible on one finger."

Stripping of his clothes, he reveals a body that makes me feel like I'm dying from the torture of the pleasure it brings. But of all the beautiful places my eyes can feast, it's the sparkling sapphires on his face that command my attention as he crawls back into bed next to me. That is, until it drifts back to the little red box.

"Are you just going to stare at it, or are you going to tear into that box like I know you're dying to?"

"You think you know me so well. I'm going to enjoy my breakfast first," I say while starting to dig in.

"Yeah, right. We'll see how long that lasts."

"You're such an ass."

Donovan chuckles as my fork *clanks* in abandonment for

the box.

I let out a little *gasp* at the contents. Inside is a necklace with a silver pendant in the shape of an infinity symbol. Its unique character boasts a dazzling sparkle resulting from entwining sapphire and tanzanite strips. Its elegant representation of who we are has me awestruck.

"I wanted to give you something with real significance so you would always remember how much I love you and how special we are. The symbol reminded me how, after all we've been through, we still manage to hold together. No matter what transpires between us, in this life or in any other, I will be with you, always. You really are my soul mate. We have traveled together before, and we will travel together again."

48

"My God," I scream while laughing. "You're going to get us kicked out! Will you stop?" Donovan has picked me up and stood me facing him on the back of a shopping cart, barricading me between it and his body. Now he's running me down the isles of the grocery store at lightning speed.

"Only if you keep squealing like a three-year old." He ceases pushing and takes a step back, causing me to fall into his arms.

"I can't believe no one stopped you."

"It's after midnight, and everyone's half asleep. We could stage a watermelon fight and no one would notice."

His lips taste like ambrosia. The delicacy makes me dizzier than the ride. "Yum ... That feels nice."

"Lily!" he softly growls under his breath then looks around as if too much caffeine has set in. "We can't do this here."

"School just ended for the summer and everyone's probably gone home. Besides, I suppose you think that no one would've looked at what you just did and not thought it was innocent."

Stern eyes and a firm jaw are his only reply.

"You're right. Let's get this over with and go home. But first come here." Following my motion, he bends down with trepidation. I whisper in his ear, "Whenever we're together but must be apart, just know I'd give anything to be able to show the world how much you mean to me."

A glow emits from his face as his lids drop to conceal his emotions. "What's next?"

"A gallon of milk and some cereal."

"You get the milk. Whole milk," he scorns while strolling

off. "I don't trust you with the cereal."

"Really?" My hands flail up in disbelief before I head off for the milk.

After rounding the corner and opening the door to the dairy case, the brash tone of a familiar voice chokes me.

"Hey, slut!"

Hesitantly my hand unfolds its grip on the case door. Fear of the wild animal that's ventured into my kingdom drives me backward. Standing before me is one of the last people on earth I ever want to see again; It's Bob, Al's little brother. How did Donovan not learn that Bob is attending Syracuse?

"Hi, Bob," I announce in hope Donovan will hear and stay away.

"I thought you moved with that Australian guy. Who was that dark-haired dude I saw you making out with?"

Crap! Of all of the people in the world who could find out Bob is one of the worst. As per our emergency plan I whip out my phone and text Donovan. *"Abort. Leave NOW!"*

"Well, Bob, it was nice seeing you. Have a good night." My phone beeps with Donovan's acknowledgment. While spurting away, Bob clutches my arm. "Get your hands off of me!" I scream loudly enough so that everyone in the store can hear, but Bob is not intimidated by my actions. He continues his pursuit.

A strong pair of arms delivers me from harm's way. Donovan throws Bob against a row of canned beans and barks, "What the hell do you think you're doing? Leave her alone!"

Bob shakes off the impact before snickering. "Donovan? Seriously! You were the one making out with Lily? I can't believe it! We all knew you were fucked in the head but your own slutty sister?" Bob breaks into resounding laugher just before Donovan's neck becomes corded. His head twitches, and his eyes grow wide and dark.

Monsters used to scare me when I was little. I thought then that I knew fear, but this creature is truly bloodcurdling.

Donovan looks like a rabid panther ready to strike as he advances towards Bob. "What did you call her? What ridiculous things did you just say?"

Grabbing Bob by the collar, Donovan puts Bob's face within inches of his own. "Come on, Bob. Show me how tough you really are." Bob cowers with the fear of death in his eyes. "I thought so. You have a ten second start. I suggest you use it."

Bob sprints out of the store like his life depends on it. I fear he's right as a foreboding of death wisps in like a frigid zephyr invading my spine.

Donovan turns to me. His motions are like those of a clockwork beast—his eyes reminiscent of a time bomb counting down. His head cocks with a snap of detonation. "Time's up."

Donovan sprints after Bob with me behind him, unable to keep up. I catch him just as he's getting into the car and beg him not to go. Coldly he stares before granting me a kiss echoing eternities of love—a haunting kiss signaling finality in this life. The emotions seem foreign to this vicious creature, and I fear it's Donovan's last grasp at reality. When he pulls back, a monstrous expression still dominates his eyes.

"Goodbye, Lily."

He speeds off to what I fear is his demise. His fishtailing through the parking lot almost takes out a garbage can and two other cars. The sound of screeching tires softens as he flashes onto the freeway and out of my sight.

ॐ

While bursting through the apartment door my voice screeches, "Donovan! Donovan!"

Frantically, every room, closet, and cabinet—any place he might hide or leave a sign that he's been here—is investigated. My whirlpool of desperation leaves me empty handed.

"Okay, ma'am," the police officer says. "We'll keep searching and let you know what we find. Meanwhile, if you hear anything at all, please call this number." The kind officer, who has been of little comfort, despite his best efforts, hands me a card with a direct line to the sergeant's desk.

"Please find him. Please, please find him."

The pleas are useless. There's only so much anyone can do. I've been dysfunctional in my assistance in tracking down the man whom I know better than anyone—the man whom this officer thinks of only as my brother—the man who is the center of my universe.

Grabbing my laptop and cell phone, I sit on the living room floor while facing the coffee table on which Donovan has rest his feet on more occasions than can be remembered. There is nothing in my surroundings that isn't a painful reminder of the complexities of my love for him. Silent prayers are again said before opening my laptop.

Dear God, please do not let him die, harm himself, or harm anyone else. And please have Christopher answer.

After what feels like hours of waiting, Christopher finally responds. "My God, Lilyanna. Why are you up at this hour? You look peaky. All right?"

"No. Nothing is all right. Dear God, somebody please help me."

Christopher looks as if he wishes he could jump through the monitor and rescue me. "Darling, what's wrong? Did somebody pass on?"

My head is throttled into my hands at the potential truth of Christopher's words. "It's Donovan. He—he lost it tonight. Just totally snapped. He left me at the grocery store when he went after Bob. He—he—"

Christopher tries to guide me into calm breathing. Illogical sentences escape me in my attempt to babble out everything that's happened. Finally, the admission of my worst fear ends my outburst. "I'm afraid he flipped and is going to drive over a cliff. I'm all alone. I don't know what to do. I told the police everything, and I just feel so helpless while I wait to hear he's dead."

Christopher has been staring at me through eyes that scream he is pleading with God for assistance in my plight. He hurriedly writes something on a piece of paper before seizing his laptop and running with it. "Keep talking, darling. Keep telling what happened."

I'm still unable to calm myself. "I called the police. They took a statement and are searching. I've prayed and prayed. All I can do is wait for him to come home or to get a call that I need to ID the body."

"Hold a moment, luv. Don't leave me." He talks to someone with urgency before again facing me. He resumes walking but with more control reflected in his eyes. He sets the laptop back on his desk, and his revised tone guides me into a calmer state. "All will be right, luv—one way or another. Promise." He kisses his fingers and extends his hand toward my image. My hand goes to my cheek where his would be if he were really here. I close my eyes and wish my life wasn't so complex.

Suddenly Christopher burst with excitement. "Do you have any board games?"

"Huh?"

"Oh, don't tell me that now you can't understand me. Do—you—have—an-ny—board—games, Jennifer? Come on. Monopoly maybe?"

"Nothing."

His eyes dart back and forth as if comically thinking too hard. "How about a pair of dice or a deck of cards?"

"I think there are some dice in the desk. I've no idea why they're there."

"Grab them. I'll keep you busy."

When I return Christopher is talking to a woman. She hands him a piece of paper. He sets it down and looks to his watch.

"All right, luv. Draw a Monopoly board. Ten squares by ten squares. Which piece do you wish to play?"

"The top hat."

He nods in acknowledgment. "All right, I will be the happy puppy dog and follow you around." Christopher looks up again and someone hands him a Monopoly game.

"What's going on over there?"

"We're playing Monopoly. You're going to roll and tell what you get. I'll move your piece while you instruct what to do on your behalf. You can track everything on that piece of paper you have. Find something to use for tokens."

"Who's that lady I keep seeing?"

"Dad's secretary. She comes here every now and again to help Mum. I have her working on something for me." He stops to think aloud, "I've never done that before. I feel rather powerful. All right, roll."

I view the clock on my computer and check my cell phone for the zillionth time. "Christopher, I'm really scared. I wish you were here with me."

The false cheer he has tried so hard to maintain for my benefit falls. "I know, but I'm going to take care of you. Try not to worry too hard. Now keep wishing, and roll those dice."

ॐ

Nearly three hours after Donovan sped off, my cell phone finally rings. The worst is feared as I turn to face Christopher whose gape reflects the terror slinking in my spine. Our eyes lock on each other as the caller tells of Donovan's fate.

It's a nurse from The Harley Rehabilitation Center in Irondequoit, New York. Donovan checked himself in, requesting I be informed he's safe. My subtle work trying to convince Donovan to get true professional help somehow got through to him. This is probably the best-case scenario.

But the news is not all rosy. Apparently my mother is involved and will be there this afternoon to make financial arrangements. My designated arrival time is ten, and I'm only allowed a few minutes to see him. After that it may be months until Donovan and I lay eyes on each other.

Months ... The notion makes my gut wrench. Closing my eyes I steady myself between the sofa and the coffee table. I try to keep down the contents of my stomach as Christopher is relayed the news. "He's at the rehab center you helped me find. I need to be there in a few hours and pack a bunch of Donovan's stuff before that. I'm not going to be able to get any sleep. I'm so confused and alone."

"Darling, you're not alone. Not for long. I've a plane leaving here in an hour and a half. It's the fastest we could get a pilot. My bags were packed while we played Monopoly, and there will be a car waiting on your end. I should be on your doorstep in about ten hours. If you don't want me, you can send me home. But please, at least let me try to help."

49

The lobby of the rehab center is surprisingly womblike. But the ambiance does nothing to help me process the thoughts that plague me. How I arrived is hardly remembered, though the keys in my hand tell I drove. I know Donovan's things were packed because I just handed a suitcase to a nurse. Traces of our life together were removed so Christopher doesn't walk into what he may perceive as hell. Beyond that, nothing is certain.

"Miss Beckett?" A short, well-groomed, upper-middle-aged gentleman with glasses and a dark mustache stands before me. His voice is delicate yet reassuringly strong. "I'm Dr. David Coe. It's nice to finally meet you in person. The nurse called me when your brother arrived last night. He refused to talk to anyone other than the doctor his sister had been speaking to. I appreciate your faith, and Donovan obviously believes you don't give it haphazardly. Please come with me."

The doctor leads me into a cheery room with a small version of a dining room table in its center. An entire wall is a window overlooking a lovely flower garden that is enclosed by a skyscraper of a link fence boasting a barbed wire crown. The site of the piercing obstacle shocks reality into my system. Is Donovan again being dominated?

"Miss Beckett, I am sure this is very awkward for you. Donovan informed me that merely a few hours ago the two of you were extremely happy and that things changed rapidly. Is this true?"

A bob of my head is the only response given. Donovan and I vowed to never talk of our relationship with anyone. This necessary exchange feels a betrayal. In conversing with the doctor previously, the private details were omitted.

"Donovan shared your relationship, the years of perverse treatment that damaged him, and how you've tried to help. Please know that if you hadn't acted, he would not have survived last night's ordeal. Instead he arrived in a state of anxiety, yet was able to communicate clearly and rationally. Apparently he was not like that when you saw him a few hours before. Is this true?"

"I thought he took off to kill himself."

"He did. Miss Beckett, this is a very serious situation. Donovan has been through a lot to be with you. It is very impressive, yet very sad. He is well aware of the social stigma attached to the love you share and is unable to reconcile moving forward in the type of relationship that you both desire while providing for your needs. He can turn around. But frankly, his goals are difficult and will only work with your full support."

As the doctor's implications are absorbed, a balloon that won't cease inflating enters my throat. "What is he requesting?"

"To use his words, he feels you are his soul mate. He wants to maintain the bond you share but has accepted the need to let go of the romantic love to ensure your happiness. He desires to go back to that time when you were friends who shared affection but nothing more. I advised against any physical interaction, but he was adamant before signing himself in that we try. Do you agree to try to meet his desires?"

I can't believe that after all we've endured he's leaving me. "Yes. That's exactly as before."

"Normally a visit this early in care would be supervised, but Donovan has requested he speak to you freely. In light of the situation I will allow it. You should expect that it might be several months before you see him again. Are you ready to see him now?"

Not at all. "Yes."

The bile building in the back of my throat is gulped

down before it escapes me. Regaining my focus on Donovan's health, I force a bitter-sweet sigh of relief in knowing the right doctor sits before me—the one who will keep Donovan's heart beating and bring his mind back. Nothing else matters.

"Miss Beckett, please keep in mind that you are almost as much of a victim as Donovan. You too have suffered from his abusers. The big difference now between you and him is that Donovan is getting help. I encourage you to do something for yourself."

The events of the last twelve hours are taking their physical toll. Why is there no water or a window that can open?

My internal commotion is distracted by the sound of a doorknob's turn. Donovan enters looking like he's just pressed the red button for an atomic bomb and destroyed all of earth's beauty. He tries to make light of the situation. "You look like crap. Were you up all night worried about some loser?" he asks, flashing a poor excuse for a grin that leaves me without even the lamest of rebuttals.

How am I expected to act? Ungainly moments like these were supposedly abolished forever. If this is the end, I'll be dammed if my last memory of us physically together will be a terrifying kiss in a parking lot before his near demise.

Fleeing into his arms, he wraps them around me. I fall apart just feeling his heartbeat. "I could kill you right now. Do you have any idea how much you scared me?"

"I'm so sorry. Do you have any idea how much I scared myself?" Ironically his embrace feels more secure than ever. "Sit with me. We only have a few minutes, and a lot needs to be said."

Enrobing my hands in his, he speaks with unwavering eyes that send a signal to my core that they will always watch over me. "I owe you my life. If it hadn't been for your forgiveness, I would've been lost long ago. If you hadn't researched this place, and had so much faith in it, I would've driven my car over a cliff last night. If you hadn't arranged for Mom to come by on Christmas Eve, and don't pretend you didn't, I never could have called her to pay for this. You saved me, Lily.

"Mom's going to take on the burden of arranging my affairs so you can get on with your life, *and don't argue with me about it*. Hold on to my savings because I plan to go back to school the second I'm able. But if an emergency arises, don't be afraid to use it. You would never need to pay me back. Think of that money as me looking out for you.

"I love you, Lily. I fought so hard to be with you, and it was worth every smile, every tease, every bit of harassment, and every morsel of every moment. Those people out there who say we're sick and shouldn't be together, they're the sick ones. If us standing by each other all these years isn't the definition of love, then one does not exist."

He's right, but that doesn't keep the situation from being wrong. "It's not fair. We deserve more time together. I don't want this to be the end."

"It's *not* the end," he assures me. "Nor am I trying to forget. I'll never fail to remember a moment we've had or a word you've said. But I need to do this for us—for the people we're going to become, the children we'll have, and the future that lies ahead. We either do this or give up things we never should only to live in shadows. I can't wake every morning knowing I'll never be able to fill your voids no matter how happy you tell me you are. Besides, I can't hide anymore, and I can't come out into the sun either. I need to fix me, but no matter what I'm always going to be in love with you. Nothing will change that."

"My turn?" I ask.

"Yeah."

"I love you in so many ways, and I will never release any of them. But I'll honor anything you want as long as it's you talking and not some freak that thinks he knows what's best. I have no intention of ever losing you, just a part of how we express what we share and only because that is what you ask. I'm always going to be in love with you. Nothing has ever extinguished that fire and this won't either."

A tear falls from his eyes. "That's exactly what I want. I promise there will come a day when you and I will be together as we should. I don't know how or when, but we *will* have our time." Before departing he permits us one last indulgence—kissing me like a man in love should. "Goodbye, Lily. I so wanted to call you my wife."

50

How did I get here? Maybe last night was just a nightmare. That small ruckus coming from the kitchen must be Donovan.

Jolting up, I find myself on the bed, fully dressed, with the comforter pulled over me. The waves of my memory crash back.

Donovan. I left him in a rehab center and returned home to be sure all traces of our beautiful relationship that landed him there were erased. Sleep must have conquered me while sitting on the front steps searching for a way to comfortably greet Christopher.

Christopher. That's the noise outside. My last memory is him helping me inside, lying next to me, and wrapping his arm around me.

Christopher's reappearance into my life is ill timed. There were so many occasions that him hopping on a plane would've put me over the moon. But how can Christopher be faced when I'm waking in a bed shared two nights ago with another? I'm not ready for him now and probably won't be until he's long gone.

I slip into the bathroom for a shower. Each drop that falls brings forth renewal like a great cosmic force cleansing my sinuses after a bout with the flu. I remind myself that little is of true importance now: Donovan is safe. Christopher came to help. Decisions I am not ready for can wait. I will survive Donovan's shattering of my heart again, much like how a doctor will re-break a bone in order for it to set properly.

With my mind claiming it's ready for anything, I enter the kitchen—but I get far more than expected. My eternally immaculate galley resembles the inside of a small ship tossed about at sea. Upon seeing me, the frazzled captain races to pour coffee and hand it to me, gallantly. "Good morning, luv! I'm sorry to turn your kitchen all pear-shaped." Christopher scratches his head and eyes the disaster he's created. "I could tell you were about to wake. I knew you'd be famished."

"How did you know I was about to wake? It's three in the morning."

His head dips, and he looks to his shoes, just like the day we met. "Well, I don't know if I should've done this, but when I helped you onto the bed you held onto me shirt and kind of tugged, so I curled next to you. Just before waking, you used to always put your head in the crease of me neck and start nuzzling. As much as I was rather enjoying it, I—" He stops to observe my clasped lips. I slip my hand over my mouth to hide my grin. "Oh, bloody hell! Your stomach was making an awful racket! When's the last time you ate?"

The animated bouncing of his disheveled hair pushes forth my chuckle and propels my arms around him. Dawn has broken after the apocalypse. "Hi, Christopher. It's been such a long time."

"How are ya, luv?"

"So much better now. I can't believe you're here."

"Oh, stop crying. Now you got me started." Christopher pulls away and looks over the room, keeping his face from view. "Bloody mess I've made, eh? Sorry. I tried to make you breakfast but some boiled eggs are the best I could do. How do you live with no food in the house?"

My eyes close. I wish I could block out the memory. "I tried to go shopping, but I ran into some bad luck."

Christopher's eyes scrunch and turn to the ground. "I'm sorry, luv. I forgot that."

"It's fine. Let's get these eggs in our stomachs then find a place to eat. I feel a little weak."

附

To my burning eyes the dimly lit diner feels it belongs on the Vegas strip. My head tries to force my body down while it flips my stomach up. Thankfully, Christopher sits with one arm around me and the other helping me remain upright, else I might discover how much gum is stuck under this table.

"Everything feels like it's going to make me sick," I say.

"Here, drink more water." Christopher again hands me a glass. "If you get sick, you get sick, but you need water and a little more food in you."

"Don't say food." My moan sounds as abrasive as sandpaper on cement. "Talk to me about something to help me get my mind off of how I'm feeling."

Christopher has no idea where to begin as he's rapidly finding many subjects are off limits for evasive reasons. "All right, how's your job?"

"I quit yesterday. When I called out for a few days, they weren't too appreciative even though they knew the messed up reason. Since I need out of this place immediately, I bailed." My dizzy head raises just enough to catch a glimpse of Christopher before needing to crash down again. "Christopher, how is it that you're here?" Quickly I squeeze his hand. That sounded harsh. "That came out wrong. What I meant was, what about school, and how did you get here so quickly? Every time I looked at flights to you it would've taken so much longer."

The face of concern held since his arrival now glows like a small child after his first lick of ice cream. "I went to the airport and flew directly." His attention turns to the glass of water, trying to give it to me while anticipating the desire to avoid my next question.

"There are no direct flights from Manchester to Syracuse."

I watch every bit of his squirming reaction. He looks caught red handed. "There are if you have access to a private plane."

"You have a plane?" After jerking up too quickly my

265

skull falls back down with a groan.

His sinking head confesses as if he is a pacifist who has committed murder. "No, Dad's company does. I had his secretary arrange the flight and asked the butler to pack my essentials. I've never done any of the like before. I don't feel very comfortable talking about these things, but I'll tell you. I should've told you so many things yonks ago."

"You have a butler!" If the next thing he says is that he has a den of exotic animals, I'm deeming him delusional and putting him in the cell next to Donovan.

"Yes. Jeeves." He bounces his head in jest, forcing my chuckle. "Actually it's Gerald, but we all joke and call him Jeeves. Nice chap, really. He's worked for us for donkey's years."

"I'm really glad you're here. I'm not in a good place now, but if you have the time to be here, I really hope you'll stay and give me a chance to get my head together so I can appreciate you."

"I didn't know if I should come, really. I'd been so upset for not coming when you first told me of Donovan's problem, but I was tied up with—Well, when you come right down to it I was just pissing around not knowing what I was doing." His shoving motion attempts to discard frustration before his enigmatic smile flashes. "But I'm here now for as long as you want me to be."

Allowing my muscles to relax, my focus alters to the remnants of my breakfast only to feel ill again. As painful as it is to let go, this disaster needs to be closed out so I can move on—quickly.

ॐ

My head is surrounded by porcelain. My brain spins as if I didn't know when to stop mixing cheap tequila and ripple. Christopher, who has been on the floor next to me while lending support, looks as green as I feel. Thank God he's here. I can't imagine how much worse this would be alone.

When the vomiting finally ceases, my Mancunian nurse practically drags me into bed. I just pray that soon he's not taking me to the hospital. Hopefully my stomach will retain the sleeping pills he claims the doctor gave him. They remind me of Grace's words about how he has his own problems. When this ordeal is done it will be my turn to play hero.

Blissfully, the drugs knock me out cold.

Over fourteen hours later, just as I stir, Christopher walks into my room with a cup of hot coffee gripped in his hands.

"Did you—" I look to find the other side of the bed untouched. "How did you know I was about to wake? It's two in the morning."

"Well, usually after you get done nuzzling me neck you let out a very specific little moan and stretch a bit, meaning you're just about to open your eyes. I slept on the sofa outside your door and heard you, so I ran and got the coffee. I hope you don't mind my coming in."

The warmth of the steaming cup in my hands is no match to that of the man who took a private plane over three thousand miles to get to me as quickly as possible. For the first time it hits me that he's really here, and I remember the effervescent joy he brings. I'm truly blessed that he ever graced my life. "I can't believe you noticed something like that."

The luminosity of his heart shows he has missed me too. "Come on, luv. Let's get you some brekky then attack that room. You've got big things ahead of you."

ॐ

"I always thought those posters were ridiculous," I say. "At least they're all that's left along with a few things in the closet."

"I'll manage those." Christopher claps his hands together and jumps to the task.

The closet door flies open, and the blend of Donovan's musk and cologne rushes over me. The engulfing aroma pulls me close to him again, tempting me to mourn our loss. But the battle over tears is won as I choose to let this fragrance be a reminder of his strength, thus renewing my own.

Upon finishing the closet I scan the room, knowing it's empty sans two remaining posters and a few things in the desk. Christopher is meticulous with Donovan's belongings, and the process is taking forever. Even if able, I wouldn't have the heart to tell him this stuff is all a joke.

I've just finished emptying the desk when Christopher approaches. The look on his face tells me he fears he is about to be the messenger of newfound misery. "Lilyanna, I discovered this just now. It was attached to the wall behind a poster."

In Christopher's hand lies a sealed envelope with my name on it. The dizzy feeling of yesterday returns in full force. The earth's rotation drags as I take the envelope and move to the living room sofa. The enclosed letter is dated this past January. Donovan must have stuck it to the wall when he decorated the room.

Dear Lily,

I fear that someday you will find this because if you do, it means you are cleaning out my belongings, and I finally snapped. I feel it coming. I know you're fighting to save me, but I may be too damaged by the hate of others. None of this is your fault.

You have sacrificed too much loving me. Don't try to fool yourself. You're making yourself ill, and you don't see it. It's time you look out only for yourself.

Go make your dreams come true. I'm adding you to the signature cards on my bank accounts as soon as you move in, just in case I do something to make you find this someday. Take that money and do great things. It's not much, but use it as seed money to start that bakery you always wanted. But before you do anything else, track down Christopher. Give him one last chance to be in your life. I don't know if he's worthy, but I saw how much he loves you, and God knows you're still in love with him.

I love you. You really are my soul mate, and I've been a happier and stronger person because of it. All that is good in my life is because of you.
Donovan

My trembling hand holds Donovan's letter openly toward Christopher who watches over me from afar. "It's all there. The abridged truth of everything that happened and him thinking that someday he'd kill himself. I need some air."

The note lays open on the coffee table for Christopher to read at his own risk. If he deciphers the code and gets the real story, it will be because deep down inside he knows the truth and it's already too late.

The world seems grey again. Donovan was right. My sacrifices for him grew each day. For years I've given him so much love and understanding that it drained me. The overall situation has brought about my physical illness, leaving me nothing to heal with.

How do you move on when nothing of you remains but an empty shell? How do you begin filling again when you may have lost your desire to put in any love? I've longed for Christopher since he left, and now that he's finally by my side I'm closed off. It's more than mourning the loss of Donovan. I'm locking myself away.

When I muster the fortitude to return home, I find my car loaded and Christopher frenziedly packing the kitchen.

"All right, luv?" he rushes over to ask. Despite his racing heart, he seems overtly focused.

"Yes. All right?"

"No. I want you out of here. I'm taking Donovan's things to the storage house down the road. When I come back we'll put your belongings in there as well. Have a suitcase packed with your essentials. We can buy anything you need along the way. We leave as soon we finish here."

Christopher smacks the tape gun in his hand onto a moving box, grabs my car keys, and leaves me behind—

stunned.

51

"Which direction is Donovan?" Christopher asks.

I reply simply, "West."

"Your mum?"

"South."

"Then we head north-east."

The turn of Christopher's personality is astounding. Within moments he transformed from the sweet and loving, albeit slightly awkward, guy I've known for years to a strong and powerful man on a firm mission.

An hour into our journey I'm still unaware of our destination. "Okay, Christopher, I give. Where are you taking me?"

"Honestly luv, I haven't a clue in the world. I just read that letter and knew I had to get you far away. We'll find some nice little inn and take a few days to get your head back into shape. After that we'll decide what's next."

Nine hours and two quick gas and food stops later we enter a deluxe suite in one of Maine's finest inns, high on a cliff over-looking the Atlantic. Christopher immediately draws me a hot bath before ordering dinner. I'm still not sure I recognize this driven man.

The warm water relaxes my soul, and Christopher's motivation becomes clear—he's evolved into a survivor. Taking advantage of having a staff so he could tend to me must be how Paul acted when Grace needed him. The one time Paul didn't, Grace packed up and left the country, taking Christopher with her. Paul thought he'd lost them both forever.

By my invitation Christopher barely cracks the bathroom door to announce dinner has arrived. Inside the sitting room a lovely candlelit dinner waits in front of a roaring fire. By the time our meal is finished, the Christopher I've cherished for so long has returned.

"How are you feeling, luv?" He kisses his fingertips and reaches them across the table.

Reciprocating the gesture, my fingertips touch his. "Safe. Loved. Recovering." My hand extends further, interlacing our fingers. "It's about time I could do that. Thank you. During that walk today, I felt lost forever, like I would never be full again, let alone ever give again. That's changing now."

"You should get some sleep. We need you to keep healing." He leads me to the bed and tucks me in before kissing me goodnight on the forehead and heading off to the sofa.

"You're not joining me?"

"Not now. You've just gone through a huge shock. Give yourself some space. I've all the time in the world to wait for you."

"You learned this with your mom, didn't you?"

"Her problem was that she never took the time to heal even a little. I'm not going to let you make that mistake. I'll be right over here, should you need me."

๛

The muted sound of waves crashing into the rocks on the shore below makes for lovely music and proved to be the perfect lullaby to put me into a blissful sleep. The captivating view of the Atlantic resides on one side of me while the even better view of Christopher approaches on the other.

"Good morning, luv." He bends down to kiss my forehead, and his scrawny body is all too easy to catch off balance and smack down beside me like a bag of feathers.

"Good morning!"

"Blimey! I'm glad I didn't have coffee in my hands. Why the tussle?"

"Yesterday I let you be in charge. Now it's my turn. You

flew over thirty-three hundred miles to see me. All I've gotten out of you is a peck on the forehead, brief hand holding, and one night of cuddles that I slept through. I demand nuzzling." Christopher looks like the marbles in my head just sprayed all over the floor. "Whaaat? Cat got yur tongue? Gobsmacked are ya?"

"Oh, your Cockney needs serious work! You should be bloody ashamed." He curls with me in his arms.

"You're right. I could use a little more time. Meanwhile, I have questions."

"Is this an inquisition?"

"Yes. I demand answers. It's the least you can do after kidnapping me."

"Blimey! All right, shoot. I mean, *ask*. After that last little row I don't know how much I trust you."

"Ha. Ha. First question: Why are you here for as long as I need when your finals are this week? Full answer please."

"Bloody hell, Lilyanna." He looks miffed and knows he won't get away with an evasive response. "Okay, I'll tell part now and part later. You can't know it all now because I need to see what happens over the next few days or weeks or whatever."

"Blimey! Don't get yur knickers in a twist!"

He looks at me in exasperation. "Really, it makes you sound sick. Wait. Are you trying to sound like you're from Liverpool? Anyway, remember how you called your job in need of caring for yourself, and the boss gave you a bad time, and since you were eventually leaving you decided to quit? Well, that's what I'm doing."

"Why? I thought you always wanted to go to school there?"

Christopher rattles his head like he's shaking off a pesky fly. "Remember I suspected me dad arranged for me to get in? I was right in that, but I wasn't when I said I could've gotten it on my own with proper notice. Turns out I've a pretty limited range of what I can do. I swear those people can play any piece on any instrument. For me, if it doesn't have strings, I lose it. Heaven help me if those strings require a bow. I'm bloody awful! And dear God, don't ask me anything about music theory!"

"I don't believe you."

"Too true. Anyway, I'll tell you the rest later, but I was pretty sure I was going to bugger off after this term. I'm much happier being with you, even under these dastardly circumstances, than being *there*."

"Is that why you really came here? To escape?"

He rolls in closer, placing his cheek on my forehead. "You know, I've asked meself that a few times. Truth is, when I saw you hurting I reacted without thinking, and that's how I got here. Everything else was kismet. Any more questions?"

"Yes, but I'll save them. I've something very important I can't put off."

ॐ

The tops of the cliffs over-looking the ocean are generous enough to share their phenomenal view. The colors of the foliage behind me fill my spirit while the wind that gusts through my hair seems to blow away some of the pain previously believed inescapable.

Sitting merely inches from the cliff's edge, I try to steal some of the sun's glow for myself while feeling both spectacular and torn. Nature's metaphor isn't lost as I admire the contrast of the clear Maya blue sky with the deep azure and sapphire of the ocean. The smooth and unclouded sky is much like the serenity of Christopher's eyes and the love with which he fills my heart. The complex colors of the ocean's cresting waves remind me of the passion Donovan's eyes often flash, and how I've learned that with who he has become I'm drowning.

The jagged rocks below share their voice as well; reminding me how harsh Donovan's spirit has turned at the hands of those who spread hate. How dare they intrude upon the wave's glorious ride? Though those rocks may be immobile, what they haven't the courage to admit is that they slowly erode with each crashing surge. Eventually those rocks will succumb to the power of the wave's will and turn to mere pebbles. But even now, as the surf washes over those vicious rocks, it leaves behind a spectacular shimmer, reminding me it refuses to lose the war.

Donovan, I know you will prevail. You will dissolve those rocks. But can we really get through this and find a relationship we both feel is right? I want to check on you, but I won't. I deserve time to heal, too.

God, I accept it, but it's unfair. I accept that Donovan and I are in love, but it's unfair that people think it's wrong. I do accept that because of those people we would have to give up things no one should. I ask that you help us through this so that we can be together in a way that makes us both happy and fulfilled. But please Lord, in the next lifetime, spare us this issue. Either bring us together properly or give us time apart. But please, never let us repeat this hell.

Stretching my face up to the sky, I'm jealous of the birds that grace through it.

Sky, it's been far, far too long since I've faced you. Please don't break my heart again.

ಚಿ

While the complexity of the colors and sounds experienced on the cliff had been stunning, they can't compare to the way the simple sight of Christopher sitting on the balcony while reading a magazine tugs at my heart.

"Come on," I say, giving my hand to him.

"Where are we going?"

"We'll both know in a moment."

Upon reaching my previous spot on the cliff I tug Christopher to sit with me before looking out over the water. Someway, somehow, I'll see my Donovan again.

"I have that last question now," I say. "Breathe deep, 'cause it's a doozy." Turning to Christopher, the freedom of the sky is reflected in his eyes. His lovely locks flow like birds in the breeze. "Are you still in love with me?"

Christopher's answer comes as if presented on a cloud. "Yes. I never stopped. Not for an instant."

"Do you still want to marry me someday?"

"I'd do it in a heartbeat." Taking my left hand he strokes my ring finger—just like he used to.

"If that happened, could you promise me a stable life? Could I open my shop and know I'm secure? Could you promise that someday we'd have children together?"

"Yes, to all of those and anything else you could ever want."

"I used to think I knew so much about you, but now I realize there is far, far more than I ever imagined. If you're really serious about us, I need to learn more before I risk losing my heart again."

52

"I thought you lived in Manchester. According to my phone's locator we're as close to there as we are Liverpool."

Christopher looks as if he has suddenly gotten a case of the dreaded lurgies. "Luv, don't ever look at that map again, especially while in a moving car with me window open."

I'm finally about to ask why I've endured so many Liverpool jokes when the driver turns off of the main road. An imposing country manor appears in the distance, stealing my attention. "You know, Lilyanna, I always thought you'd love this place. So many times I've nearly sent snaps, hoping to sway you to move, but I couldn't do it. I've been incredibly unfair. You completely brought me into your world, yet I hid mine. I can only imagine how it must be for you seeing how I kept secrets. I hope you can understand and someday forgive me."

Unable to face him for the reality of the words, my head snuggles into his shoulder. "Sometimes people maintain silence for very important reasons. There's nothing to forgive."

Grace runs out, acting like a pre-teen at a boy band concert. At least it seems like Grace. The lady standing before me appears so much more refined and happy than I've ever known Grace to be. "Lilyanna!" She clings to me with excitement. "Oh, how much I've missed you! I can't believe you're finally here!"

Her grip on me is nearly strangling. Mine on her is almost as strong. She makes me feel that I've returned home after a long tour of duty. "Grace, seeing you makes me know everything is really going to be all right."

"Of course it is, dear."

Inside the foyer my eyes trace an elegant, wooden, double staircase in awe. Before the driver can set down our suitcases, Grace ushers me into the drawing room where I'm introduced to two of Christopher's brothers. They seem more like jocks than they do Christopher; tall, strong, short cropped blonde hair, and the pathetic wit that I've come to loathe. From the sound of their conversation the other two brothers are much like them.

After a brief razzing and some third degree questioning, Christopher spares me with a tour of the opulent manor that boasts elegant windows and ceilings dripping with ornamentation. The vastness leaves me feeling swallowed: six bedrooms, three reception rooms, a conservatory, a breakfast room, a dining room, dressing rooms, and a staggering amount of bathrooms. The premises also include a snooker room, stables, and an indoor pool.

The sum of the beautiful rooms pales in comparison to the commanding office that belonged to Christopher's father. The imposing wooden chamber resembles a museum covered in signed photos, awards, and gold and platinum records that span decades. No space is vacant of treasure.

Christopher's boastfulness is uncharacteristic as he guides me to a scratchy black and white photo of five, handsome young men and points to the only one who doesn't look familiar. "That's me dad. The snap was taken in nineteen sixty-five, just before he quit the band and started managing and producing. He somehow had a hand in every record you see on the walls here. He helped shape music history."

"I can't believe one man touched all of this." I marvel at the surroundings before being distracted by the whimsy of a paper map taped haphazardly to the wall. Its character is completely out of place among the framed and polished gems. "Christopher, why are there darts in this map?"

He chuckles and scratches his head. "Mum put it up when they had the row of all rows. She took three darts and threw them at it. I was told to pick one and that's where we were going. It's a bloody good thing she took a choice of three because the first one landed in Ethiopia and the second in Antarctica. Dad left this as a reminder not to be stupid anymore."

I marvel at the dart that annihilated my hometown's location. It is responsible for so many things that have happened in my life, including this very moment. Venturing closer to the records on the wall, I seem to have entered the Twilight Zone. Several of the faces are ones I turned to years before when I accepted my decision not to follow Christopher. Many of my biggest moments are foreshadowed within these walls. Suddenly I feel dizzy. I think it's time to lie down.

ॐ

Despite his brothers' tormenting, Christopher insists that a guest room with a self-contained bath be set for me, asserting I need privacy after all I've been through. He's right, but he's been so respectful that had he not confessed his feelings on the cliffs of Maine, I'd deem any hope of an amorous reunion dead.

Processing my situation with Donovan is still challenging. Often the reality of our emotions, his struggles, and the mental image of him in a straightjacket send me cowering with private tears. He's the primary of two things avalanching my thoughts. The second of which is uncovering all of Christopher's dynamics.

"Is there a significance as to why you brought me here on my first day sightseeing?" I ask while sitting next to Christopher on a picnic blanket and looking over the legendary countryside. The vibrant colors of nature brought forth by England's ongoing war between sun and rain fail to disappoint.

"Not at all. I thought you might like something easy and to get some fresh air." His casual tone turns serious, almost stern. "Lilyanna, how someone could go to pastry school and lose weight is beyond me. You've turned very thin."

He's right, and joking gets me nowhere. "So you're saying I'm thin and pasty, or in other words, I look British?"

"No joke. You look ill. The only other time I've been around a girl so sick she was up the duff or when Mum left Dad for America. I know you've been through a lot, but I'm terribly worried."

His words freak the crap out of me. I'm not pregnant. A routine of doubling up on protection has me certain of it. But it's a curious subject for Christopher to bring up. He hit the nail on the head though about leaving someone I love behind. "I don't do well under stress. When you moved I barely slept for weeks." Christopher's eyes turn downward. He shudders a barely discernible wince. "Please don't feel bad. I thought I'd lost you forever. I can't tell you how many times I almost begged you to wait for me to graduate."

Christopher's head snaps towards me before sagging and appearing downright shameful. Often he's riddled with extraneous remorse, but an expression of true disgrace is surprising. "I wish you had. There's so much I'd have done differently. I made loads of mistakes I'm not proud of." His hidden features tell he's opened a vault of filth his eyes don't want to peer into. "Oh, I suppose I've stepped in it now. I'd really rather not discuss this for fear it'll color your opinion of me."

"If it makes you feel better, I've a few things I'd rather not discuss. I've no shame, but I fear you'd think badly of me as well."

Christopher's unnervingly fast to resort to his chipper self. He dusts his hands off as if to discard reality. "Very well then. Let's agree that the last two years never happened. As far as we're concerned, I came here and brought you with me. It's all we ever need to think of."

The last thing I want is to continue this conversation, but if this pact ever fails and Christopher uncovers my end, the results could be ruinous. "I'm totally fine with that. As far as you and I are concerned, the last two years didn't happen."

"Good!"

"But what if someday you learn something about me that repulses you? Are we going to ignore that?"

Again he's lightning fast to answer. "Lilyanna, I strongly doubt you've ever done anything that would make me lose respect for you. We'll promise to regard the other's privacy. I hereby waive my right to ask you about the last two years."

"I'll do the same, but first I really need to ask you something, else I may never sleep again. I'll word it very carefully, so I'd appreciate if you'd answer the question." I sense his muscles tense. He's afraid I'm onto him. "Are you, or are you about to become, a father?"

His face becomes covered in a shroud of betrayal. "No. I wish it were that honest."

My hand strokes the hair from his face. I search for understanding. His snail's pace in moving forward isn't just for my benefit. We both need time to heal. "Hey, for the record, I still think you're exactly the same, amazing person I always knew you to be. I never deserved you."

"Hey! That's *my* line! Bloody hell, Lilyanna you can't go stealing my lines!" I snuggle next to him, and he kisses my head. "I never deserved you before, and I certainly don't now."

"Get over it, because I'm beginning to think you're stuck."

A veil of relief colors his voice. "Jammy I hope so."

53

Doctor Coe sits at his office desk. His face is framed on my monitor by the degrees and awards that flood his wall. "Lily, I am sorry to have attempted contact so many times. Your mother and I were concerned, and it's become difficult to conceal from Donovan. I feel it time you two speak. Are you comfortable doing that now?"

"Wow. It's only been a few weeks. I thought it would be months." I hoped it would be months yet also feared it. Worry for Donovan is constant, which makes me feel the need to both see him immediately and avoid him like the plague.

"Donovan's a very determined man," Dr. Coe says. "You and I spoke of the four-steps to recovery, beginning with the admission of issues and accepting their implications. He is beginning the third step, which is developing survival tools. Step four will be the most challenging. He must face issues and the damage done to him head on, fix what he can, and cope with the unchangeable. That can only be done upon obtaining the truth. I will be in the room, but please speak as if I'm not. I will stop you if necessary."

A moment later, Donovan slips into Dr. Coe's seat. It's obvious that he's benefited from a little sun and exercise. The glow of the pre-abuse Donovan glints through. "Lily," he says, "I've been worried out of my mind. I knew they were trying to reach you, but no one would tell me anything."

"I'm fine." I start to blow off the trauma of the last few weeks but remember the doctor's words. "I wasn't. I was really sick. I—" My words stall with a deep breath in realization of how much I don't want to tell him the truth.

"I'm in England."

Everything, from the time Donovan sped off to the present is spilt, whether he wants to hear it or not. With each new event his expression alters, and he certainly morphs through plenty. Once all is blurted, Donovan is the pleasantly cocky version of himself; the one that's really him talking. "Okay, wait. You're telling me that Christopher is"—rapidly he blinks his eyes and rattles his head—"loaded, you're in some fancy house, and his dad was some famous guy who produced like every one of those scrawny dudes Mom drooled over?"

"And then some."

"Wow! Does Mom know this?"

"Oh God, no! If I tell her, she'll be on the next plane with the intent of shagging the two brothers who are still single."

In the background, Dr. Coe represses a chortle. I'm sure he is taking notes on that little tidbit.

Donovan looks as green as a Martini olive before earnestly turning his thoughts back to his challenge. "I always knew Christopher would be there for you, just like I knew you were torn because you still love him." His eyes divert from the infinity pendant around my neck. The ring Christopher gave me that still sits on my hand becomes his new point of attention. "Don't feel bad. I know you'll always love me too. I remember every time you ever showed it, and in every way. Even now I still see it in your eyes."

Did he have to call me out on it? His truth makes my words strangling. "There you go, shooting to the gut again. I used to wonder why you were such the jealous type yet you wanted me to stay in touch with him."

"I promised to always look out for you, so I took precautions."

"And you always have. How are you doing *with everything?*"

The question seems to enliven his spark. "A bit better since I realized we're not freaks. Did you know that ten to fifteen percent of college age people have had relations with a sibling and five to ten percent of those are sexual? There are seven thousand students in my school; so about seven hundred and twenty five had something going on at some point. Granted some is abuse or sexual curiosity, but we're definitely not alone."

"We're so not alone. The Internet is filled with stories like ours. Finding them is easy once you know where to look. But what about you, Donovan? How are you really? And please don't dodge the question."

He looks a tad disgruntled. "I still feel like a screw-up, but that's Dad yammering. The funny thing is that had Mom and Dad left me alone I think I'd be more free-spirited like Christopher. Ironic that I'd be like the guy stealing you away, huh?"

Certainly the doctor will stop me, but my pain deserves expressing. A piece of paper on the desk beckons me to watch its fibers shred as I tear it into tiny pieces while choking back tears. "Donovan, are you absolutely certain this is what you want?"

His eyes drop, slowly following the edges of the calendar blotter on the desk, then staring at the boxes as if they are a giant blur. "It's not what I want at all, but it's what we both need."

"I feel robbed." I slap down the paper and grab back his attention. Facing Donovan is the only way to start accepting the complete impact of our loss. "We didn't get a chance to last or fail on our own. I want that chance. People have raped us of our rights."

The sensitive voice of Dr. Coe emanates from off screen. Donovan's head snaps towards it as a respected source of trust and wisdom. "Maybe I can help. First, look at the things you miss about each other, and see what you can have again. Then start accepting what you can't."

My list could go on for days, but I start simply. "Every moment we had, no matter what we were doing, was wonderfully romantic. I especially miss all the notes you used to leave in the strangest places. You always made me feel cherished."

Donovan's gaze returns to the desk, again unable to face me. "Christopher doesn't?"

"He does. It's just different with you."

"I miss that too." Mental construction seems to occupy Donovan. He's trying to use those tools the doctor spoke of. "But you know, that's all right because that was us. I promise to never leave notes for anyone else, and I'm glad Christopher isn't doing that with you. It shows how special we are."

Audible relief releases from me in seeing the doctor's approach taking hold. His voice returns, but this time Donovan's focus on me doesn't waiver. "That's perfect. Also, try to find reasons to not be together. Legitimate ones that don't involve your blood relations or society. Ones where you don't feel victimized."

"That is going to be a lot harder," I say.

Donovan solemnly agrees. "Yeah, that may not be possible."

54

The sun breaking through the crack in my bedroom curtains beckons me to bounce out of bed and embrace my surroundings. I'm in England! I'm with Christopher! This is fantastic!

Already up and dressed, I'm making tea as Christopher enters the kitchen for a cup of coffee to bring to me. Racing up to him with his cup, my lips grace his for the first time in years. "Good morning, luv!"

"Cock-a-hoop! Someone must have slept well. What's your pleasure today?"

"Well, there are a few things I'd really like to do that you've been very naughty about." My carnal grin that implies his clothing is transparent catches him off guard.

"What's that, luv?" His lips are ear to ear, yet he pulls back a little as I toy with his shirt. He's not falling for my ploy.

"For years there's something I've wanted to do, and you have the power to make my dreams come true. I want you to take me to Liv—that place where The Beatles are from."

Finally Christopher, who's been guarded since he arrived at my door, animatedly returns to the man I love. "Oh, bloody hell, Lilyanna!" he cries, and smacks his cup down on the kitchen counter. "You get me all worked up and then you burst on me with that! You're a sly one, you are. Americans!"

"Oh, come on, luv. Please, please me," I beg while batting my eyelashes.

"Not on your Nelly!" You'd think I've asked him to slaughter a puppy. With one look at my pleading face, he caves. "Fine, but I'm rather gutted over it. You should have your purse taped to you. Better yet, keep your necessities in your shoe and leave your purse here. Bloody Scousers!"

Grace strolls in dressed far better than the usual day at the manor dictates. "Oh dear, is she trying to get you to Liverpool?"

"Yes. Help please!" he begs as she fixes herself some tea.

"Well, fret not too much. You need to have her back by three. Lilyanna and I have a tea reservation at four."

"Fine. Well, let's see, it's eight thirty now. By the time we get there it'll be about noon—"

I swat his arm. "Only if you drive like you're a thousand years old! We should be there in forty-five minutes so we can have brekky there. Give me five minutes to get me essentials in me shoe and we'll go."

I skip off, giggling as Christopher scorns Grace: "I hope you know you're bloody well in it for this!"

ℴℂ

After a fun-filled, albeit short and terse, visit to the land of the Fab Four, I'm finally feeling in my element while enjoying a privileged person's version of afternoon tea at a swanky hotel in Manchester proper. The delicious pastry reminds me that I am a train ride away from France, which I must be sure to visit while here—via Rome. Maybe this time I'll order the Pasta Puttanesca.

"So, tell me dear," Grace says, "now that you're with Christopher again, do you regret not coming sooner?"

That complicated question has infested me since Donovan raced off. "Honestly, yes and no. I've missed Christopher terribly, but I don't know if we'd have the opportunities we have now if I'd come sooner." Meaning Donovan and I might still be incommunicado. Now the truth is known. If Donovan's salvation was at my hands as he claims, then I did the right thing. However, if I had moved, would Mom have ended the madness and spared Donovan two years of torment? Then he may never have broken—in which case I nearly destroyed him.

Grace pats my hand. "Well, I'm glad you're here now. I certainly know Christopher is. He's trying not to get his hopes up much, or so he says, but I know you being here makes him feel there is potential for his future happiness. He hasn't felt that way much lately." Grace shakes her head. Her eyes blur while staring at the cup in her hands. Lord, what is he hiding?

There's definitely something else hounding me, though I have no idea how to approach it. "You've done so much for me, and I appreciate every bit of it. Is there anything I can do for you?"

"You're very sweet to ask. Paul's passing still guts me, but I'm much better. I'm aware that when you knew me before I was emotionally well in it, and it came out horribly. I can only imagine what you thought."

Boy, did I have some crazy ideas! But once she knew she was coming home to Paul, the damaged spirit caved way for the real Grace to emerge. I still see her now, which is a little perplexing. I fidget with my cup, and divert my eyes from hers to a plate of lemon slices. "Grace, I mean this with all the respect in the world, and I ask because the answer may really help me with something. How is it you were in such a different state before, but now—"

"You mean, how is it I was so gutted and became cheap and common when Paul and I were separated, yet now that he's gone I'm collected and normal?" She gives me a comforting smile. "When Paul and I separated, the chances of him sitting at home pining seemed slim, so how could I do that for him? I set a terrible example for Christopher. I was always on the make and half the time on the piss or stoned out of my mind. The truth is I've still no idea what Paul was doing. We made a pact not to talk about it.

"The difference is when you can admit that someone or something is dead, then it's gone, and there's no longer anything you can do about it. When I spoke with Christopher a few months after we moved, he told me that neither of you had ever said you were through. That's why I kept pushing him to call. No matter what else might be happening in your lives, as long as neither of you ever said you were done, there was hope.

"Paul and I never said we were through. Each assumed the other would file for divorce, but we never did. Now with Paul gone I know we are done, and I can go on with my life." Grace forces a smile. "Who knows, I may even remarry someday. Anything is possible for me now, but that doesn't mean I don't miss him terribly. No matter what happens, I will never, ever stop loving him. Even if I love another, I will always be in love with him and treasure every moment we had together."

Once more Grace has spelled it all out for me. I'm compelled back into Christopher's arms but can't bring myself to affirm it because I haven't accepted my romance with Donovan as dead. It died in the super market when Bob strangled the life out of it. He changed our futures along with those of everyone we will ever love. Donovan was stolen from me, and whether or not it's for the best is immaterial. We have been victimized, again.

All the while the ring that still graces my finger has been my way of never saying Christopher and I were through. I knew this day would come just as much as Donovan did.

"You know Grace, you might be the smartest person I've ever met."

ॐ

Flocculent clouds make for a spectacular pink and gold-laced sunset that lies just outside the dining room window. It draws me toward it for a moment of privacy and to catch the last of its glow.

Sitting against a tall tree, the stables serve as my backdrop while the chilly air punctuates my sorrow.

Donovan, what happened to us is unjust. I want to keep fighting, but you are right. Because of our unfair circumstances I've let myself get ensnared in a web you didn't spin but is your burden to possess—a web that we each need to escape on our own so that you can destroy it. That precious romance we fought so hard for and cherished so much, it's dead and gone. Maybe we can catch each other in the next lifetime, or maybe it's buried forever. But I will always, always be in love with you. As for the rest of what we have, we'll see that again soon. We'll make sure of it.

During my private funeral, the sun closes its eyes as if in mourning for what we've lost. My mind forbids me to return inside until its anguish is released and the night's mantle of darkness has extinguished the little bit of hope that I've clung to in denial.

After everyone has fallen victim to twilight, the love reflected on my finger draws me into Christopher's room, waking him as I slide into his bed.

"Lilyanna, you all right? Do you need something?"

"Yes," I whisper. "I need to sneak through your window, but I can't find a thirty-foot ladder. It's a good thing you left your door unlocked, else I'd have climbed the trellis."

He turns by your side to face me. I place his hand on my cheek to ensure myself his presence is not an apparition. "Walking past your window today, it occurred to me I've been so wrapped up in my own messes that I haven't even told you I love you. It's time that changed. I love you, Christopher. As much as there were times when life would have been much easier had I stopped, I have always loved you."

His lips find mine with a fury that tells me he fears my mind may change if he allows a single heartbeat to pass before reclaiming me. Finally we share the homecoming kiss for which we've both longed since the day he left years before.

"Darling, I love you so very much. I was beginning to think—"

"Shhh. Do you remember on Valentine's Day when you were the first man I saw, and you said it meant that you were the one for me? I plan to collect on that; so don't go getting any crazy ideas that I've forgotten. You're the love of my life, and we've squandered too much time already. If you'll still have me, I'm remaining by your side."

"With all my being, yes."

"Then it's settled. I'm officially yours."

55

A tattered flyer sporting a moisture ring, with the word *reserved* scribble on it, causes me to chuckle. Christopher and I take seats inside a crowded pub on the outer edge of Manchester. The crowd cheers at the football game on the TV, and I take in a sea of Manchester United T-shirts. Signs line the walls reading, "Nuke Liverpool" and "Liverpool – I'd Rather Walk Alone." As Christopher removes his jacket, revealing his own Manchester United T-shirt, the motive for years of Liverpool wisecracks smacks me in the face.

Before Christopher can notice my facial admission of ignorance, an older, slightly rugged man, approaches. Christopher immediately faces him with military attention. "All right lad, let's see what we've got. Straight up. Not too shabby, but you're a little rough round the edges, just like you should be. I suppose you're ready for battle."

"Yes sir, general sir!"

"Above all remember, you're not Britain, you're Manchester!" The man returns the salute before breaking into a jovial smile and brambly clasping Christopher. "Well, it's about time! We heard you were back yonks ago. Where've ya been?"

"I've been pleasantly occupied. I'd like to introduce you to Lilyanna. Lilyanna, this is me old mate Derek."

"So this is the famous Lilyanna! We thought he was telling porkies." Derek calls to a group of men across the room, "Hey lads, get on over. Christopher found a fit bird to pretend her name is Lilyanna."

Five, hauntingly familiar, gentlemen surround me. While I've been kept in the dark about them, judging by their welcoming grins, they obviously know about me. I'm greeted like an old friend.

"Christopher, who were those guys?" I enquire upon their departure.

"Me mates. Actually, me dad's old mates." Christopher sounds suspiciously casual, meaning they're far more important than he's led on.

"They look familiar. Were they the ones in the picture in your father's office?"

"Yes. Well, four of them were. Tommy was Dad's replacement. And having met your mother they should indeed look familiar. She'd be having kittens if she were here." He chuckles and waves a dismissive hand. "You'll figure it out soon enough. Anyway, you asked why I'm so different. That's because while Dad raised me brothers, those blokes raised me."

My eyes glue to the men whom I've just met. Paint flies onto the canvas of my mind as Christopher creates a handsome portrait.

"Dad started out as a rather terrible musician and quit before the band fired him. But he was good at producing and managing money. Knowing his friends were being swindled, he took over their affairs, changed their name, and made them famous. They owe that and pretty much every penny ever made to him.

"Seeing my parent's wonky marriage, they were there for me when Dad wasn't. Sure Dad loved me and all, but Keith, he taught me to ride a bike. Whenever Mum dragged me off during a split, Tommy took me to football games to keep me mind off things. My sense of humor came from Derek. Eric not only taught me to play guitar, he rang the states weekly, checking I wasn't out on the piss every night. He always straightens me out when I need it. Me own father never did those things. I'm far more like those blokes than Paul Eccles. They are my fathers, and I'm bloody well proud of it.

"Really Lilyanna, everyone makes such a big deal about blood, yet you say your mum betrayed you and Donovan. Those blokes would never betray me. I've heard people say that because someone is adopted they're really not a person's child. That's bollocks. At the end of the day, it's who respects you that matters. I'll take that any day over blood or genes."

Christopher's words ease my soul. Looking at him with new admiration, I display affection upon him that leaves his mates cheering.

Eric returns carrying a guitar case. There's something special about him. His electric eyes make it obvious why he'd been the one that girls flocked to, including my mother. "Sorry, Lilyanna. We can be a bit crude at times."

"It's fine. Christopher told me how you taught him to play, among other things."

Eric smiles at Christopher in admiration of his perfect son. "Yeah, I suppose I taught him a thing or two. Hopefully at least one was good. Christopher, I thought you might like to give this a go." He removes the guitar he just brought over from its case. Instantly I know it's not just any guitar. Its pentagonal shape is unmistakable—even to a novice like me.

"Aw, she's lovely!" Christopher's expression is like that of a toddler at Christmas. "You know what this is, luv? It's a—"

"Vox Phantom XII, *the* guitar of the British Invasion. Eric's famous for playing that on many of The Chestermen's early records. They're sexy, but apparently the Phantoms are a little overrated as far as playability."

Christopher shoots me a look of amazement. "Crikey! How'd you know that?"

It's one of the many little things I learned while we were apart, because I missed him more than I ever admitted to anyone—even myself.

Eric seems rather impressed as well. "You'd better keep her happy," he says to Christopher, "else I'm going to swipe in and wangle her away." He tugs the still stunned Christopher by the arm. "Come on. Join us a spell."

The improvement in Christopher's playing is astounding.

Whether it's the result of school, more time with Eric, or Manchester itself, Christopher's definitely in his element. In my mind, it's settled. While The States will always be home, seeing Christopher in his glory, along with feeling the happiness that glows within me, I see it's time to buy my own Manchester United T-shirt.

"Well, Lilyanna, what'd you think of the boy genius? Cracking, eh?" Eric and his captivating smile return with Christopher to join me. He also lets the cat out of the bag that we may be moving. Christopher's coy and immodest grin brings about cautious optimism.

"Remember how you said we could go anywhere you could find a decent job? Funny thing, Eric got me a fantastic job as a session musician for a major label. I start in less than two months. It's almost an impossible job to get."

"That's amazing! Are we moving to London?" I can totally move to London, as long as it's *with* Christopher.

"I suppose we could …"

Eric chuckles as Christopher toys with me in a transparent attempt to wind me up.

"but the job is in Los Angeles."

The chair supporting me slides away as I attack Christopher like he's unearthed the secret of the universe. "Graham!" I scream.

Eric clearly gets my joke, and lets out a bold laugh. "This girl's a clever one. Cheers, mate." With a pat on Christopher's arm, he departs. Eric's face shows a blend of pride over Christopher's accomplishments and the sorrow of releasing a son into the world.

"Christopher, do you really want to do this?" I ask. "I thought you hated America."

"I never *hated* America. I needed to learn about fitting in. I'm not some guy who formally studied music all his life like the people in school. I learned it from my fathers. Sure, some had formal training, but mostly they taught themselves before teaching me. I'm very happy this way. I'm bloody good with a guitar. I can play anything and make it sound any way you want. Thing is, when I came back and got a good look at meself well, look at who me friends are. They're great blokes, but they're in their sixties, and I'm barely twenty. So I have to ask if I really fit.

"It's time to make my own mark and earn an honest living like me mates did. I don't want to be like Dad, nor do I really want anything he left me, but I'm not stupid. I should set us up properly so we can survive on our own with the knowledge if things go balls up, there's a safety net. I've lived in survival mode for too long and so have you."

"But I thought your dad only left you something if you went to college?"

"Funny thing that." Christopher scratches his head in mock perplexity. "We lads all had the same trust funds, but the wording on mine was different. Theirs said they had to graduate. Mine just said I had to go. Apparently *someone* had it changed before it was signed." Christopher lets out a snicker. He looks like the Artful Dodger upon discovering the wallet he's lifted is loaded. "So, what do you say? Shall we go to California and find ourselves a little castle?"

Dear God, yes!

56

With nervous apprehension I honor Dr. Coe's request to visit Donovan. Being here makes me jumpy enough, but Christopher's valiant insistence that he wait in the lobby, just incase I need him, intensifies my jitters more than his three hundred watt amplifier rattles the windows.

It's been nearly six weeks. Seeing Donovan provides a jubilant, yet agonizing, reunion. Once the embracing starts, the doctor needs a crowbar to pry us apart.

We seem to astound Dr. Coe quite a bit. While we've both warned him about how we interact, seeing has become believing.

"This has gone very well. We have covered every point except one. When we all last spoke I asked you to find legitimate reasons not to be together. Have either of you had success with that?"

Donovan and I stare blankly at each other before both turning to the doctor and responding in what sounds like rehearsed unison.

"None."

Dr. Coe again raises his eyebrows. "You two have been very interesting today. Let's see if we can come up with something."

"Can we detour first?" I ask before turning to Donovan. Donovan slouches in his chair and releases a sigh of doom. "Don't get all broody on me. Spill it. I know what it is, but the doctor should hear you say it. Personally, I wish you didn't have to."

Dr. Coe continues to be stymied by our antics. Meanwhile, Donovan fidgets in his chair and then fesses up. "It's just that this isn't easy. You look fantastic, you smell great, and it never should have been this way. I should've done something—I *wish* I could do something to change it."

I take his hand. He's right; it never should have been this way.

Dr. Coe speaks respectfully of our situation. "Now might be a good time to go back to that question. Can you find a legitimate reason not to be together? One where you don't feel robbed or denied by others."

We look blankly at each other. Donovan drops my hand. "Your turn, Lil. You have a whole speech waiting to come out."

"There isn't a single reason why we wouldn't have worked, and no one can tell me contrarily unless you've had some kind of epiphany. I've accepted we're making a decision based on circumstances over which we have no control. I wasn't ready to do that before, even though you saw it and waved it in front of me like a big, red flag." The focus of my diatribe flips to Dr. Coe. "It all comes down to us accepting that we can't have the life we want together because others are close-minded."

Donovan turns to the doctor in agreement. "What she said."

&

With less than three weeks remaining in Donovan's ninety-day rehab program, I return to New York for our weekly visit. Commuting from Los Angeles has been ridiculously expensive. But as much as these visits are necessary, so is distance from my former life.

House hunting with Christopher has been a whole new kind of adventure. The intention of buying someplace cozy romanced us. But after realizing how insanely expensive homes are in California, Christopher decided to take advantage of a depressed market and put an offer on a mini-mansion to accommodate our future needs. When I asked if he desired an excuse for his brothers to stay with us, a case of the dreaded lurgies loomed before he made the head-smacking announcement that a guesthouse is required.

For all my blessings, guilt lurks at me from around every corner. It would be foolhardy to think my head is stable until the man who gave nearly everything to shield me from ugliness has healed. My liberation has arisen like a flawless flower from a pool of Donovan's blood, leaving behind a trail of thorns on which he treads.

"Why do you feel so guilty?" Donovan asks as we sit in our usual chairs in Dr. Coe's office.

"Asks the man in the funny farm to his sister/ex-girlfriend who can leave any time she wants and go home to her enchanted palace."

His head rolls back along with his eyes. "God, is that what this is about?"

My hands flail into the air like those of a puppet frog. "That and Christopher wants you to move into our guesthouse. How do I tell him you can't possibly do that without spilling why? I'm compelled to tell him everything, but that would be the mistake of a lifetime."

Donovan squirms in his chair to get a better look at me. "Trying to talk like this is." He grabs my hand, escorts me to the sofa, and sits me in the middle while he plops into the corner, facing me. Automatically, we kick off our shoes and put our feet up, our legs entwined at the knees. Donovan still holds my hand. "You tell me what we need to do. Should we tell Christopher, and how are we going to handle this if he bails?"

"I'd be absolutely devastated if he left, and I'd never, ever forgive myself for hurting him. Also, you and I have a pact not to discuss this."

"Whatever, Lil. I'm willing to let that go in this case. Just how much do you love this guy?"

Concern over fragile words when discussing anything with Donovan is a thing of the past. "I wish he'd ask me to marry him, but he hasn't because it's obvious I'm not ready."

"Why not? You've been in love with this guy for years.

What could you possibly be waiting for?"

All I have to do is look at him.

Donovan drops his head back and groans. "Lil, you're no longer allowed to feel guilty about me. It should have stopped long ago. Seriously, why are you letting the bad things that happened in the past delay you getting all of the amazing things you really want while they sit waiting?"

"I do love Christopher, but how do I move forward with him when you're in here largely because of loving me?"

He toys with my fingers. His annoyance at my dallying caves to inner sentiments no longer suppressed. "I wish it were me instead of him, but I'm glad you're getting all the amazing things you deserve. I can't help you move on without being in the way. Accepting that I can't always help you may be the toughest of all challenges."

Tears well at the comfort of just being near Donovan. For the first time in years we're talking like we always used to. I've needed him so badly for so long.

Dr. Coe clears his throat and steals our attention.

"Well, doc, what do you think?" Donovan asks. "Any wisdom for this lovely lady?"

"I think you said everything she needs to hear, but I have to ask if you have heard everything that you said. Look at the two of you. You are exactly as you said you wanted to be the day you walked in here." Dr. Coe hands two envelopes to Donovan. "I had the front desk intercept these a few days ago. I thought you might want to open them with Lily here. Congratulations."

Inside the first envelope is an acceptance letter to Dr. Coe's alma mater, Ramsey University, a private school in Colorado known for their physiological studies. It's the perfect place where Donovan can continue both school and his care. The second envelope contains a partial scholarship Dr. Coe helped Donovan obtain. It's designed for those who have overcome mental challenges. Between that and what is left of both of our college funds, Donovan is set— and then some.

"Registration begins soon," Dr. Coe says. "I've made arrangements with your mother to get you out of here early so you can get settled before school starts. Be sure to keep those grades up so I can write you that letter of recommendation next year."

"Letter of recommendation?" I ask.

"Once step at a time, Lil. I have a master plan."

Epilogue

"Thank you for letting me do this, Lil. I know it's weird, but I really need it." Donovan looks at me as if a goddess stands before him.

"Given the choice I'd rather you be by my side, but that seems awkward too."

My being surrenders to his touch as he caresses the line of my jaw. "Doesn't matter, either way the result's the same. You look lovelier than I've ever seen. The only way you could be more enchanting is if you were marrying me. Sorry, I just had to get a last one in."

He's not sorry at all. At least, I don't think he is. My nerves are so on edge that his thoughts couldn't be grasped if he glued them into my hand. "Do you think you'll ever do this with Anna?"

"Time will reveal more than can be foreseen. All I know is that since I've met her my plans are falling into place."

"Donovan, I'm so anxious that I can't hear myself think. Am I doing the right thing?"

His words are almost hypnotic, relaxing me into a near trance. "You're doing exactly what you're supposed to. You have a long and happy life ahead, and I'm going to always be with you, making sure you don't blow it. I remember all you've ever wished, and I'm going to ensure we get *everything* we've ever desired. It's all just a matter of time. You ready for us to take that walk so you can put the shackles on your scrawny dreamboat?"

"You're such an ass. I guess you really are back to your old self."

"Did you doubt I wouldn't come out unscathed?"

Time's Forbidden Flower

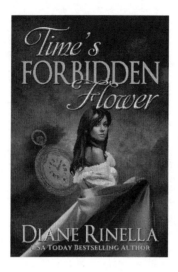

An eternity of passion cannot be quelled by society.

Once upon a time Donovan assured Lily all of her dreams would come true. But how could he keep the promise of a fairy tale when her truest goals could not involve him, though her deepest desires did?

Now, Lily has it all—love, passion, a family, and the career of her dreams—with Christopher. But something is lacking. She and Donovan have spent the last ten years living apart, and the soul mates are eager to reunite. Can Donovan keep his promise to give Lily all she desires, even with Christopher in the way?

*For Lily and Donovan, the past is a mirror to
the future that cannot be shattered.*

Donovan is convinced Lily has been his love for all eternity. Determined to unravel the past, they embark on a journey to discover where it all began. For centuries Donovan has stolen Lily's heart while forced to suffer for his love. How much can a soul endure before the breaking point is reached and a monster emerges? Can the demons of the past be combated to pave the way for happiness in the next life? Or has the abuse suffered in this life already turned Donovan hell bound?

SOMETHING TO DREAM ON

If a painting in the home of your perfect man reflects your dreams of doom, do you run, or do you dare to embrace love? While Lizetta lives a life of compassion, childhood bullying over a few extra pounds have caused this sparky woman to lose sight of the beauty of her soul.

Jensen's recent past is filled with substance abuse, shady morals, and loose women. A brutal wake up call forced him to find his way back to the gentle soul he once was; however, there are some whose futures depend on the return of the demon.

Souls can heal, but how long can they fight the forces that seek to destroy them? If one of those forces is the person who shattered your self-image, and she is determined to take down the one you love, could you still believe that everyone deserves a second chance?

THE ROCK AND ROLL FANTASY COLLECTION

One Christmas, Darla was given a mystical gift, along with an ominous message. Years later, meeting Chris puts her head in a spin. Could it be that gift from long ago holds the key to their happiness?

The Rock and Roll Fantasy Collection is a set of standalone novels and novellas. The novels revolve around characters whose deep-seated love of music is a driving force of the story, while the novellas focus on the supporting characters that you can't help but love.

THE ROCK AND ROLL FANTASY COLLECTION

*A fantastical romance involving a woman,
the music that fuels her, and her Ouija board.*

Rosalyn seeks acceptance, but is always ridiculed for her eclectic wardrobe and unconventional music collection. One fateful night, Rosalyn bewitches Niles, a stylish man whose quirky character is the perfect complement to her own. Unfortunately, Niles has a secret flaw that always ensures relationship suicide—and he can't hide it much longer.

During a tango with a Ouija board, Rosalyn summons the ghost of Rock and Roll deity Peter Lane. Peter entices Niles with the key to saving his relationship with Rosalyn. When Niles hears the price is avenging Peter's murder, how far will he go to secure Rosalyn's heart?

THE ROCK AND ROLL FANTASY COLLECTION

For Jacqueline, a second date is as rare as a unicorn. She's beautiful. She's intelligent. So why is she experiencing a string of first dates that leaves her ducking behind bushes and running for buses? Contrary to her nature, trading in her heels and curling iron for an easy chair surrounded by cats sounds appealing. Is she cursed, or can she find the man who will steal her heart?

Queen Midas In Reverse is a standalone novella that takes place in the Rock and Roll Fantasy universe, alongside Scary Modsters and its prequel, It's A Marshmallow World.

THE ROCK AND ROLL FANTASY COLLECTION

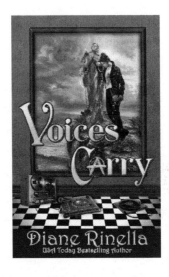

*An incredible romance involving a man,
the music he craves, and the voice that haunts him.*

Rock and roll turns Brandon Wayne into a juvenile delinquent in all the best ways—crazed, ambitious, and with a slip of danger nagging at his hips. His marketing job at Endeara Candies and hunting down classic vinyl nirvana at Warped Records make his world seem ordinary, but there is another side to his life.

As an anniversary of tragedy approaches, odd occurrences riddle Brandon's mind with questions. Whose voice is suddenly materializing in his head? Is he fabricating a psychic who looks like one of his favorite rock stars? Why is he having retro dreams involving welded beer cans, disco, and a punk rock girl? The puzzle seems never ending.

Have the musty fumes at Warped Records and the terrible candy at work rotted Brandon's brain? Has he crossed into the realm of insanity? Or is the reason for the madness beyond his comprehension?

Voices Carry is a standalone novel that takes place in the Rock and Roll Fantasy universe.

THE ROCK AND ROLL FANTASY COLLECTION

Can unseen forces nudge you onto a new path?
If so, Dale and Bailey might get shoved!

When Dale seeks the help of a wine-loving psychic, he has two things on his mind: "Where is my dream girl? And why is a ghost following me?" Five hundred dollars later, he has a cryptic clue and a song stuck in his head.

Across the continent, Bailey is the answer to Dale's prayers. However, her sleazy boyfriend has her over a barrel. Someway, somehow, she has to outfox that snake and escape his hold—even if it means diving into mischief.

When a long-sought opportunity arrives, will it lure Dale off course? Or will otherworldly intervention get him and Bailey dancing cheek to cheek?

Moonlight Serenade is a standalone novel and companion story to *Voices Carry*. Both are part of *The Rock and Roll Fantasy Collection,* a mystical world where rock and roll will save your soul.

ABOUT THE AUTHOR

Enjoying San Francisco as a backdrop, the ghosts in USA Today Bestselling Author Diane Rinella's one hundred and fifty-year old Victorian home augment the chorus in her head. With insomnia as their catalyst, these voices have become multifarious characters that haunt her well into the sun's crowning hours, refusing to let go until they have manipulated her into succumbing to their whims. Her experiences as an actress, business owner, artisan cake designer, software project manager, Internet radio disc jockey, vintage rock n' roll journalist/fan girl, and lover of dark and quirky personalities influence her idiosyncratic writing.